# *W*hat the critics are saying...

ഔ

*Five hearts!* "ANGELS ON CRUSADE is a wonderfully written story, filled with all kinds of historical figures. The characters are richly embellished...If you like time travels and have an interest in French history, ANGELS ON CRUSADE is a book you must have!" ~ *The Romance Studio*

"Samantha Winston's Angels on Crusade is historically accurate. The pageantry and political intrigue of the Crusades is dead on. I ached for Isobel and her possible punishment because I just knew she was destined to fail. The book held more surprises than I expected. At the end I found myself sighing with pleasure when, out of the depths of despair, love bloomed." ~ *Joyfully Reviewed*

"Samantha Winston gives great detail in this story. History is alive for the reader to enjoy. *Angels on Crusade* is a well written story with a few shocking twists that will surprise you. Ms. Winston has done a fantastic job with this story. I look forward to reading more of her stories to come." ~ *Fallen Angel Reviews*

"Author Samantha Winston's books are outstanding for their vivid characters and fast pace. Isobel's perceptions and emotions were so clear to me as I read, that I could almost see a web of connections between my nerve system and hers. When Isobel realizes what special punishment her assignment was designed to inflict on her, I had tears in my eyes...Readers take note, ANGELS ON CRUSADE is not the place to look for pageantry.

Thirteenth century France has come down to earth." ~ *Reviewer's Choice Reviews*

"ANGELS ON CRUSADE is an exciting time travel tale that seems so realistic especially when Isobel meets the teenage Jean and finds he is nothing even remotely close to his dossier. The story line is exhilarating as Isobel seems like a displaced person moving back over fifteen hundred years yet is the perfect selection by the omnipotent TCF because her prison time has made her submissive enough to fit at home in the past. Fans of medieval tales with time travel twists will appreciate this powerful story that hopefully leads to more TCF angels on the prowl." ~ *Harriet Klausner*

# Samantha WINSTON

# Angels on Crusade

Cerridwen Press

A Cerridwen Press Publication

www.cerridwenpress.com

Angels on Crusade

ISBN 1419955462, 9781419955464
ALL RIGHTS RESERVED.
Angels on Crusade Copyright © 2005 Samantha Winston
Edited by Ann Leveille

Electronic book Publication December 2005
Trade paperback Publication December 2006

Cerridwen Press is an imprint of Ellora's Cave Publishing, Inc.®

# Also by Samantha Winston

&

*If you are interested in a spicier read (and are over 18), check out the author's erotic romances at Ellora's Cave Publishing (www.ellorascave.com).*

# About the Author

&

Samantha Winston is the pen name for Jennifer Macaire, an American freelance writer/illustrator. She was born in Kingston, NY, and lived in Samoa, California, and the Virgin Islands before moving to France. She attended Parsons School of design for fine art, and Palm Beach Junior College for art and English literature. She worked for five years as a model for Elite. Married to a professional polo player, she has three children.

After settling in France, she started writing full time and published short stories in such magazines as Polo Magazine, PKA's Advocate, The Bear Deluxe, Nuketown, The Eclipse, Anotherealm, Linnaean Street, Inkspin, Literary Potpourri, Mind Caviar and the Vestal Review. One of her short stories was nominated for the Pushcart Prize. In June 2002 she won the 3am/Harper Collins flash fiction contest for her story 'There are Geckos'.

Samantha welcomes comments from readers. You can find her website and email address on her author bio page at www.cerridwenpress.com.

# *Author's Note*

∞

For those interested in history, the Crusades were a rich tapestry of events that contributed a great deal to our culture. Architecture, science, astrology, religion, stories and dealings suddenly flowed between two civilizations that had been static for many years—Good and evil came from those wars, but one thing is certain, without the Crusades, the world would never have been the same.

King Louis IX, or Saint Louis as he is known, was born in 1214. Under his rule, the kingdom of France captured the Maine, Poitou, Normandy and Anjou. In 1249, he took part in the Seventh Crusade, but he was captured by the sultan of Egypt. Obliged to buy his freedom, he returned to France in 1254 and vowed to become an exemplary monarch. He built the Saint Chapel in Paris and reorganized the government, instating the fundamentals of parliament. His devotion became legendary during this time, and he gained a reputation of having 'healing hands'. In 1270 he decided to go on the ill-fated Eighth Crusade to Tunis to try and win the King of Tunis to his side and to construct a fort from which to attack Egypt. He died soon after debarking. He was canonized in 1297.

His son, Philip III, ruled but a short time before dying in battle in Perpignon in 1285. Philip IV, the son of Philip and Isabella of Aragon, was called Philip the Fair. He is considered France's first "modern" ruler, as he opposed the pope, separated church and state and favored the development of judicial and administrative institutions. He made the role of the parliament and the chancellery stronger. Yet he wasn't perfect. In need of funds, he turned against the Templars, seized their wealth and had them all burned as heretics. In 1312, the last of the Templars burned at the stake, accused of witchcraft. As he burned, he cursed Philip and his descendants. He foretold Philip's death within the year, as well as the deaths of his three sons and all their families. He prophesied that Philip's dynasty would end and that France would go to war for one hundred years.

After Philip died, his sons reigned, but they died one after the other. Their sons also died, and the only living member of Philip's family left was his daughter Jeanne, married to the king of England. She immediately claimed the crown of France for her son, thus starting the Hundred Year's War. The curse of the Templar had come to pass.

Nearly three hundred years later, Henry IV was the first of the Bourbons to rule France. A Protestant, he inherited the throne in 1589, after the three sons of Henry the II died without heirs. (Henry IV was married to Henry II's daughter, Marguerite). He converted to Catholicism and managed to restore peace in France, ending a bloody war that had opposed Catholics and Protestants. A popular king—dashing, handsome and romantic—he was also a shrewd diplomat. Under his reign, France prospered as he introduced silk-making, new agricultural practices, and turned the finances of France over to his minister, Sully. He was assassinated in 1610.

His son, Louis XIII, is famous for being the young king depicted in the story, "The Three Musketeers".

# ANGELS ON CRUSADE

# Chapter One

*Angels on Crusade*

ɛ୬

The nurse in charge of freezing my molecules inserted a glowing needle into my arm and had me count backwards from ten. I got to zero and stared at her, perplexed. "Now what?"

"Again."

I obeyed without question. Ten years of prison had left their mark.

Then a cold wave washed through me. I felt my blood freeze. No one had told me it would be so painful. My teeth chattered and the place where the needle was inserted into my arm ached and ached. The pain grew. Frost bloomed in silver flowers on my hands and face.

The pain was so intense I passed out. My last thought before I fainted was wry. The program was going to lose their corrector. I was dying.

\* \* \* \* \*

I didn't die. I woke up lying on my back in the middle of a large mud puddle. Rain pelted my face, and my body convulsed with painful tremors. For several minutes, I felt so awful I wished I had died.

Groaning, I rolled over and propped myself up on my forearms. My clothes were drenched and filthy. I tried to stand up, but my legs wouldn't hold me. I crawled off the road and collapsed behind a large bush. I had no idea why I'd been beamed into the middle of a road. I could have been killed. I looked closer at the road and sighed. If anything were going to come down it, it would probably be an ox plodding before a heavy farm cart. The farmer would have been able to stop in time.

Unlike me. I hadn't been able to stop my car in time. I'd killed a child, and I'd been punished with life in a reproduction prison where I spawned one-hundred-and-twenty possible children. Every month an ovule was taken from my body and fertilized and the egg was implanted into an artificial womb. For ten years, I reproduced. I lay on a metal table once a month and donated an ovule, and in between, I worked at the prison library, copying ancient paper books onto gel matrix for safekeeping.

Then I'd been given a choice. Go back in time and change a mistake, or continue to live in a prison, in solitude, where my only jobs had been to produce eggs and reproduce books.

My mission now lay before me. I closed my eyes and tried to remember exactly what it was I had to do. Unfortunately, there seemed to be an empty space in my brain where all that information was supposed to be. I couldn't remember the first thing about it. I shivered with panic and cold. If my mission failed, the Time Correction Foundation, the omnipotent TCF, would erase this portion of time and I'd be erased along with it.

I took several deep breaths and calmed my nerves. All right. It was coming back to me. I had to convince a young boy not to join the ill-fated Eighth Crusade and therefore save the future crown of France.

I huddled in the gorse bush and wiped the mud off my dress as best I could with my hands and thought of my mission. It had all happened because of a mistake. Time travel was reserved for a select few — highly trained journalists chosen to go back in time and interview famous people. The journalist who'd caused the error I'd been sent to correct had spoken of the crusade in front of a boy who should never have heard about it.

The careless man had taken holograms, as the regulations instructed, but he hadn't checked to make sure nobody else listened to his interview with Queen Marguerite. Jean de

Bourbon-Dampierre had been near enough to hear. On the hologram, he looked up from his reading as the journalist began to speak. Because of what he'd overheard, the boy had slipped out of his bedroom one night and run away to join a ragtag gaggle of youngsters on their way to save Jerusalem.

Jean would not do anything of note during his life, but his descendants would eventually rule France. By running away, he changed the course of history dramatically. I was supposed to find him and bring him back. If I succeeded, I'd be allowed to live the rest of my life in the thirteenth century. If not, I'd be erased, along with all the mistakes the journalist had wrought in only two sentences.

Just two little sentences, which had been approved for the interview, for the queen, but not for Jean de Bourbon-Dampierre, visiting with his mother and sister at the court. "My Queen Marguerite, what have you heard of the crusade your husband, the king of France, has embarked upon? What about the group of youths calling themselves crusaders who have nearly reached the sacred Cathedral?"

The words had echoed weirdly around the room, and that evening Jean packed his meager belongings in a leather bag and clambered nimbly down a castle wall in search of adventure and a way to get out of his Latin studies.

\* \* \* \* \*

My mission was simple — get time back on track.

Shall I tell you how this system came to be to the best of my limited knowledge? It's not as if the TCF or the Tempus Program allows their secrets to become common knowledge, but as a corrector, I was privy to some small information.

Time travel was invented in 2300 and used for short trips into the past. At first, trips were only possible with inanimate objects, primarily those made of quartz crystal. When it was perfected in 2900, Tempus University, already an elite institution, started their reporting program. Because their time in the past was limited, researchers and historians had to make the most of it. It was decided they should act as journalists and concentrate on interviewing famous people. Some early experiences were resounding successes — Shakespeare, Julius Caesar and Marie Curie gave fascinating interviews. Other interviews were failures — Jesus, for example, remained elusive. Some trips simply didn't work out because the journalist was in the wrong place or the wrong time, but they usually came back alive.

The science of time travel is kept deliberately fuzzy, I think, so that the Tempus Program will never face any competition. Not that they'd allow it. As far as I could gather from my own experience, two enormous magnets are placed above and below a chair made of pure quartz crystal, which is located in a specific place on the Earth's surface. When an electric current is passed through the beam of magnetic pull, the resulting "force field" is able to send whatever is in that chair to another place and time. I gather it has something to do with the particular resonance of the quartz molecules, but that's just from overheard conversations. Nobody felt they needed to explain it to a mere corrector, especially not one taken out of the prison system.

But I digress.

When I started the mission, I was skeptical. Selected out of thousands of prisoners from my background in history, I still didn't believe I could make a difference. There were other ways of correcting a major mistake. The TCF could have erased a large enough portion of history to accommodate the changes the journalist had wrought. However, the electrical and nuclear energy expended in such an endeavor was enormous and cost an astronomical sum. Erasing history meant going to the point where the change occurred and taking out a chunk of time. It's the last resort. Don't ask me how it's done, it's used only in dire need. Mostly, they use correctors like me to set time right.

When a journalist is sent back in time, he — or she — is left there for exactly twenty hours and then brought back with the molecular magnetic beam to fame and fortune. When a corrector is sent back in time to correct a mistake, he's left there to fend for himself forever. The job is not coveted. Usually the "volunteer" is taken out of a prison program, like me.

I'd had one year to learn everything I needed to know to survive in a world two thousand years removed from my own. I had a limited chance of survival. That didn't bother anyone—besides me, that is. I had no family, I was sentenced to life imprisonment and if I did my job well I'd receive full pardon and my name in the roster of Humanitarian Awards. What an honor! From a criminal to a hero in the space of a day. This was how long it would take the TCF to verify my work in the Vacuum History Book, located at the North Pole.

How could anyone know if time had actually been changed, you ask? If you changed the past, you automatically changed the future, right? Wrong. Well, almost wrong. Most of the butterfly theory is correct. Little things can have enormous consequences. However, big things, things you assume would alter history, are usually swallowed up in what scientists call the "Molasses Theory of Time". Time follows its schedule like inertia, starting slowly and then flowing like a bottle of molasses tipped over on a table. The molasses is thick, torpid, but it flows. To stop it one must be very quick. Otherwise, the sluggish, sticky stuff will ooze all over the table. It follows its own schedule, just as time does.

To make sure time isn't changed in any irrevocable way, scientists placed a detailed history book in a permanent molecular magnetic beam located in the exact center of the magnetic pole of the Earth. The beam doesn't send the book anywhere, but it does keep it from becoming altered in any way—no matter what happens when someone goes into the past and modifies time. A replica of the book is kept in another room, in a normal environment. After each time trip the books are compared. The differences show up within a day. Any discrepancies are fed into a computer and the results analyzed.

If there is no danger of time moving from its flow, then the book is closed and everything continues blithely on its way. If, however, the changes are major and deviate the flow of time, then something is done to put it right. Within a year, a "volunteer" corrector is found and trained and sent to live and die farther away from home than most people ever imagine. A year to train a corrector and pray the mission is a success. After that, the possibility of correcting time becomes improbable and likely to influence the present in calamitous ways. Or so it's theorized. Possible time change has never been allowed to go that far. The TCF always erases it.

Because of the high cost, little alterations to the continuum are ignored, and time, like thick molasses, keeps flowing, as it should. Those changes never affect our present because the flow of time tends to glide over flaws without a bubble in its surface. Nor does the history book have the name and date of birth of every human being who ever lived on Earth. The faceless mass remains anonymous. A person could go back in time and fade into the background, and no one would ever be the wiser if they did their job well.

\* \* \* \* \*

I got to my feet, wrung my skirts, and made my way down the road. I had no idea if I was going in the right direction, but I knew I'd eventually find out. Besides, I had to go somewhere, right? At the first crossroads a sign would likely tell me which way to get to Chartres, where I had to find a certain Jean de Bourbon-Dampierre.

I walked all day. The city of Chartres, a prosperous town of about a thousand souls, was on a flat plain, and the cathedral was visible for miles. Unfortunately I'd started in the wrong direction and it was only three hours later that I discovered my mistake and had to retrace my steps on the rutted dirt road.

Seven hours of walking in perfect freedom after ten years of prison life. Seven hours of walking in a straight line, more or less, after ten years of walking around and around a courtyard. There was grass and blue sky, although the grass was still dead, it being early March, and the sky was a frosty, gray-blue that promised cold weather. I didn't mind. I was free. The feeling was intoxicating. The road stretched empty to my left and to my right for several kilometers. The very tip of the cathedral showed in the distance. I thought perhaps there were ten more kilometers to walk.

My head spun, and I had to sit down. I gazed ruefully at my feet in their thick leather shoes. They were well broken in because I'd walked with them for six months in the prison. It wasn't that my shoes, or my feet, hurt. It was the fact my stomach was empty and hunger was making me dizzy. I would have to wait until I found an inn though, I had nothing to eat with me. I had nothing but the dress I wore, a warm cloak, my shoes and a small, leather pouch full of coins and a few trifles the historians at the TCF had allowed me to take.

I groped for my purse and nearly had a heart attack when I didn't find it right away. The relief when I finally grasped it made me even fainter, and I put my head between my legs so I didn't pass out. My heart pounded and sweat pearled on my upper lip.

I drew a shaky breath and sat up straight, trying to still my wildly beating heart. Most of my panic came from the thought of meeting people and trying to fit into society. I bit my knuckles and tried to empty my mind. It was easier to bear if I just didn't think about it.

When I recovered, I dug the purse out of my deep pocket and opened it. The coins inside were supposed to last me a year. There were two heavy gold ones, some silver and many, many copper and bronze coins. I took the gold coins out of the purse and weighed them in my hand. They were worth quite a lot, and if I lost them or if anyone stole them, I'd be doomed. I didn't know how likely theft was, but I didn't want to take a chance.

I searched in my leather pouch for the sewing kit. It was an antique, probably from a museum. The TCF historians had approved some of the items on the list of things I'd asked for, and this was one of them. I sewed the gold coins into the inside seam of my skirt. Perhaps I should have done it before. It hadn't occurred to me then, but now the reality of my situation had hit me. I spaced them evenly and made sure that they were secure. Then I did the same with the silver coins, sewing these into the hem of my shift. One silver coin I put back in my purse.

I didn't have many belongings. In my leather pouch, worn tied to my belt, I had the sewing kit, a change of undershirts, a deck of cards, a cake of soap, a bottle of perfume, and some makeup—kohl eyeliner, face and hand cream and powder. I had a few pieces of gold jewelry hidden in my belt, which I could sell if need be. I had nothing else. No passport, nothing with my name or photograph on it, and even my fillings had been replaced by an ivory composite that wouldn't betray my strangeness.

The only thing unchanged was my face. The car accident that had cost the child his life had also cost me my face. A huge scar jagged down one side from temple to chin, sectioning my lower lip and ending halfway down my throat. It was a fearsome scar, but I had refused all offers to have it erased.

* * * * *

As I walked toward the city of Chartres, the tip of the cathedral spire grew like a pine tree pushing itself out of the ground. Then the rest of the town's buildings sprouted around it. Rooftops and chimneys rose out of the gray fields, and stone houses grew like squat mushrooms. Black shrubs and winter gardens appeared. Only a few people were outside that day, hurrying through the gathering dusk.

The road I walked went straight across the flat plain. Chartres crouched in a slight depression upon the banks of a narrow river. The last things that came to my view were the main street, winding around the base of the massive cathedral, and the sullen, black river flowing sluggishly under the bridge.

I wanted to find an inn, eat something hot and lie down in a soft featherbed. At the entrance to the town the gatekeeper directed me to the only inn, a large, stone building near the church. To my relief, his words were easy for me to understand.

The historians had done their job well, and I'd had many holograms and tapes from this period to learn the language and familiarize myself with the environment. The tight knot in my chest eased somewhat as I approached the tavern and peered inside.

A huge caldron simmered inside the great chimney and the scent of roasting meat made my mouth water painfully. I rapped my knuckles on the lead-paned window and waited until a woman opened the door.

"I'd like a room for the night and some food, please," I said.

"No rooms left here, and the dinner won't be served until after vespers." The voice was quiet but firm. Before I could open my mouth again the door was shut, the latch dropped and I found myself leaning against the wall in order to stand upright. For a moment I wanted to cry. My face screwed up, and I pressed my cheek on the rough stone and closed my eyes.

"Pardon, mademoiselle?" The voice came from behind me, and I turned wearily. Two blue eyes stared at me from beneath thick, black brows. Two deep blue eyes in a peaked face lined with lines of hunger and suffering. The crevices made him look ancient, although I doubted the child was more than ten years old.

He stepped closer. "If you're hungry the Church has food for the crusaders. They're arriving and they want bread. Come with me, I'll show you. That's where I'm headed." His voice dropped confidentially. "I'm joining the crusade."

"I see." I eyed him warily, but he didn't look like a thief. The fact that he was joining the crusades didn't amaze me. From what I'd learned, everyone wanted to go. The crusades had been the world's first publicized event. Recruiters were everywhere.

His face suddenly tightened. "You won't be saying anything to Madame Latrainée, will you?"

"I don't know who she is." I peeled myself off the wall. "I just arrived in the city."

"I know, I saw you coming down the road. I've been watching," he continued, speaking as we walked. "I've been watching since yesterday, waiting for the crusaders."

"And you've seen everyone who's come into the city?" I asked him, suddenly interested.

"Of course I did. At first I thought you were one of them, but you're all alone."

"The crusaders in this group are nothing but poor peasant youths," I said. It was my memorized speech. "They're heading straight for their deaths. Listen to me, what's your name?"

"Charles." The boy looked at me sideways, his eyes a deep, navy blue.

"Sharl," I pronounced it as he did. "Listen to me. This crusade is ill-fated. Most of the crusaders will never make it to the Holy Land. They'll be sold into slavery by merchants and ship's captains in Marseilles. They will tell you the boat is heading for Antioch, or Tyre, and they'll take you straight to the slave markets in Africa."

His steps faltered, and then he shrugged. "What difference will it make? A slave here or a slave there, what difference? Here I sleep in the stables, I have food when the master remembers to feed me and I have clothes when I can steal them from the washerwomen at the river. Otherwise I am just a slave, 'do this, do that', and no hope to do anything else." His voice broke and he frowned. "I was thinking of running away to Paris, taking a chance there, and then I heard of the crusade. Maybe I'll have a better chance with them. At least they get fed when they come to town."

I looked at my companion and for the first time noticed how dreadfully filthy he was. His hair was matted, snarled, probably crawling with lice. His face was not only peaked, it was pale and unhealthy. He held himself stiffly. I wouldn't be surprised to discover old greenstick fractures on his limbs from beatings he'd obviously suffered. When he walked, he limped. I bit my lip again. Children made me cry. Whether they were healthy and happy or miserable, they were all reminders of what I'd done.

My knees trembled and I grabbed a lamppost to stay upright. I took a deep breath. "Sharl, I, I…" I hesitated. What could I do to save him?

What would happen when I saw the doomed children all massed together, their white faces drawn and illuminated with the fervor of their faith and a terrible hope? Hope for a better life, hope that would be completely shattered.

My hand slid down the lamppost as I sank to the ground, and my eyes brimmed with tears. It came to me just what punishment the TCF had devised for me. I turned away from Charles. I could not, simply could not, go to the church and see the children. I hadn't seen any since the accident. I closed my eyes and tried to shut out the images that haunted me.

"Are you all right? Shall I get help?" Charles sounded anxious. He poked my arm, then, when I failed to respond, pounded me on the back.

"I'm fine, I'll be fine." I got to my feet and stared over his head at the huge church spire. It was nearly obscured by darkness.

Suddenly, the bells began to clang, shockingly loud. The air shook with each clang. Each hard ring broke the sky into a puzzle of gray pigeons flapping whitely through the evening. Each thunderous toll shook me from the soles of my feet to my head. My face vibrated with the sound.

Charles' little face blanched and he swallowed convulsively. "Vespers is starting," he said. "We won't get anything now until it's over."

"Well, we might as well sit down in the church." I sniffed and wiped my face with the back of my hand. "Let's go, shall we? Maybe our souls will be saved."

"God forbid," said Charles and crossed himself neatly.

I looked at him askance, surprised by his wry voice, but he just shrugged and took a rather shaky breath before leading me into the great, stone cathedral.

# Chapter Two

ॐ

The cathedral was full. We arrived at the last stroke of the bells and just managed to squeeze onto a bench. Charles was as slight as a wraith and I wasn't much thicker, though I was tall. We were packed in, but the press of bodies kept me upright, and it kept me warm. The only thing still cold was our feet, the floor was stone and the chill seeped up our legs.

In the front of the church, the noblemen and rich families had thick rugs under their private benches and braziers smoked warmly next to their pews. In the middle part of the church, townspeople had mats made of woven rushes underfoot. Here in the back were the peasants and the poor. Some of them even had animals on their laps or at their feet to keep warm; we sat next to a goat. Our breath made white clouds in front of our faces as we chanted in Latin. The crowd of people all around me made me feel lightheaded, almost panicky, and I clutched the wooden pew in front of me to steady my nerves.

I tried to take my mind off my panic by staring at the stained glass windows and stone carvings. I already knew that the cathedral in Chartres had been rebuilt after a fire destroyed it. The relic it housed, the virgin's cloak, believed to have been lost in the fire and found miraculously intact after four years, had roused the builders to a fever pitch. They had finished the vaulted ceiling in less than twenty years. Now, nearly finished, the cathedral astounded me with its beauty. There was nothing like this where I came from, nothing so solid or majestic.

The setting sun lit up the west side of the church, making the windows glow. The red glass became molten ruby, the yellow fire. Figures etched into the colored glass seemed to come alive as the last rays of the sun flickered over them. I fixed my eyes to the magnificent windows, each worth a fortune.

The night grew steadily darker as the evening service wore on. The stained-glass windows lost their bright colors and faded to black. I tried to hear what the priest was saying, but it was nearly impossible. We were in the back, and microphones had yet to be invented. Once I thought I heard 'suffer the children', but I pinched myself hard and the darkness faded from before my eyes. I must have fallen asleep and dreamed it.

Then the bells rang again, louder from inside the church. Half-deafened, we made our way through the crowd outside to the barns in the back of the cathedral, where thirty young crusaders prepared to sleep in the hay.

Women in warm cloaks doled out supper to the raggle-taggle bunch. They stood over steaming caldrons of cabbage soup and carved thin slices of smoked ham. The crusaders crowded around the hams, snatching at the slices as soon as they were cut. They had rarely eaten meat, I think.

There were youths of all ages, though most were in their late teens. They huddled together close to the largest woman, who was busy filling their bowls. They wore rough woolen robes over leggings of the same stuff and some had sleeveless tunics made of leather or sheepskin. Their clothing was poorly made with patches and rents and crusted with filth, and I realized that these people were the unwanted ones, the ones who could be spared, and who would not be spared. Their faces were pinched and white, but in their eyes dark pools of hope glimmered. People were actually feeding them here.

As I watched, the woman in charge handed a child a bowl and made to pat her fondly on the head. The child flinched. Then she hugged the soup to her chest and ate voraciously, first dipping her fingers in it to fish out bits of cabbage.

Another group stood in a circle, chatting in hushed tones. They were older, and among them was a youth who stood out despite his efforts to blend in. Everyone else suffered from starvation or ringworm, neglect or abject poverty. This boy was straight as a young elm, his hair was cut well around his head, and his ears didn't have the black coating of dirt the others' had. His clothes were rough, but of good quality, they were dyed and his wool tunic was tightly woven. Moreover, his eyes had none of the painful hopefulness the others had. He looked around with the gaze of a hawk, keen and appraising.

I heaved a sigh of relief. I had found my assignment. I recognized him from the hologram the journalist had brought back with him. Now all I had to do was to get him back home. But first, I had to eat or I was going to faint.

Charles took my hand and practically dragged me over to the soup. The ham was a thing of the past—not a scrap of meat was left.

"We have no bowls," he informed the woman.

"You'll have to give them back." She dipped a ladle into the caldron and served us two bowls full of steaming soup. "Good appetite."

"Thank you, Madame," said Charles. When I didn't say anything, too overcome with the odor of food to speak, he jabbed me with his elbow.

"Thank you, Madame," I echoed.

We sat on a pile of dry straw to eat. Another woman handed out bread. There were no spoons, knives or forks. Napkins were our sleeves. We drank our dreadful soup and sopped it up with bread. When the first edge of my hunger was gone, I had a hard time finishing it. It was simply cabbage boiled with ham bones, unsalted and unseasoned. The cabbage was tough and the bread was stale.

The crusaders ate voraciously. They probably got one meal a day when they were in a town, but what did they eat along the route? My heart squeezed in my chest. They looked so frail— their arms and legs too long, the soft covering of childhood prematurely stripped away, leaving their bones and sinews exposed and vulnerable.

My hand shook, the bowl I held dropped and rolled in the straw. Charles sighed and picked it up. "The soup's gone, but there's some cabbage left," he said.

"Take it." I noticed that no one was offered a second helping of soup, and the smoked ham was nothing but a bone. Judging from the way the children gnawed on the pieces they had, it was inedible anyway, as hard as shoe leather. I shivered. Perhaps shoe leather tasted good to these poor creatures. Perhaps it would taste good to me after I'd been here for a while. My stomach heaved with anxiety and I clenched my teeth to keep my meal down.

Nothing I'd ever experienced, nothing I had studied on the holograms, could have prepared me for the reality of this time, I thought, my head aching. Not for the cold that penetrated the buildings, the poor food, the clothing, or the hard life the people lived. Our shelter was made of stone, had an earthen floor, and the only heat came from the three fires in the center of it. The smoke rose to the rafters and swirled around before escaping through the many holes in the roof. Rain would probably come through those very holes, soaking anyone underneath, so I prayed it didn't rain. The straw prickled, and the food was nearly inedible. I folded my arms over my knees and rested my forehead on them. I hated this century. I'd only been here a day and I already hated it. Moreover, I was stuck, stuck here for all time.

Nevertheless, I didn't cry. I hadn't cried in years. I wasn't about to start now. I had money, more money than all these people had ever seen in a lifetime, with the exception of Jean, the young lord. I could rent a room, a bath, and sleep soundly in relative warmth. I looked at Charles, beside me. The food had put color in his cheeks and his head nodded sleepily. His eyes fluttered closed, his long lashes sweeping his cheeks. His face, in repose, lost its lines of suffering. In the firelight, he looked again his age. His cheeks smoothed and his mouth softened, and his face seemed surrounded by a nimbus of light. I blinked, sending tears down my cheeks, and his face came sharply back into focus. So much for my not crying.

I wiped my face and got stiffly to my feet. "Stay here, I'll be right back," I said to Charles. I took off my cloak and covered him with it, making a bed for him in the straw. He didn't protest. With a small yawn, he snuggled into its warmth and two seconds later he was sound asleep.

I made my way outside to the public latrines, small wooden sheds sticking out over the river. Through the hole in the bench where I was to sit, I saw swirling black waters. Afterwards I went back to the barn and sought out the young lord. Jean de Bourbon-Dampierre, recently of Paris, runaway.

I waited until he was finished arguing about whether or not they should leave the next day at dawn or let the youngest children rest a bit, and whether or not they should go toward Orleans or Le Mans. When that was settled—they would leave the next day, and they would head for Orleans—I stepped up and tapped Jean on the arm.

"Excuse me, my lord," I said deferentially. "Your father has sent me to bring you back home. Your mother is suffering greatly from your leave and would have you return."

The historian in charge of my education had insisted that Jean was very close to his mother. He'd been sure that a few words to Jean about his weeping mother would send him running back home. Historians can be such fools.

The boy looked at me scornfully. "He sent a woman to bring me back? Why not the guards? Who are you, anyway? Where is my father? Has he decided to show an interest in me at last?"

I held his gaze. "I was sent, yes. The guards have better things to do, don't you think? My name is Isobel. Your parents will both be pleased to see you safe and sound back at the court."

He hesitated, expressions of anger, confusion and distrust chasing themselves across his face. Finally he said in clipped tones, "I am sorry to inform you that I have decided to join the crusade. We are on our way to the Holy Land to free…"

"To free Jerusalem from the infidels. I know, I know." I launched into my prepared speech. "Nevertheless, your crusade is doomed. The children you see here will most likely be sold into slavery. They have no money, no way to insure their safe passage. Did you really think you'd be able to get a boat to take you across the inner sea just because of your faith? Or that you could actually fight?"

Jean lifted his chin. "Of course I will fight. I intend to join the king's army."

I pointed. "Look at that child over there, he's only five, maybe six years old. He walks ten kilometers a day. Then you must carry him because he's exhausted. Poor food and neglect have weakened him. He knows nothing about the Holy Land. What he needs is food and rest and someone to care for him. He's never had that. You don't have any excuse. You have a family, warm clothes, and have always had good food in your stomach. Don't throw it all away. Be thankful for what you have."

"How do you know all this?" Jean's eyes hardened. "Are you a soothsayer? A witch?"

"Don't be ridiculous," I said. "I have eyes, I can see and I have common sense. You have it too, so use it."

"I cannot," he said, looking suddenly sad, surprising me. "I cannot abandon my companions. We've marched from Paris together. What will they think of me if I just leave them?"

"Whatever they think, they won't think it long. Half of them won't live to see the next harvest, or they'll become slaves working in the silver mines. You wouldn't survive as a slave so they'd sell you for ransom perhaps, or kill you. You're too proud to submit to chains." My voice was sad too, and very quiet.

I couldn't keep my eyes away from the tiny, dirty child. Jean followed my gaze. "His name is Antoine," he said. "He comes from Lille. He has already walked so far. I only carried him a little ways."

"We can carry him back to Paris if you wish. I'll find someone to care for him."

Jean searched my face, not speaking for a long moment. "You look so innocent," he said finally. "You seem so sure of what you say, and yet so afraid. You speak of the future as if you really know what will happen. Your eyes are as clear as an angel's, but you have a fearsome scar. Are you a seraph? One of the fallen ones? Have you come to warn me of my fate?"

"I am no angel, believe me. Neither am I evil. I have simply come to take you home."

"Tomorrow," said Jean. "We'll speak about it tomorrow. Tonight, I'm tired, and I would sleep now." He spun on his heel and left me, walking quickly through the crowded barn. I didn't follow him. I was too tired to follow anyway. Instead I went back to Charles, who slept deeply in my cloak, and I lay down next to him.

With a deep sigh, I too fell asleep, despite the prickly hay. The day had exhausted me.

The night was cold and the damp seeped into my clothes and made me shiver. I woke up at least ten times. Each time I peered blearily around, panicked, forgetting where I was and why I was there. My chest ached — stress always gave me pains there. I took slow, deep breaths and tried to calm my fluttering heart. The night seemed to last forever. It was never still. Children shifted in the straw, spoke in whispers or cried out with nightmares.

At five in the morning, the church bells began ringing again. Some got up and went to Mass. Charles didn't stir. I raised my head and saw that another fire was being lit beneath the great iron caldron. Women, dressed warmly in thick cloaks, breathed clouds of white in the frosty air and prepared breakfast for the crusaders.

I thought the children would be welcome to stay a few days, but I also knew the townspeople really wanted them to go on their way. While they were here, the militia was on the alert. It was a time when a child of ten would be thrown in prison for stealing a loaf of bread, and prison meant certain death. The militia, freemen culled from the townsfolk, stood guard around the barn and made sure the older boys didn't slip into the town to steal.

I was standing in line to be fed, Charles right in front of me, when I heard a depressing tidbit of information. Two of the women who ladled the soup spoke to each other in low tones.

The youths around me didn't even glance at the women as they gossiped softly. I tilted my head to hear them better.

"They must be off by noon, poor dears. Look at that one — skin and bones he is. He won't get far."

The other woman who wore a red cloak, snorted. "Do you really believe they're crusaders, Jeanine? They look more like villains to me."

I started, then remembered that villain was a word employed to describe the poorer peasants or serfs in that time.

"I can't see them freeing the Holy City, that's the truth," the woman called Jeanine said with a sigh. "But I admire their faith. Remember when the last crusade came? King Louis was so young and his men were so handsome, and the horses so bold. I was only seventeen, but I remember seeing the king as if it were yesterday."

"Now he's old and so feeble they say he must ride in a litter."

Jeanine crossed herself. "Poor King Louis. His three sons ride by his side, and they will give him strength."

"Jean-Tristan was born in the Holy Land during the last crusade," said the woman in the red cloak. "They say he's a handsome man and nearly as pious as his father!"

"They failed to free the Holy Land from the infidel," said Jeanine as she doled a ladle full of soup into a bowl and handed it to a thin boy dressed in sheepskins. "Perhaps this lot has a chance. Some say it isn't a question of might, but of faith. What did you think of the prophet, that boy from Cologne? Do you think these children are following a false prophet as well?"

The other woman pulled a face and shook her head. "I don't think these young villains are following anyone. The one from Cologne whom some call St. Nicholas now is gone, lost at sea. These mites aren't part of his crowd, may God bless them. I wish them well. At least they'll escape the worst of the winter's chill if they hurry."

Jeanine nodded. "And hurry they must. At noon the militia will be here to escort them from our town."

"Seems hard to cast them away like that. Would some want to stay? I cannot see that child over there walking all the way to Marseilles, and even less freeing Jerusalem from the infidel. Saladin's name be cursed! Now there was the devil, the very devil himself." The woman in the red cloak shivered.

"Died in Damas, he did. My mother was alive when the news came. She stood up and danced on the hearth and her over sixty."

"I remember that. I was a young girl then and madly in love with a knight I'd seen leaving on the Seventh Crusade." The woman sighed and shook her head. "I wonder if he ever came back. In any case, he never passed through this town again."

"That small child won't even make it to the next village." Jeanine shook her head. "Perhaps someone had better keep him here."

"Who?"

"Why not you? Your brood is grown and you've a place at your hearth," Jeanine said persuasively.

"I couldn't. Who knows where the mite is from, or who his people are? Perhaps he's a changeling. I wouldn't dare take him home."

It was my turn now to get my bowl of watery soup and chunk of hard bread. I'd been listening carefully to the whole conversation. Now I spoke up. I hoped the lie I was about to tell would be believed.

"Excuse me, mesdames? The child you speak of is named Antoine. He comes from Lille. He's no changeling. He was simply one child too many in a poor family. They couldn't feed him, so they sent him on a crusade. The village priest blessed the child before he left and gave the family a sack of grain for their efforts. If you take him in you'll be sparing him a certain death." I spoke quietly with my eyes cast down. I was afraid the women would take offense, but they didn't.

The woman in the red cloak handed me my soup. "I'd take the child to spare him the long walk to Marseilles, but I'd need a coin to feed him and clothe him. We're not rich folk."

"If you take him, I'll give you money," I said. "If you promise to treat him well."

"Do I look like a cruel person?" She sounded indignant.

"No, I apologize." I took my soup to my place in the straw and sipped it slowly. Believing Antoine would be cared for here in Chartres reassured me. I felt a small measure of peace. Charles sat beside me and ate noisily, pausing now and then to wipe his mouth on his sleeve.

"I heard what you said to her," he said, pointing with his chin.

"Do you think that I did the right thing?"

"Perhaps. Who can say? I know that woman, she has a good reputation. She helps feed the poor when the church asks her to. She's here now, and that says much for her. I think Antoine will be treated fairly if you can give her a coin. Can you?"

"I can." I opened my purse and dug out the silver one. It was a nice, heavy coin and I knew it could feed a small child for half a year. "This should do, don't you think?"

Charles looked and his eyes grew wide. "A coin indeed. I think that will do nicely. You have just bought Antoine a home. Pray he appreciates it."

"I will," I said.

When the woman saw the coin, she raised her eyebrows. "That's quite a sum. I'll take the child home with me. I have a pallet for him there. I promise he'll never want for food, and I won't make him sleep in the stables."

"I believe you," I said. We looked at the subject of our conversation, Antoine. He sat by himself, his bowl in his lap and his face pinched with fatigue and ill health. I wondered if he would last the winter.

The woman must have sensed my unease. "He'll be all right. He has nothing a full belly and warm clothes won't put right. I won't make him work hard until he's full-grown, and if he proves himself able, he'll have a place in our workshop. There's always work there. My husband cuts stone. He's working on the cathedral."

I nodded, reassured. I knew the cathedral would be under construction on and off for at least two centuries. Fire would destroy it twice. Workers would always be needed for it. If Antoine became a stonemason, he would be lucky indeed.

As if to reward me, the sun came out. Its bright rays lit the barn's dim interior. We ate breakfast and then crowded once more into the cathedral to hear mass before being escorted out of the town. The priest spoke for so long a plague of yawning descended upon us. I could barely understand what he was saying, but a few words caught my attention.

"The road to Marseilles is long and arduous, and the Moslem awaits with his army of infidels. When you get to the Holy Land seek the tomb of Agnes de Courtenay and pray for aid. She will surely help you on your quest."

Agnes de Courtenay had been the mother of the defunct king, Baudouin IV. Would her spirit, even if it were able, really help a mob of rag-tag children? Doubtful. She'd never done anything except help her own cause. I sighed. The priest droned on and on, and finally the bells rang, liberating us.

No one was spared the vicissitudes of fortune's wheel. I had been well off and happy, a carefree student one day, a convicted murderess the next. And now I was here, standing on the cobblestones in front of a magnificent, half-built cathedral.

I managed to find Antoine in the crowd, and I told him I'd found him a place to stay. As I paused on the steps, the woman with the red cloak approached.

"My name is Dame Sara," she said, taking the boy's hand. "Will you come with me then, and see your new home?" she asked, her voice kind.

Antoine nodded, his face pinched with worry.

I went with them, too, as it wasn't far from the cathedral. The house was large and well built. Its floors were planked with wood, and the stone walls were covered with heavy cloth to keep the chill away. There were three fireplaces, one in the kitchen, one in the great room, which served as a living, dining and bedroom for the family, and one in the annex, a large room where the workers slept. Behind the kitchen was the larder, where several smoked hams hung amidst other salted and smoked meats.

The family was evidently prosperous. They certainly didn't need my silver coin, I thought wryly. But then I realized that anything could happen in those days. A dry spell, a sickness in the livestock or crops, and all was lost. A silver coin would guarantee Antoine food for a year.

I followed Sara around her home without a word and tried to keep as much out of the way as possible. Antoine was kindly received by the other occupants of the house. Sara's husband nodded and smiled. He was a tall, well-knit man with huge hands that looked as hard as the rocks he cut. Sara said she had two daughters, married and living in neighboring villages.

A gray cat sat in a curl next to the fireplace, and as we opened the door and let in a flood of watery sunlight, an old woman looked up and blinked at us.

"Grandmother, this is Antoine. He'll sleep next to you and keep you warm this winter." That was Antoine's introduction to his bedmate. He stood uncertainly, his finger in his mouth, but the old woman put her knitting down and motioned him near. She peered at him and touched his cheek gently.

"A fine lad." Her voice was still strong. "Antoine is your name, and a good name it is. Do you see the cat? Have you ever touched one? No? Well, you must pet her gently or else she'll scratch. Her name is Grisette. If you're quiet, you can hear her purring."

Antoine forgot to be shy and was soon seated near the fire stroking the cat. His face, which had been pinched and gray, relaxed, and color came back into his cheeks.

"He looks better already." Sara nodded and I handed her the coin I'd promised. She took it and tucked it into a small purse tied to her waist. "I won't lie to you. This will buy him a year with me. At the end of that time, if I find he's a good boy and willing, I'll keep him. However, if he causes trouble I'll turn him out."

"He's but five years old!"

The woman shrugged. "I'll do my best. I'll treat him well. It's up to him now."

I knelt next to the small boy and took him by the chin. "This woman is giving you a chance to stay with her, and with the cat." His hand tightened on the animal's fur. "For your own good you must obey her. If you're a good boy you can stay here and learn a trade. You must promise to be well-behaved."

Something in my voice must have reached him, because he put his thin hand on my arm and squeezed it. "Don't worry," he lisped, "I'll be good." His eyes were huge in his starving face. They were lined with red and had deep bruises of fatigue around them, but they were bright eyes, deeply knowing for such a young mite.

I nodded. "Farewell then. I wish you well."

He didn't reply, and Sara escorted me to the door. "Don't worry, young miss. I'll tend to him. You can go to the Holy Land now and free Jerusalem. May God protect you. I'll care for your child."

That gave me such a shock I was speechless. She hadn't believed the story I'd made up about Antoine. However, I reflected later, it was just as well that she thought he was mine. At least she thought she knew his mother, and that the child wasn't a feared changeling.

Once I left the house, I found Charles waiting patiently for me on the street. "The others have already left," he said.

I was surprised to see him. "Thank you for waiting," I said, strangely touched.

Charles jostled my arm. "We better be off," he said in his deep, raspy voice. "The villagers won't want us staying around."

Yes, we were off, and my assignment still unfinished. Now I had to find the stubborn Jean de Bourbon and escort him home. I picked up my skirts and hastened down the road. Townsfolk lined up along it. To wave, to wish us well, to make sure we were really going. I felt a pang of terror and prayed that Jean would listen to me when I caught up with him. I had no wish to go on a crusade.

# Chapter Three

❧

Charles and I crossed the bridge and took the road leading south. As if to reward me for taking care of Antoine, the sun came out. Its bright rays lit up the town of Chartres and the outlying countryside. In the fields, serfs labored picking up the omnipresent rocks and stones. It was late March and it was time to plow, to harry, to rake and to prepare the fields for planting. In the vineyards, men were cutting the grapevines back and burning the twigs. Smoke rose from small fires in thin spirals and disappeared in the clear air.

We caught up to the crusaders after about an hour's walk and I searched for Jean. He wasn't visible in the crowd but I wasn't worried. I'd wait until we'd gone a ways from the city before I spoke to him.

Along the way, the crusaders talked and chattered to each other. In the daylight I could study the crusaders better. It was a relief to see that Antoine had been by far the youngest of the group, and aside from three or four spindly children, most were robust youths or young men and women in their twenties. Crusaders, I had learned in prison, were not all valiant soldiers. The Church urged all common folk to take part in a crusade. They were expected to fight with sticks or their bare hands, I supposed, for none were armed. They were poor, dressed in tatters for the most part, and I felt almost too well dressed with my thick woolen cloak. Many of them had acne scars, peaked complexions and chapped cheeks and lips. They looked, overall, unhealthy. And though none had the slightest bit of grace or brightness in their faces, almost all had the fervent expressions of fanatics, with eyes that burned and voices that rose to a high pitch when they spoke of the Holy Land and of killing the infidel.

I started to wonder if the crusades weren't a ruse to get rid of undesirables in some towns. I could picture the mayor, or whoever was in charge, going to the local group of hoodlums and describing the delights of disemboweling the enemy. He'd urge them to do their sacred duty and off they'd go, caught up in a fervor of bloodlust and faith—a powerful combination in any time.

I stumbled on a rock and stepped on my hem. Before I could fall, a strong hand caught my arm, and I found myself staring into Jean's keen eyes.

"You've been searching for me," he said, tossing his head like a strong-willed colt might.

"That I have. Will you follow me to your home now?"

"No. I've decided to go to the Holy Land to fight the infidel, after which I plan to join the order of the Templars as a soldier. You can go back and tell my mother I'll buy her some souvenirs from Jerusalem. My father should be content to have me out of the way for a year or so. Tell him I'll be back to claim my inheritance."

My throat constricted and I thought I'd probably faint. I had been expecting to find a lad. Sixteen was, to my thinking, still a child. However, Jean was at least a head taller than I was, and his expression was that of a grown man's. I had rarely seen such determination in anyone's eyes before. We stopped walking and the rest of the group flowed around us like water in a stream. Charles glanced back, saw we weren't moving and trotted to join us. I motioned for him to stay away, and he sat on a clump of grass to wait.

"I heard what you did for Antoine." Jean's eyes softened just a bit. "It was a good deed, and I'm sure your soul will be judged more kindly because of it when you die."

I licked my dry lips. "I didn't do it for my soul. Jean, I can't let you go to the Holy Land. I'm sorry. I must bring you back to your home. My life depends upon it."

That gave him a pause. "What crime did you commit to merit that punishment?"

I shook my head mutely.

"I won't go back home until I've fought against the infidel and won a place for my soul in paradise. Then I will buy a relic from a souvenir vendor in the Holy City and bring it back for my mother."

"Your mother is desperately worried about you, Jean," I said. "She's making herself sick with anxiety. You must come home now."

"I won't go back until I'm a soldier, and then I'll take my place at the head of my family. I won't return until I can usurp my father's position and prove to the whole world what a coward he was to refuse to go on this crusade."

"Perhaps he has good reasons," I said. "Did you ask him?"

"He thinks far too much of material things and not enough of his soul. The pope has blessed us all, and while we are on the crusade we will be exempt from communion or confession, despite the last council."

I frowned. This was not going as planned at all. According to the TCF historians back in my time, my mission was supposed to be simple. Jean, they'd told me, was a dutiful, submissive child. They obviously had been wrong, I thought bitterly. "You're too young to fight," I snapped, my nerves fraying.

"It's true we're quite young, but the Templars have need of soldiers now, and I have money with me to give them. They will certainly accept me in their order." The last words he spoke were whispered in my ear although we were quite alone now, the group having passed us by. Charles was dozing on the side of the road.

"Please, Jean, forget this folly. I'm sure the army has already left and there are no more boats to take us to the Holy Land."

"I told you, I have money. I will pay my own way." He shrugged, and his green eyes glinted with excitement. "Come, we're falling behind."

"Charles?" I called. The boy sat up and rubbed his eyes, yawning. He got to his feet and trotted over to me.

"I'm with you." He shoved his hand into the crook of my arm. His eyes, however, followed Jean's broad back as he marched down the road.

I gritted my teeth. This wasn't how my mission was supposed to go. I'd intended to bring Jean back home, and I would, even if it took longer than I'd previously expected. There was no time limit to my mission. All I had to do was make sure Jean went back home, married and had children. I was stuck here for the rest of my life, so unless something went radically wrong, I wouldn't be erased.

We walked all that day, not stopping for meals, and we slept when we came to a small hamlet that offered us the shelter of its hay barn for the night. The next morning we ate boiled cereal prepared by the villagers, and we walked some more.

The days passed in a blur. I was starving half the time. My stomach, unused to the coarse food, revolted. I didn't have the energy to do anything but stagger along the road. The crusaders prayed and I prayed — but for different things, I can assure you. I wanted decent food and a chance to talk Jean into going back home, but Jean had taken to hanging out with a group of hirsute, unsavory-looking characters. They were a rough lot, and Jean often got into arguments with them. I didn't like their looks and stayed by myself. Charles kept close to me, my little shadow.

Charles was a godsend to me. Thanks to the idiot TCF historians, I had been woefully unprepared for this mission. He made sure I was all right and gave me tidbits of advice.

"I don't like the looks of them either," Charles said to me. We were sitting in a washing shed. It was raining and this was the best shelter the village had to offer. But my spirits were raised by the scent of cooking meat. Someone had offered a whole suckling pig to the group and it was roasting on a spit beneath a tree, not far from us. Tending the fire were Jean and another young man. The group of rowdies sat at the other end of the shed, playing dice and squabbling among themselves.

"I'm hungry," I said. That was about all I thought of anymore. Eating and sleeping. "Where will we sleep tonight? There's no straw here."

"The villagers will bring some, don't worry." Charles patted my arm.

I worried anyway. The washing shed had a good roof and four planked walls, but the middle of the floor was taken up by a stream-fed pool, surrounded by stone slabs that slanted toward the water. We had scarcely the space to sit, much less lie down.

Just then a cry rang out. "Supper is ready!" There was a rush toward the tree. Some fell in the washing pond with resounding splashes. One, a girl, hit her head on the stone and slipped underwater.

The water was only knee-deep, but the girl was unconscious. I grabbed her and tried to pull her out, but her clothes were soaked and heavy, and I was weak.

"Charles, can you help me?" I cried.

He did, and we managed to haul her onto the floor. She sputtered and got to her hands and knees, water streaming from her mouth and nose.

"Shall we take her to the town?" Charles asked me, worry in his voice.

"Can you walk?" I asked the girl.

She nodded, and we took her arms, helping her to her feet. Blood flowed from a nasty gash on her temple. No one else paid the slightest attention to us as we left the shed.

"It's still raining," muttered Charles, wrinkling his face. "We'll be walking through mud tomorrow."

It was already muddy. The cow path to the village was sodden. By the time we made it to the cluster of houses we were soaked and filthy.

"Call for help," Charles suggested, and I did. Heads poked out of houses, and one kind soul trotted over to us. He was a sturdy young man with a thatch of black hair and black eyes. Rainwater streamed from his felt hat.

"Where are you from?" he asked the girl, but she was too muddled to reply. "She isn't a Cathari, is she?" The man frowned at us.

I had no idea what he was talking about, but Charles shook his head vehemently. "Of course not! We're crusaders!"

The man looked closer at the girl. "Is she married?"

The girl, dazed, shook her head and collapsed in his arms. He carried her into a small cottage that, despite being tiny, was well built and warm, thanks to a roaring fire in a large chimney. There was no glass in the windows and the roof was thatched, but it was clean, the floor was planked, and there was even a curtained bed and an oaken chest in one corner—signs of prosperity.

Charles and I waited to make sure she'd be all right, and then we left. I was reluctant to leave the cozy farmhouse, but there was hardly room for all of us in the main room.

"I don't think we'll see her again," Charles predicted.

"Did you see how the farmer was looking at her?" I asked.

"As if she were a fine, fat heifer," said Charles with a grin, and then he sighed. "It must be nice to have a house for one's own. I never lived in a house." He glanced back over his shoulder at the humble dwelling.

"Never?" I was shocked.

"No. I was born in a barn and lived in the stables. I've never slept in a bed," he added with a shrug.

"Charles, what are Cathari?" I asked. It wasn't a word I recognized from my language lessons.

"Shh!" He looked shocked and glanced about to make sure no one could overhear. "Cathari are part of a heretic sect that broke off from the church. There was an uprising in the south, and all the Cathari were massacred. No one talks of them, and if you're suspected of being a Cathari, you're turned over to the authorities and they...take care of you," he said. "Don't let anyone hear that word from you, and pray you are never accused of being a Cathari. It's almost as bad as being a sorcerer." With that he crossed himself, looking grim.

We slogged through the pasture and arrived at the washing shed. All that was left of the pig was a pile of white bones without a scrap of meat. I swayed and had to grab the tree to stay upright. Next to me, Charles swallowed hard, his face wan.

"How could they?" I cried. I peeled myself off the tree and staggered to the fire. Nothing. There was nothing. I picked up a rib and gnawed at it, then tossed it into the sputtering fire. I felt like screaming.

"Don't worry," said Charles, an angry glint in his eyes. "I'll get us some coin, and we'll buy food from the farmer."

I paid him no attention, too absorbed in my bitter disappointment. I stared at the bare bones and was fighting back tears when I heard an angry cry.

Charles had been caught dipping his hand in Jean's purse.

"You thief!" Jean cried. He grasped Charles by the arm and would have sliced his hand off at the wrist if I hadn't intervened.

"Stop!" I grabbed Jean's hand, where a wicked-looking knife glittered.

"Stop!" echoed Charles. A bony little knee went straight to Jean's crotch.

Jean dropped the knife and doubled over, gasping. "I'll kill you," he hissed, when he got his breath back.

Charles danced out of his reach. "You're wicked to be so well-fed and strong while we have to beg for each morsel of food. Look, Isobel is starving right before your eyes. How do you think you can earn a place in paradise if you can't even help your companions? Will you let her starve while you stuff your face? You finished the whole pig while Isobel was helping someone. You should be ashamed."

Jean sheathed his rapier, all the while backing away from him. He opened his mouth to retort, but I watched him too. When he noticed my regard, he flushed an angry red. With a curse, he turned on his heel and walked away.

The next day, Jean approached us and apologized. He even gave me his breakfast, a bowl of watery gruel. I took it and shared it with Charles. I was still angry. My stomach hurt constantly.

"Are you all right?" Jean took my elbow as we left the washing shed.

"I'll be fine once I get something to eat," I said. I was seriously considering taking one of my hidden coins and buying food for myself, but I was terrified the loutish group would learn I had money and steal it. "You should watch out for those men," I said, nodding in their direction. "They're nothing but trouble."

Jean shrugged. "They're fighters. They're going to war."

"They're thugs," I said. "Jean, you have to go back home. These others aren't your equals in anything. Look at them!"

I called our companions "the others", which didn't endear me to them. I had trouble remembering their names and I couldn't talk to them about anything. I found their fervor offensive and their zeal embarrassing. When we came to a new village, I cringed on the periphery of the group while they spoke to the persons in charge and insisted on food and lodgings.

Although I had money sewn into my hem, I never let on I had any coin at all. I told anyone who asked that I'd given all my money for Antoine's care. The villages gave us shelter in the form of barns or haystacks, and the people gave us food as well, even if it wasn't good food.

If I succeeded in my mission I'd be here for a lifetime, and I'd need all the coins I could get. I'd taught myself how to sew, if

I could find a little farmhouse like the one in the last village, I could settle there, and maybe Charles would stay with me and we could raise chickens or something.

Though it was a time of peace and safe borders, the people had only just begun to prosper. A middle class made of talented and trained artisans would slowly flourish and create new towns and villages. The farmers, too, would eventually find a steady market for their goods and prosper as well. France would have another hundred years of peace before wars and the Black Death tore through the land. The state would grow stronger, and education, art and literature would flourish. A small, golden age was approaching, if I could live long enough to enjoy it.

I eyed Jean sourly. Because of him, I was about to embark on a disastrous crusade and probably lose my life, or he would die and we'd all be erased. Not a very cheerful thought.

Jean caught me looking at him and he frowned. My expression was not the most amiable at that moment. "What is it, Isobel? Did something bite you? Is your stomach aching? I'm sorry about not saving you a bit of meat last night. Is that why you're upset?"

I glared at him. "Why can't you simply go back to your home?"

He didn't reply. It was a question I asked him at least twice a day, and he'd taken to ignoring it. "You'll never believe what I heard in the village," he said.

"I don't suppose you heard that they've called the crusade off."

"No, the king is going to Jerusalem to fight. He means to free Antioch."

"The king is elderly and shouldn't be making the voyage." If I remembered my history correctly, Louis would die in the Holy Land. I scratched my head. Confusion and lice made me do that often. "Where will he embark?"

"In Aigues-Mortes, the port he built the last time he left France to fight the infidel." Jean looked pleased with himself. "I heard he is pledging free passage to all those who will come and fight with him."

"Wonderful," I said. I looked at Charles, who hadn't missed a word of our conversation. "What do you think, young sir?"

"A free ride from the king is better than begging a boat from a slave trader." A spark of mischief lit his eyes. "Now that we have free passage, we're sure to reach the Holy Land. I can't wait to see it!"

I sighed. "I suppose we have no choice but to go. But you," I said to Jean, "had better not get killed. If I don't bring you back safely to your family, I'll be burned alive."

Jean's eyes widened. I made that part up, but it was convincing. Since Jean hated his father and thought him capable of anything, he believed my story. I'd embellished it as we marched, acting as though I allowed him to drag the frightful details out of me. I added bloody tortures and a wild chase through the darkened streets of Paris until I was caught by soldiers. My life truly did depend on his wellbeing, he heard that ring of truth in my stories.

* * * * *

Both Jean and Charles, like anyone in those days, adored stories and songs. They were important in that time when entertainment was rare and only came from troubadours or storytellers. I had made up a good story, and Jean fell for it. Not to the extent that he was willing to give up the crusade, but I'd persuaded him not to enroll in the archers, to leave the fighting to the trained soldiers and only to make the pilgrimage to Jerusalem to pray for the deliverance of the Holy Land from the infidel.

At least he wouldn't be in the thick of the fighting, though I didn't plan to let him out of my sight. He had a quick mind and an even quicker temper. If he changed his mind, I was afraid he wouldn't hesitate to sacrifice me.

Charles stayed near me. He didn't like the other travelers any more than I did. His wry humor was worlds away from their fervor, and I tended his minor cuts and bruises without comment. One time they weren't so little, and I knew that one of them had thrashed Charles, although he never told me who.

When we walked, I was careful to lag behind the rest of the group and keep Charles with me. Jean walked behind with us, silent and deep in thoughts he rarely shared. A more prickly person was hard to imagine.

* * * * *

After a month, we reached the south of France. The weather became warm, and I took my cloak off and folded it, tucking it into my belt. I had hated the rain and cold, but the heat was unbearable too, with sweat making a prickly rash on my body. I itched and stank and most days I found myself wanting to strangle Jean and just get it over with.

On one particular day, the sun hammered us mercilessly and my mood was black. Jean walked alongside me without speaking, and his presence grated on my nerves. "Are you thinking such lofty thoughts that our words would interrupt you and bring you crashing to Earth?" I said.

He looked at me warily. If Charles had dared the same statement he would have riposted with a quick insult, but he was more circumspect with me.

I wasn't finished. "Does your silence mean you have taken a vow? Will you decide on obedience or celibacy? You can't have both, you know. You're far too unyielding."

"Why don't you leave me alone with my thoughts?" he asked.

"The road is long and I'm bored. I'd like you to tell me a story for once. Charles has none to speak of. While your king traipses off to the crusades, sick with dysentery, his lady wife pines for him. Shall I tell you a secret, Jean? Your king won't come back alive."

Charles, who had overheard, gave a sharp gasp.

"Don't speak evil of our king," Jean snapped.

I think I was a bit mad that day. The sun beat upon our bare heads and the road was white, dusty and devoid of shade. I gave a bitter laugh. "Truth is not evil," I said.

"If you weren't a woman I would thrash you," he said, after thinking about it for a while.

"I'd like to see you try." I clenched a fist and waved it at him. I'd never been in a fight in my life, not even in prison, but I wanted to hit him. Why wouldn't he listen to me and go back home?

His face darkened and he took a step forward, but Charles caught his cloak. "No, no Jean!"

"It's *my lord* to you, villain!" He turned on the unfortunate child and raised his hand.

I darted in before he could strike. "If you want to hit someone, hit someone bigger and stronger than you are." With that, I swung my arm back and hit him across the face in a rousing punch.

He sat down in the dust, more stunned than hurt, and stared as I hopped about, hugging my bruised knuckles to my chest. "What demon has possessed you?" He let Charles haul him to his feet.

"Is there a demon called frustration?" I asked.

He took my hand and examined it, rubbing the red spot on the knuckles and shaking his head. "Didn't anyone teach you how to hit?"

"Heavens, no!" It was so unbearably hot. I plucked at my sweaty shift, wrinkled my nose at my own sour body odor and burst into tears.

Jean and Charles looked at each other. We had fallen so far behind the others that the dust from their footsteps wasn't even visible. There was a small dip in the fields, and a copse of dark trees seemed to beckon.

"Let's go over there and see if there's a stream or a spring." Charles jutted his chin at the woods, and we agreed. Jean took my arm at the elbow, and helped me across a dry ditch and onto the plowed field. We walked the distance in silence. The only things we heard were the liquid notes of a thrush.

"A thrush means water," Charles said, with evident satisfaction.

We stepped into the shade and I sighed. The relief of being out of the sun was sublime. A small, swift stream gurgled and splashed between banks of fern and nettle. We found a small, sandy beach and sat down. I took off my shoes and put my feet into the water. Jean and Charles stripped and washed themselves. I waited until they were finished and left me alone. Women in this time were expected to be modest, though the people were far from prudish.

The boys soon finished and told me they would be right out of sight, but within hearing. "If anything bites you, call out," said Charles.

I took off my clothes and plunged into the stream. With handfuls of sand, I scrubbed myself. I had a cake of soap in my purse, which I used with delight. I washed my clothes as well, scrubbing them with sand and rubbing them on a flat rock to remove the grime. Afterwards I carefully hung them on branches so they would dry quickly.

A hot breeze eddied through the woods. I was surprised; it was May in France, albeit the south of France. I hadn't realized that the sirocco, a hot wind straight from the Sahara, could be felt as far north. However, the air blew hot and dry as if from an oven.

In a few days, we would be in Montpellier. Our long march was almost over. The arid lands we trampled through were nothing like the desert we would soon see, though. I wondered what I would do for clean clothes and baths where we were headed. The thought of no bathing made me cringe.

Well, it could be worse. I hadn't yet had my period, which was a blessing, but I assumed it was because the TCF doctors routinely sterilized their correctors. One day they'd taken me to the prison medical building and the doctors had put me to sleep. When I woke, they informed me that I was now sterile, that my appendix was gone, that my tonsils were out, and that I'd been vaccinated against every sickness I could think of.

Their words replayed in my head as I sat with my feet in the water. I would never have children, and I was stuck here. The hopelessness of my situation sank in. I was alone in a dreadful century with a recalcitrant runaway, a waif and barely enough money to buy me a year of decent living. And my soap was half gone.

I lay on the beach and sobbed, heedless of what anyone would think. After a while, I sat up and dried my tears. Several nervous coughs from a deep thicket made me nearly smile.

"Oh, you can come out. I don't mind if you see me naked."

"We mind!" It was Charles, his voice indignant.

"Why? I saw you!"

"It's not the same."

"Wait a second." I picked some leafy branches and covered my sex, sitting with my feet in the water and my head in a spot of blue shade.

The boys came out of the bushes in single file. Charles grinned at me, but Jean refused to glance in my direction. His ears were very red.

"If I were you, I'd wash my clothes and dry them."

Jean snorted. "Wash my own clothes? Who do you take me for?"

"An intelligent person. Obviously I was mistaken." I said. "If you won't wash, you'll pest."

"I pest already." He shrugged. "I'm crawling with lice and I stink. So what?"

"Horrors! I'll wash them for you," I said. "I prefer walking next to someone who doesn't smell like sewage."

"So do I, but I don't mind if you pest," he said. He glanced at me then looked away with a frown. "Is it so important to be clean?"

Charles made a face. "When the dirt's gone from behind my neck I catch cold easier."

"Good Lord, Charles, let me see your neck!" I exclaimed.

After I saw his grime-coated neck, I made him shuck off his clothes and bathe again, scrubbing this time with sand and my soap. Jean did likewise, but only after chiding me never to take the Lord's name in vain again.

They didn't ask why I'd been crying. People were always crying then, from exhaustion, from hunger, from despair. There were so many reasons, but they'd never have guessed the real one. Charles glanced at me once or twice, a question hovering on his lips, but that was all. Jean seemed bothered by my nudity and wouldn't look at me until I'd put on my shift. Afterwards, he looked at me, tilting his head to the side.

"You should always wear your hair down," he said, as I struggled to comb out the tangles.

"I want to chop it all off." The mess of tangles and snarls exasperated me, though I'd spent the previous year allowing it to grow long so I'd fit in here. In prison we kept our hair short.

"No!" He pushed my hands away and smoothed my hair over my shoulders. "I used to braid my sister's hair, but hers is dark. Yours is fair and thick, like a sheaf of ripe wheat."

I was flustered, but Jean's hands were deft and he soon had my hair in tight braids. "Thank you," I said.

His hands lingered a minute on my hair, and then he shrugged and stepped back. "I miss my sister, that's all," he said.

I gritted my teeth. The TCF historians hadn't said a word about Jean's sister. What else hadn't they known?

After our clothes dried, we dressed and made our way through the dusk to the next town, where the crusaders had already requisitioned a hay barn and a large, simmering pot of soup.

Like me, Charles was always famished. The smell of the soup brought a flush to his thin cheeks. Jean waded into the crowd and fetched two bowls, one for him and one for me. His chivalry didn't extend to Charles, but the boy was used to that and had elbowed himself to the front of the line.

"Thank you," I said, as I took the soup from Jean.

He frowned and looked down at his bowl, then sat down next to me. "Isobel," he said.

"Yes?"

"How did you get your fearsome scar?" He asked the question in rushed tones, his face slightly reddened.

I sipped my soup and peered over the rim of my bowl at him. He stared back at me, not eating. His cheeks were flushed, whether by the sun or temerity I couldn't tell. His eyes sparkled, flashes of green emerald. His hair, newly washed, was as shiny as a raven's wing. "I fell through a window," I said, finally. I didn't know how to tell him I'd shattered a windshield with my face.

"You could have died," he said.

"I nearly did. It's horrible, isn't it?" My hand strayed to the scar and traced the line of it from my temple to my throat. When my fingers reached my lip he caught them.

"No," he said.

I was surprised. "No?"

"Who saved you, a fine physician? Was he a monk?" Jean's fingers tightened around mine and I looked at our hands, entwined. I shook my head and wondered why I was suddenly so lethargic. I should pull my hand from his grasp, my mind said. My hand tingled strangely. His touch made my chest tight.

My mind scolded, but my spirit had stopped listening. Warmth crept over me. The hay beneath us was soft and fragrant. My breathing quickened. I felt my cheeks grow hot. I didn't dare meet his eyes.

"What are you doing?" Charles bounded over and seated himself cross-legged in front of us.

Jean whipped his hand away as if it was burning, and I cupped my shaking hands around my bowl of soup and tried to compose my thoughts.

"I asked Isobel to tell me about her scar," said Jean, after a moment. He gave a shrug. "She cut herself on a glass window."

Charles gave me an appraising stare. "Glass can be very dangerous if you're not careful."

Jean yawned. "After tomorrow we should arrive in Montpellier. Then it's just a short ways to Aigues-Mortes." He folded his cloak around him and snuggled into the straw. A few minutes later he was asleep or feigning sleep. With Jean, I never knew for sure.

Charles collected our bowls and returned them to the village women gathered around the fires. I made my way to an outdoor latrine pit and searched for something to clean my teeth. Hygiene was the biggest problem I'd faced so far, hygiene and hunger. When I found a small hazelnut tree, I broke off a few twigs to use. In prison I'd read of an ancient toothpaste recipe that came from Egypt and was used by a certain princess, but for that I'd need ground chalk, a pinch of ashes, oil of clove, and the urine of a young virgin.

I contented myself with the twig and an occasional vinegar rinse.

# Chapter Four

ဆ

The night was agitated. Rodents scurried about in the hay in search of food, barn owls hooted, dogs barked nearly constantly, and at around three a.m. a fight broke out between some of our fellow crusaders. Shouts woke me. I sat up, blinking and trying to see through the darkness. Next to me, Charles emerged from a pile of hay. He yawned loudly.

"What is it?" he asked, scratching his head.

"I can't see," I answered. The fight was getting louder and others woke, peevishly calling for some quiet.

There was a sharp scream and then came the sound of a body hitting the earthen floor. A steady cursing sounded now and agonized wails. Someone was hurt, apparently. Somebody else blew on the coals in the brazier, adding straw to coax a flame. The brazier was set in the doorway of the barn to keep out the chill. Now it cast a reddish light over the scene. The noise had woken the village, and a constable and guards with torches came within minutes.

The squabble was over a girl. She sat in a pile of hay, her black hair a tangled mess, and pulled at her lower lip with dirty fingers as the constable tried to get her version of the story. The two young men who'd fought were both dead. They'd been fighting with knives, and mortal wounds had been dealt by both of them. I recognized the fighters as two crusaders I liked to stay away from because of their irascible tempers.

The girl stared dumbly at the carnage on the floor and wouldn't say a word. After a while the constable led her away. Some villagers loaded the bodies upon a cart, the torches were doused and we were left alone in the barn with the coppery smell of blood and the echoes of screams in our ears.

I don't know if anyone got any sleep after that. I certainly didn't. When the light cracked the sky open I huddled in a corner, trying to will myself back into the twenty-fifth century.

It didn't work. A touch on my shoulder, and Charles was whispering that we should leave. "The townspeople will want us gone, after last night's fracas," he said. "Jean is waiting for us at the gate. Come."

I unfolded my stiff limbs and walked slowly out of the barn, avoiding the black stains on the floor. The other crusaders slept or preened like chickens in the straw. I hardly glanced at them. My blood was iced with horror.

It was time to go. I wanted only two things, to get Jean back to Paris and then to slit my wrists.

*   *   *   *   *

I could barely keep myself together that day. Perhaps it was the fight—more likely it was just depression settling over me. The dusty road wound between huge cliffs that cast a deep violet shade. Above our heads, the sky was raw blue. The cliffs were red, and the grass was yellow. In the distance was the sea. I could smell it now. Salt in the air left a faint glitter on our skin.

Fatigue made my head spin, made me clumsy. I stumbled repeatedly. Charles grabbed my arm and urged me on. When the sun was straight overhead, Jean spotted a recess in the rocks, and we climbed a narrow goat path to a small cave. Other travelers had left a pile of tinder, but we had nothing to cook so we lit no fire. I simply sat and shuddered as the full horror of my situation registered on my mind. Charles watched me closely for a while then said he'd go find water. I think he'd decided I was dying of thirst.

Actually, I was parched, but it made no difference to my mood. All I could think about was suicide, and soon. My mission started to fade into the background, I could hardly remember it anyhow. What was I supposed to do? Why? Why bother? I was going to die anyway. I might as well be erased so none of this would ever have happened.

Jean slid over to me and took me in his embrace. Immersed in my own thoughts, his actions took me completely off guard. The feel of his arms around me was like an electric shock. No one had touched me in so long, aside from the doctors in prison. I turned to him and clung, pressing my shivering body to his.

His hands slid down my sides and his breathing deepened. My head spun. I didn't realize what was happening until he'd already lifted my dress over my head. By then it was too late to stop. Desire rose within me, sharp and compelling. All thoughts fled at his touch. Surprise and longing took hold of me. I arched my whole body toward him and offered myself wantonly.

It was over very quickly. Just the touch of my bare skin made him cry out. I hardly had time to draw him into me before he shuddered and spent himself. His breath was ragged, sweat stood out on his brow.

I couldn't move, completely under the spell of raw passion. My body had been wakened by Jean's touch, but my mind was strangely lethargic. Locked in a tight embrace, the stuffy heat in the cave making our bodies slick with sweat, I couldn't think of anything but assuaging my desire. After a minute, he hardened again and we made love once more. This time I took control of the situation and showed him how to give me pleasure. It was soon done—a violin string couldn't have been drawn tighter than my lust. We cried out in unison, he in surprise, I in release.

He rolled off me and lay panting on the floor. I sat up and drew my blouse over my breasts. With hands that shook, I smoothed my dress down over my legs.

Jean watched me with a puzzled expression, as if he couldn't quite place me. "I'm sorry," he said. "Did I hurt you?"

I closed my eyes. I wanted the silence to become visible, to cloak me and cover me in darkness so I could melt away.

"No, Isobel, look at me!" Even his pleas were stern. Perhaps he couldn't help it. He was used to giving orders.

I put my hand out blindly and touched his face. Slowly I drew my fingers down his cheeks, over his chin, then back up to his forehead. I searched his face with my hand, looking for something, some sort of salvation, but all I felt was the smooth cheeks of youth and fuzz on his chin where a beard should have been. If only he'd been older. Sixteen! Oh God, I'd just lain with a sixteen-year-old. I was thirteen years older than he was. No, I shook my head. Who was really older? He'd been born more than thirteen centuries before I had—I was younger than Jean by nearly a thousand years. A giggle burst from my lips. I buried my face in my hands and, for the first time in two weeks, started to laugh.

"Isobel!" Relief, and a hint of anger, colored in his voice.

I raised my head and looked at him. "I'll be all right," I said.

"I don't know what happened, I felt, I wanted…" He moved closer to me and gripped my arm. "Will you marry me?"

"Oh, Jean." I sighed. My sorrow was lessening. I could feel its weight easing off my body, and I could move without the feeling of lead in my limbs. "You don't have to marry me, for heaven's sake. All we did was make love. You can't go and ask the first girl you lay with to marry you. You have to get to know the person, fall in love with her, want to spend the rest of your life with her, have children…" My voice tapered off.

"Will you have a child?" he asked, his eyes very bright.

"No, I will not," I said. The depression departed, but I was exhausted. My head ached. "Let me sleep now. I won't marry you and I won't have a child. We can make love again, whenever you want to. It's better to ask first, instead of just falling upon me, though." I yawned. "It's all right, don't worry."

"Why are you crying then?" He pulled my head down to his lap and stroked my cheeks.

"I don't know, I think I'm just tired."

"Then sleep, Isobel, sleep." His voice, I realized, could be very gentle. I slept.

* * * * *

All my life I'd been prone to depression, but prison had made it worse. Sometimes it was all I could do to get dressed in the morning. When I was depressed, everything seemed wrong. The sky was too bright, the trees too close together, even my feeling of touch was altered so that things were too rough or too slick. My mind and my body would get out of synch, and I would struggle to keep an appearance of calm while fighting rising tides of panic or crushing waves of sorrow. The efforts drained me, and I would finally fall asleep from sheer exhaustion.

From experience, I knew these bouts of depression never lasted long, although they were crippling. I didn't try to fight them anymore. I only tried to ride through them. The next morning things would be better. From prison doctors I'd learned how to deal with my condition, and so I slept. Whenever I drifted awake Jean still held me lightly and stroked my temples and hair. It was comforting to be touched by another human being.

When I woke fully it was night, and there was a small, bright fire. Charles had snared or stolen a rabbit from somewhere, and the smell of grilled meat tickled my nose. I sat up, blinking sleepily. I felt nearly normal again. The healing powers of sleep had worked their magic yet again.

Jean and I looked at each other, and our smiles were twin flashes of white. His eyes sparkled, and I'm afraid to admit mine were probably glowing as well. We didn't speak. I stood up and made my way out of the cave toward a clump of bushes. A clean, white bathroom with running water would have been my first choice, but I'd have to be content with a shallow hole dug in the ground and, hopefully, a small spring or stream to wash up in.

In the darkness, I stumbled into the bushes. On my knees, I dug a hole using a stick and when I finished using it as a toilet, I covered it with dirt again. The gurgle of water alerted me to the presence of a stream.

As I searched for water after doing my business, my mind wandered. It usually did that after a bout of melancholy. I remembered Jean's arms around me and I stopped, tipped my face to the stars and took a deep breath.

It had been so long since I'd been in the arms of a man. The last time had been just before the accident. My fiancé and I had made love in his apartment. Afterwards I'd looked at my watch, sighed deeply and told him I had to hurry or else I'd miss my flight. I'd slung my bag into the trunk of my car and turned once more to wave at him as he leaned out the door. The hiss of steam from the engine in the deep, tranquil night air had hypnotized me, already relaxed from our lovemaking.

Why had that child been outside in the dark? Why hadn't his parents kept him in his bed? A butterfly net had been clutched in small hands and a collection jar hung over his shoulders. He had been intent on his prey, the nighthawk moths that floated like white ghosts in the heat of the summer's night.

So intent was he that he never noticed my car's headlights. I had been thinking of my fiancé and his soft groans as he thrust into me. I'd closed my eyes for an instant, better to imagine his face. When I opened them a second later, I swear it was only a second, another face stared at me. A white, moon face, trapped in the blinding glare of my headlights, paralyzed by the vision of the car rushing toward him.

The shock had been terrible. I'd swerved in a last, desperate attempt to avoid the child, but the corner of my fender caught him on the chest and flung him into the night. My car hit a tree, and I crashed through the windshield. Steam had escaped from the cracked boiler in a white, billowing cloud. As I faded into unconsciousness, the child's parents had rushed out of the house. The screams of his mother accompanied me into hell.

I woke in the prison hospital, three weeks later. My trial had been held 'in absentia' while I lay in a coma, though they'd waited to pronounce the formal verdict when I awoke. Considerate of them, yes? I was found guilty and sentenced to life in prison, life in a tiny, private room with a narrow bed, a plastic chair and a wooden desk, and a window that looked straight at a tall, brick wall. In silence. I had no physical contact unless you count the cold steel of the doctors as they probed for my ovules each month. In the library I worked in the back rooms where automated machinery hummed and clicked, but where few people ventured. I received no letters from my fiancé, no mail from my family who had, like most of my fellow prisoners' families, decided to forget all about me. For my crime I'd been erased from their lives as surely as the TCF could erase me from time if they wished.

I shook my head sharply, chasing away the bitter memories. In the dark, I saw the glint of moonlight on water. I approached and found a small, bubbling spring. The water was icy. Shivering, I washed with my dwindling sliver of soap then heard Jean calling me.

His voice floated over the right. "Isobel! Isobel!"

I rinsed, dressed and went back to the cave, braiding my hair as I walked. My shoes were in the cave, but my bare feet were getting tough. I didn't notice the sharp rocks anymore. Once inside the cave I was nearly overcome by the warmth of the fire and the rich scent of roasting meat. I swayed.

"Are you feeling better?" asked Charles, a wrinkle of worry between his brows.

I nodded. I didn't trust my voice yet. The memories were still too sharp, but time was slowly eroding the edges. Soon I'd be able to remember my trip into hell, and then, perhaps, I'd be healed.

\* \* \* \* \*

We arrived in Montpellier late the next day. The sun was setting, casting a red glow over the ancient city. Montpellier had been founded by the Romans as a trading post. Now it was French and perhaps the most important seaport they owned. Temples and churches abounded, and as we arrived, the air was split by the sound of ringing bells. Charles made a face.

"Vespers," he said. "I suppose it will be a two-hour wait until dinner."

We straggled into the nearest cathedral and sat while the priests chanted mass. The wooden bench was very hard, and I couldn't help shifting about on it. Jean sat very still, his face like carved marble, his eyes fixed upon the priest, his lips moving silently along with the Latin prayers. On my other side, Charles struggled against hunger and sleep in resigned silence, his head nodding now and then. I heard his stomach growl and he shot me an amused glance from beneath his long lashes.

"Shh," hissed Jean.

When the service was over, we filed out of the church to search for lodgings. I'd persuaded Jean to take rooms in a hotel and distance ourselves from our fellow travelers, whom we'd managed to avoid for two days now. I admit to selfishly wanting to spend a night in a real bed, with a hot bath and some decent food. The other crusaders could fend for themselves, my mission involved only Jean. I wondered if I could seduce him into forgetting the crusade. I'd try, at any rate. As we walked our hands entwined, and I felt almost happy.

As fate would have it, we stumbled upon the other crusaders as we passed the great, gilded doors of the church. A shout, a rough hand shoved me aside, and a loud voice said, "Is this the man?"

"Yes, it is!" The shout came from one of the louts Jean had often argued with along the way.

The crowd drifted out of the cathedral and pressed around, obviously looking for entertainment. Women pulled their children out of the way as the crusaders jostled one another, and Charles and I found ourselves in the midst of a shoving match between townsfolk and crusaders as they tried to get a better view of what was happening.

Jean struggled gamely, but he was held tightly by an armed guard. They wore cloth badges sewn onto their tunics. I assumed they were town constables.

They held his arms, not his mouth. "What do you want of me?"

"You killed two men near Orange, and then you fled. Have you forgotten already?" One of the crusaders, a tall man I knew by sight, stepped forward from the crowd and pointed at Jean.

"I did nothing of the sort!" cried Jean. "They killed each other. I protest my innocence!"

Charles yanked on a constable's arm. "It was a brawl between two knaves for a bitch in heat!"

I too stepped forward to intervene, but there were too many people shoving, shouting and milling about. All I could do was watch, impotent, as Jean was led away, kicking and struggling.

When the crowd let me pass, I had lost sight of Jean, as well as Charles. Several bystanders told me Jean had been taken to the city prison, which, as I discovered, was a dismal building near the port. Just past its black turrets, I could see the tips of tall masts, and the scent of salt water came in gusts from the sea.

Charles slumped glumly on the steps. The guards on each side of the door didn't even glance at him. They ignored me as well, and I motioned to Charles to follow me. We stood in a nearby alley and spoke in whispers.

"What shall we do?" he asked.

"I was about to ask the same of you. How can we see Jean?"

"We could ask the prefect," he said. "But I think he'll want money."

I darted a glance at the prison. "Let's go find lodgings. Perhaps we can get help there." Before we left, though, I did go to the prefect and ask for the name of a lawyer. I also warned him that Jean was related by marriage to King Louis and that I planned to go to the king's camp and report Jean's arrest.

Jean had doubtless told the same tale. The man listened gravely, gave me the name of a 'fine lawyer, well schooled in defending murders', and told me the faster I saw the king, the better, for Jean's trial was for the morrow. I was taken aback at the pace of justice, but my studies hadn't delved into the intricacies of murder trials. I knew that animals could be tried for murder, but I hadn't known that trial followed arrest so quickly.

My heart pounded painfully in my chest as I nearly dragged Charles through the city looking for a likely inn. Once settled, I sent a message to the lawyer and invited him to meet me for dinner.

The inn was large and expensive. I had wanted something decent, and now with Jean in prison, I needed to impress a lawyer. I wanted him to think we were nobility and therefore try his best. The doubtful looks the innkeeper cast upon Charles and I disappeared when I pulled my purse out. I paid for a week with one of my heavy silver coins. Included in the price of the room were a maid, all the hot water I required for bathing, dinner and breakfast for myself and Charles—my valet, I told the innkeeper—and the services of a messenger. The innkeeper agreed and respectfully asked what else I'd need.

At that time, it was not unusual for a woman to travel alone. The innkeeper showed no surprise and led us to a large room with a four-poster bed, a large fireplace, a chest for clothing, a desk for writing and a straw-stuffed pallet on the floor for my valet. I bid the maid to bring a table and chairs for supper in my room, as well as a hot bath. Soon, to my delight, there was a large tin tub in front of the fireplace. Servants carried buckets of steaming water to the room, and I made Charles wash as well, much to his disgust.

I ran a sponge over my body, used the perfume I'd brought with me, brushed my hair until it shone, and pinned the braids in two rolls over my ears. Luckily for me, the styles of the times were elementary. Women wore dresses that reached their ankles and their hair in braids, tucked into a hair net or pinned to the head. Some wealthy women wore tall, pointed hats with scarves attached, but the TCF hadn't provided me with the trappings of wealth.

I pulled on my baggy stockings and tied them around my waist with the ribbons attached to the tops. Then I put on a fine linen shift with long sleeves. Over that went a sleeveless dress. There were no underwear and no bras. The clothes were made of wool, and, if I hadn't worn my linen shift, would have itched horribly. The TCF had given me clothes that put me in the upper middle class. Nothing too fancy, but everything was good quality and the dress had some embroidery on it. I put my belt on, and I tied a gold ring to a green ribbon, looped it around my neck and hoped the grass stain on my hem wouldn't show in the dim firelight. I scrubbed Charles' face again and told him to act the part of my servant.

"Your servant?" He frowned. Before he could argue further, there came a knock at the door.

"Answer!" I whispered, "And ask who's calling. Then announce him like royalty." I pushed him toward the door with an imperious nod.

"Who's there?" called Charles, shuffling his feet and rolling his eyes at me.

"Monsignor Houdebert, *avocat de la cour*," was the response.

I raised my eyebrows at Charles. "Lawyer for the court?" I mouthed. He shrugged.

I waited until Charles opened the door to my room before standing and offering my hand to be kissed. The lawyer, Monsignor Houdebert, bowed over my hand, kissed the air several inches above it, and smiled without showing his teeth. He wore a short robe made of good quality cloth, dyed deep blue. His belt was leather, set with eagles cut out of shiny brass. His short beard curled around his chin. His eyes were blue-gray and very deep-set under fair brows. His hair was auburn, streaked with gray, and he wore it cut square and just touching his shoulders. It was straight, but he'd crimped it sharply with curling irons at the ends.

"Thank you so much for coming so promptly," I said. "Please be seated. I have taken the liberty of ordering our meal. I hope you appreciate grilled sardines. I was told they had arrived fresh this evening on the fishing boats."

"That will be perfect." He seated himself on a chair and leaned forward upon his cane. I suspected that he carried it more for show than for use, for he was still a man in his prime and without any serious limps I could see. Perhaps it held a hidden weapon to use if set upon by thieves.

I looked at him closely.

He met my gaze seriously, in silence. Finally his wide mouth curled in a smile — the corners had been smiling for quite some time. "Do I meet your expectations, Mistress de Bourbon-Dampierre?"

I blinked, then remembered I'd given Jean's name to the lawyer.

"You are younger than I thought you'd be," I said, feeling flustered.

"I hope that doesn't disappoint you." The dimples at the sides of his mouth deepened.

A knock sounded on the door. "I believe our dinner has arrived," I said. Charles uttered a loud sigh of relief and opened the door to let in our maid, laden with a tray and a pitcher of wine.

The dinner was simple but good. As the cook had assured me, the grilled fish was fresh. There were no vegetables — we ate our fish plain, with bread. Creamy goat's cheese and dried figs were our desert. The wine was not bad at all, a light rosé the lawyer told me was made in the hills behind Marseilles. I let Charles have a glass, and right after dinner he curled up in a corner on my cloak and fell asleep.

Mr. Houdebert and I looked at each other. I poured him more wine, and he sipped it, settling back in his chair and plucking at an imaginary speck of dust on his stockings. "So, your cousin has been arrested for the murder of two men?" His voice rose in question and I nodded.

"That is correct," I said. "Jean is innocent. We were sleeping soundly when the fight broke out. By the time a lantern was lit, one man lay on the ground, dead with a knife in his craw, and the other man was trying to staunch a wound that proved fatal for him."

Mr. Houdebert folded his hands underneath his chin and stared at me. "Why do you suppose that your cousin," he seemed to hesitate slightly, "was accused?"

"I believe it was because the other travelers in our group disliked him. You must realize that he isn't of the same class, and he can be quite arrogant at times. The other voyagers accused him of hoarding money for the trip to Antioch. Jean denied this and cited King Louis' promise to take the crusaders free of charge, but that didn't change their attitude. They argued, and I think they wanted to punish him."

"What more can you tell me about the night of the killings?"

I was glad he'd stopped saying murders. "A woman was involved. I saw her today in the crowd, so she's still with the crusaders. She wouldn't say anything in the barn, but perhaps she was in shock."

"I will speak to her tomorrow," promised Mr. Houdebert. "Right after I've seen to Jean de Bourbon-Dampierre."

"That would be a good place to start." I stood, intending to dismiss him.

"I don't know about that," said Mr. Houdebert. He gave me another one of his appraising glances. "I think the best place to start would be right over there." He indicated the high bed with a small jerk of his chin. "If it pleases you, my lady."

I was stunned, although I tried not to show it. Another particularity of this century, I remembered, was that people didn't think of sex as a sin. On the contrary, they believed that it led to good health. The more the merrier, so to speak. Jean had asked me to marry him, but it had nothing to do with sex. He'd become infatuated, that was all.

Fornication was not only tolerated, it was encouraged. The Church was just flexing the young muscles it would use in another two or three hundred years, culminating with the war between Protestants and Catholics. Right now, the Church and its Inquisition were still fledglings.

The crusades were the first holy wars it had fought, and Church and state, though closely linked, were not yet inextricably united. The Inquisition, an ecclesiastical institution used to suppress heresy, was gaining the power it would wield for the next five hundred years, but its main concern right now, as I learned from Charles, was with the Cathari and with sorcery.

King Louis, later known as "Saint Louis", was the first truly pious French king. The results of his leadership would be spectacular in several ways, provided I could turn Jean on the correct path.

Right now, though, the king was ill with dysentery, cranky with lice and eager to be sailing toward the Holy Land where he would die. He didn't know that, of course. But I did.

*     *     *     *     *

"Your skin is as smooth as the finest silk," murmured Mr. Houdebert. He was a skillful lover, lithe and thoughtful, unhurried and absorbed in his delight.

I arched my back and shivered. It had been so long, so long, and suddenly, in the space of two days, I'd had two lovers. My body ached with pleasure. I caught my breath as he bent over my nipple. A hard throbbing started deep within me and I abandoned myself, my hands holding tightly to Mr. Houdebert's narrow hips.

He chuckled appreciatively and nipped my shoulder, then quickened his movements as his own passion swept over him. The heavy curtains surrounding the bed muffled his groans. I hoped he wouldn't wake Charles because I wasn't up to explaining my method of hiring a lawyer.

Afterwards Mr. Houdebert dressed, bowed over my hand, kissed it firmly this time, then turned it over and kissed the inside of my wrist. He left quietly, drawing the door shut behind him.

Mr. Houdebert! I bit my lip, torn between laughter and tears. What was his first name anyway? Dare I ask? Or would I go through life thinking of that skillful lover as Mr. Houdebert, *"avocat de la cour"*?

Satisfied I'd done everything I could to obtain Jean's freedom, I tugged my covers under my chin and slept deeply.

\* \* \* \* \*

The bells for matins rang through the city and woke everyone with ears.

Charles unrolled himself from my cloak in the corner and yawned. "How did you sleep?" he asked.

I peered at him closely but decided it was an innocent question. "Very well, thank you."

"Mr. Houdebert seemed very proficient," he said.

Thinking about the lawyer brought a furious blush to my cheeks. Instead of responding to his comment about the man, I asked Charles to fetch a servant to draw my bath.

I bathed while Charles devoured breakfast. Then I dressed with care and took one of my gold coins from its hiding place. I showed it to Charles, and luckily he'd finished eating because he nearly choked.

"It's for Jean," I said sternly. "Mr. Houdebert said I'd have to pay for his food in prison and his linen, and I must buy a proper dress in which to go see the king. There will be enough left over to pay the lawyer and bribe a magistrate if things go badly in court."

"I should think so," said Charles, awe in his voice and eyes. "May I touch it?"

# Chapter Five

**ഔ**

Charles and I bought fine robes, one for each of us and one for Jean, still in prison. The magistrate in charge let us bribe him in order that Jean have a good meal, a wash and a chance to put on his new clothes before the audience. Then I hired a man with a white donkey to lead me to the king. It wouldn't impress him if I arrived on foot in the army campground.

His camp was on the road to Aigues-Mortes, about a four-hour ride from the town. There were far too many people with him to lodge in the city, so Aigues-Mortes, a port on the far end of a dead-water bay, was expanded to launch the crusade.

The donkey trotted all the way, and the weather was fair so I made good time. I arrived at noon, just as the king was finishing his second round of prayers for the day. My fears of not being able to approach him were unfounded. He received all visitors according to rank. I was dressed in a good robe, my hair was clean and I must have looked like nobility, for I only had to wait a little while before my name was announced.

King Louis was elderly and frail, and his hands shook as he motioned to me to advance into the cool shade of his blue tent. His eyes, though, were full of kindness. I don't think I ever saw such a compassionate regard. They were blue eyes, pale now and cloudy with age, but lit from within by a munificence that seemed to confer a glow to his whole face.

Once in front of poor, doomed King Louis, I felt very timid. I bowed as was the custom and addressed his feet when I spoke.

"Sire," I said, choosing my words carefully. "Your cousin, the Sire de Bourbon-Dampierre, has asked me to look after his son, Jean. As his guardian, I have followed him on this crusade. He is determined to fight the infidel at your side. Jean is headstrong and brave, but he has gotten into trouble with some scoundrels in Marseilles. He has been unjustly accused of murder and needs your help."

"Ah?" The king raised his eyebrows. "That is a grave accusation. I will write to the magistrate at once. How did Jean come to be in Marseilles?"

"He heard of your new crusade and wanted to join it. His father, your cousin, forbade it, but Jean climbed out the window and ran away. When Sire de Bourbon-Dampierre found out, I was sent after him."

The story brought a smile to the wan face. "It does my heart good to hear of such enthusiasm in a boy," he said. "I'm proud to hear he wants to join my crusade. I will make room for him in my cortege as soon as this unfortunate incident is cleared up. I'll dictate a note for the magistrate, and you can give it to him. Did you appoint a lawyer?"

A tall man seated next to the king wrote the letter. The royal scribe, I surmised, as I noticed his inkwell, parchment and quills. After, he sealed the latter and handed it to a page who then handed it to me with a little bow.

The king sank back into his cushions and waved his thin hand. "Go now, my child, and have no fear for Jean. I shall look forward to seeing you before we leave. We will have a grand adventure and free the Holy Land."

"Amen," I said, my heart sinking. Saving Jean from prison only to have him shipped off on a doomed crusade was not the best of plans, but I could do nothing else.

I mounted my little donkey and the driver took her bridle and led her off again at a smart jog. We were back in Montpellier well before sunset.

* * * * *

I thought my adventures were over for that day, but unfortunately, they were not.

When I entered the prison for the third time, a man claiming to be the magistrate's page led me through a dim hallway to a small room. I should have known better. The man was far too old to be a page.

He didn't waste time. First, he hit me, and then he took advantage of my shock to throw me to the ground. Underwear being nonexistent in those days, it took no more than a second to lift my dress, and he was upon me like a rutting pig.

In my first year of prison I'd been beaten by a sadistic guard. When I'd tried to tell the warden, the beatings grew worse, so I'd learned to close my eyes and wait for it to finish. When this man knocked me down, my first reflex was to submit. I quickly realized I was being raped, so I screamed, earning a cuff on the nose. Apparently my panic excited him for he soon grunted, finished his loathsome business and stood up.

He leered down at me. "If you say a word to anyone, I will personally go into Jean's cell and stab him to death. And no one will be the wiser," he ended with a coarse laugh.

"What about the letter?" I asked in a voice that shook. All I could think of was getting the king's letter to the magistrate. I don't think I fully realized what had happened to me. I still lay on the floor, my face numb where the man struck me and my robe bunched around my waist.

He adjusted his breechcloth and licked his lips. "Don't worry about that. I consider myself well bribed. Don't bother coming back again, unless you'd like another go." With that, he took the letter and left.

I pulled myself to my feet and stood, shaking violently, before I vomited all over the floor.

I was in shock, so I'm not quite sure what I did next. I remember going to the inn and asking for another bath, which made the innkeeper mutter balefully. Then I sat in a large tub of boiling water, but perhaps that part is just wistful imagination.

My face was bruised, my whole body was sore and I couldn't stop trembling.

I crawled into my bed and huddled under the covers. That was where Jean found me after they set him free.

The trial wasn't a trial at all. Jean told me that the king's letter went straight to Maître Houdebert, who presented it to the prefect, who gave an order and Jean was freed within the hour. A very efficient system indeed.

Jean sat on the bed and pulled the covers back. He saw my face and frowned. "What knave hurt you?"

I just stared at him. Shock made speech impossible.

He cursed very fluently, took me in his arms and stroked my hair. "I will kill whoever did that to you."

That jarred me out of my shock. "No, no, please," I cried. I had visions of Jean in prison once more, and the thought of approaching that horrible place again made me shudder. "I fell down the stairs, my robe caught on a...a something. It's nothing, I promise."

"My poor Isobel." His voice was tender again. His hands, caressing my back and my head, strayed toward my bodice and I felt his breathing deepen.

A sort of blind panic took over me then. I can't explain it, but it must have been an aftereffect of the rape in the prison. I screamed and thrashed, pushing him right off the bed. Then I dove under the covers and sobbed so hard I started to choke.

Jean was stunned, though not into immobility. He reached under the covers to drag me out. I wouldn't be comforted, drawing in huge gulps of air and sobbing between each breath. He sent Charles to get some brandy. I also heard the word leeches, but that didn't sink in until I saw the innkeeper's wife standing over me holding a shallow bowl full of black, slimy worms.

"Poor lady, she's in a bad way." She shook her head and clucked. "I wondered about her when she came in near sunset, all bruised and pale. Looked to me she was about to vomit. If she had a bad fall, it's the shock. If it's her liver, the leeches will set her right. Hold her up now and give her a glass of that brandy."

A cup of burning liquid was poured down my throat, then I watched numbly as the innkeeper's wife rolled up my sleeves and applied the leeches.

Voracious creatures, they latched onto my arm and seemed to swell immediately. Though I believed in my twenty-fifth century wisdom that leeches would only hinder my recovery, I hadn't the slightest bit of strength left to protest or struggle. If I'd been in my right mind, I would have screamed, but I'd been beaten into docility long before my voyage through time. Now I simply sat, my arms on pillows in front of me, while the leeches did their work.

They drank their fill and dropped off. The innkeeper's wife plucked them off the covers and plopped them back into a wooden bowl full of water. She waited until they'd all finished, then she dried my arms, wiping off the ribbons of blood. "She'll be fine tomorrow," she said. Then she cocked her head. "The bells will start soon. It's nearly vespers."

Charles heaved a huge sigh, whether of relief or annoyance, I don't know. Then he perched at my side and stroked my cheek. "Are you well now?" he asked.

I nodded. I did feel better. My head felt as if it were full of helium and would float right off my shoulders any second. There was no more blood in my veins. I felt as light and pure as an angel. I smiled. The brandy didn't hurt either. I'd ask for another cup, as soon as I got the power of speech back.

Jean stepped forward, though he didn't get too close. "Was it my fault?" he asked, hesitant. Though the bells pealed outside he made no move to attend vespers.

I shook my head slowly and mouthed the word "no". Then darkness swooped upon me. Drunk, bled to faintness and numb with shock, I slept for two days.

\* \* \* \* \*

When I woke Charles told me, as he helped me to my feet and laced my dress up, that Jean had been to see King Louis and that we all were to accompany the king on his voyage. We would be in the secondary court, not on the same level as the nobles, of course, and we'd pay our own way, which meant buying a tent, bedding and pack animals to carry everything. However, we'd have the protection of the royal guards, and Jean would benefit from that as well. He wouldn't be in the infantry, marching to battle. As part of the court, he'd be expected to stay near King Louis.

I was relieved and terribly worried at the same time. The chances of dragging Jean back to Paris before we embarked for the Holy Land were growing very slim indeed. The future hung from a thread, and I was supposed to make sure nothing changed. That thread grew thinner every day, and worry sometimes gave me blinding headaches.

We spent another two weeks in Montpellier at the inn, and during that time, I didn't see Maître Houdebert again. He wrote me a charming letter and reproached me for not visiting him, *"pour le remercier"*, but I was still in shock and it took days for my bones to stop aching. Of those two weeks, I remember only bits and pieces. My mind took steps to protect itself, protect its ability to function. The same fog had numbed me when I killed that poor child with my car, and still did to an extent.

Jean chafed at waiting. He had grown up in the court and knew the king's youngest son, Jean-Tristan. They hadn't seen each other since they were ten, and Jean was worried that his friend had forgotten him.

"I was ten the last time I saw him," he reminded me for the twelfth time in one day.

I looked up from the game of solitaire I'd been playing and tried to look interested. "I'm sure he hasn't changed much. Now, can we talk about maybe going back to Paris?"

He ignored me about Paris. He usually did. "No, he's changed. He's a knight now, he has his own troop of archers, and he's got a warhorse." His voice cracked and he frowned.

"He hasn't got a wife, though." He brightened, and the look he gave me was downright lascivious.

"Go see him and stop bothering me. I'm sure he remembers you. Didn't you say you both went to Nevers one summer?"

Jean scratched his head, and then looked at his nails. I'd realized not long after I came here that most people did this to check for lice, automatically, like you or I might check for dandruff. He heaved a sigh and nodded. "I'll go today to speak to him. Of course he'll remember me. We were friends, once." Despite the confidence of his tone, his face puckered with worry.

When he left to find Jean-Tristan, I shuffled the hand-painted deck of cards that the TCF had provided for me and tried not to worry. I wanted Jean to find his friend, but I was sure that if he did he'd never return to Paris. He'd want to fight with the prince's regiment. That would be better than if he fought in the rank and file, but I still hoped I could convince him to go home.

He came back that evening glowing. When I saw his face, I knew.

"You saw Jean-Tristan," I said.

"He gave me this!" With a flourish Jean whipped aside his cloak and held out a helmet. A jaunty, red plume waved at me as my heart plummeted to my feet. "I'll even have my own shield. Jean-Tristan has asked his own smith to paint my arms upon it."

I touched the helmet and smiled at Jean. "You want to be a knight, like Jean-Tristan, don't you?"

He nodded, too excited for words. Then he set the helmet carefully on the wooden chest and turned to me. His fingers fumbled my laces and he leaned into me, burying his face in my neck. "He's a knight, but I have this," he whispered hoarsely, and his hands reached into my dress and cupped my breasts.

Jean hesitated. "Are you feeling up to making love to me?" he asked, his expression worried. He hadn't tried since I'd pushed him away. In reply, I pulled him to me and kissed him.

My body tingled with delight as his eager hands undressed me. Jean loved to make love to me whenever he could, and his enthusiasm was contagious. I hugged him to me and gasped as his movements quickened.

"When you become pregnant, then you'll have to marry me," Jean said as we lay side by side on our bed.

"No, Jean, and stop asking me." I frowned. "I hope we don't run into that group of crusaders again."

"Who, the ones that accused me of murder?" Jean nuzzled my neck. "Don't worry about them. Maître Houdebert had them banned from Marseilles. I hear they've left the city."

"That's a relief." My heart had given a little flutter at the mention of my charming lawyer, but Jean's next words chased him out of my head.

"The boats are coming to Aigues Mortes. The king has sent messages to the crusaders to join him there. We'll be leaving tomorrow."

"Are you sure you won't reconsider?" I brushed a lock of hair from his face and looked into his eyes. "Please? Can we forget this and go back to your home in Paris? Your mother misses you."

"Will you marry me then?" he asked, his face suddenly stern.

"Will you go back to Paris if I say yes?"

He thought about it for a minute, then his mouth quirked into a grin. "No, I suppose not. I'd rather go fight with King Louis than get married. Once we return, we'll marry."

"I cannot marry you," I said gently. "You don't understand now, but you will someday." He had to marry someone else, someone who could have children and found a dynasty, but I couldn't tell him that. I knew he wasn't in love with me. If he had been, I was sure he'd have given up his dream about going off to fight a war.

He shrugged and kissed my shoulder. "We'll talk about it later. Right now I have to go get our supplies ready."

\* \* \* \* \*

Finally we joined the huge encampment and marched to Aigues-Mortes. The crowd had grown to such proportions that the road was clogged with traffic. Upon arriving in the bay, every parcel of dry ground was taken up by tents, horses, people or carts. People were even obliged to camp in the marshes, resulting in a plague of illnesses.

Jean, with his usual arrogance and forcefulness, found us a decent spot to set up our tent. It was the first time we'd done this.

Charles and I proved to be totally inept at setting up a tent. I put the stakes in backwards, so that they shot out of the ground at the slightest tug. Charles tangled the lines and managed to poke a hole in the roof with a tent pole. Jean sighed, pushed us out of the way, and soon had our little tent standing jauntily. I unloaded our belongings and Charles took care of the donkey. The tasks were thus distributed — Jean set up the tent, I took care of the baggage and Charles led the little donkey to graze and to water.

Our tent was very nice, except that hole, I guess. It was made of green velvet and the material was thick and well sewn. The tent poles were ash and very straight, and we had an awning that gave us shade. Jean bought a rug for the floor and a small brazier for cooking and for warmth.

We stayed only a short time in Aigues-Mortes. There were too many people there. The grazing land was soon stripped, and the water became rank with waste. As soon as possible the ships were organized and everyone loaded.

My hopes for escorting Jean back to Paris vanished altogether when we stepped onto the ship that would carry us across the Mediterranean Sea. From the upper deck, I watched Aigues-Mortes dwindle in the distance. I trembled in fear. The thread holding onto the future was stretched to the breaking point. We were heading toward certain death, defeat and disaster. How could I save Jean? If I couldn't, erasure would cost me my life and the lives of everyone in this portion of time. My thoughts were in turmoil. The boat plunged into a trough, rose with its bow toward sky, plunged again, veered, rocked, and half the voyagers rushed for the sides.

I stood a moment longer and felt the wind whip my robe, tease my hair out of its braids and shred the last of my hopes for a successful mission. I turned my face to the sun and decided to face my own future with courage. Then the boat plunged again, and I too rushed to the side and lost my breakfast.

By dinnertime, I was ready to die. I considered throwing myself right off the boat. The deep blue swells looked more inviting than the rough wooden planks of our cramped quarters. But Jean kept me inside the cabin and wouldn't let me commit suicide.

"You'll feel better in a few days," he said sympathetically, while I retched miserably into a wooden bowl. He handed the bowl to Charles and waved him away.

Charles gave him a look that would have singed Jean's hair, had he noticed, but he took the bowl and emptied it anyway. He'd been busy doing that all day.

"Have another salt cracker," Jean said.

"You're a loathsome sadist," I said, when I could unclench my teeth.

"What's a sadist?" asked Jean, though he didn't bother to listen for an answer.

I remembered belatedly that the Marquis de Sade hadn't been born yet, but I also recalled Jean hated Latin studies. "It's a Latin word," I said. "Didn't you learn it?"

"I despised Latin," he said. "The sailors told me you'd be better after a good night's sleep, and they said to eat a cracker after every bout of sickness. Have some water now and then try to sleep. It's dark now."

"How can you tell if it's dark? There's no window here. It's always dark, from what I can see," I answered peevishly. Jean just shrugged, too excited to be on a boat bound for the Holy

Land to notice my ill temper. He'd much rather be on deck getting in the way than attending to me, but the exasperated sailors had ordered everyone below. So I ate the cracker, drank the water and was ill once more.

To take my mind off my seasickness, I thought about King Louis. In the eyes of the king and the rest of the court traveling with him I was Jean's legal wife. There was nothing odd about that because most people married very young, and I supposed I looked young to them, with my clear skin and fair hair.

Too, there was the fact that Jean had introduced me as his wife, which left me gaping longer than I would have liked. The king thought I was a "charming" and devoted wife to have come to see him while Jean was locked in prison. He paid me several very flattering compliments, waved his royal hand and I was led away.

Later, when I asked Jean what in heaven's name he was thinking, he merely grinned.

"I have decided to make you my wife," he said. "For one thing, it will make my father absolutely furious. You did say he wanted to kill you, didn't you?"

I gritted my teeth. "I prefer a more romantic reason to marry someone."

"Well, I'm sure we'll find one," he replied, with a cheerful leer.

We shared a tiny, cramped room in the pitching boat. Charles slept on the floor, and Jean and I huddled on a narrow cot that folded down on leather hinges.

I was sick for a day, but as Jean had predicted, I felt much better when I woke up. This lasted until I found out there was no fresh water for bathing, brushing my teeth or washing my clothes until we arrived in Sardinia, our first stop. We had to wash in salt water, our clothes were rinsed in salt water and salt permeated everything on the boat, even our skin, with a fine, silver dust.

Jean and I sailed with the secondary nobles. It was fitting, Jean explained, that we shouldn't be with the villains. First came the king's boat, and nobles took up the next fifteen boats. Jean would have preferred to be with his friend, Jean-Tristan, but he was in a separate ship with his troops. Soldiers and archers piled into twelve other boats, ten boats carried supplies, although I knew from my research they would prove woefully inadequate, and there were even boats full of curious fishermen, sailing alongside for a while.

The rest of the crusaders—the commoners and probably the group we'd traveled with, if they hadn't been sold into slavery—were packed in thirteen other boats. We spread out upon the ocean, not so close as to bump into one another, and made our way the best we could.

Caravels with deep keels and swinging booms hadn't been invented yet. The boats in the thirteenth century were wide, had very short keels and rolled like corks on the sea. Their sails were square, like the ancient Viking ships, and I wondered at times if our prayers were what kept us afloat. We were at the mercy of the wind, and when it blew contrarily the sails were lowered and the anchors thrown out to stop us from being blown right back to France.

Only two days after we'd set sail, two storms rushed across the water, sweeping over our flotilla and sinking three of the boats carrying our fresh water. Another boat, loaded with horses, sank right after a storm. The sailors were picked up and loaded onto another boat, but not the horses. I watched, horrified, as the poor creatures thrashed out of the debris and then swam after the boats, whinnying pitifully. They could swim nearly as fast as the boats sailed, and being strong swimmers, they followed us for hours. One by one, though, they grew exhausted and drowned. Their plaintive neighs echoed in my ears for days.

The storms were brief but violent. After each one, the sun came out and scorched us. We would make our way to the deck and search for the king's ship then the others. Our mouths moved as we counted silently to see how many had been lost.

After eight days of this sort of "two steps forward one step back" movement across the water, we arrived in Cagliari in Sardinia, our first stop.

The boat docked, and we all got down on our knees and gave thanks. The prayer went on and on, but for once I fervently agreed with everything the priest said.

We were the eighth boat to arrive. Next came the knights and their horses, loaded on boats that smelled like manure. The villains arrived the next day, and the king anxiously scrutinized the horizon for his best archers, all on another boat.

I thought the old adage "never put your eggs in one basket" could be changed to accommodate archers and a boat, but they all arrived safely after two days. Twelve other boats sailed into the harbor, ten with infantry and the others loaded with more rag-tag villains and crusaders. Everyone fell to their knees as soon as they reached dry land, then fetched their belongings and merged into the squalor that was the encampment.

The natives didn't appreciate our coming. They retreated into a large fortress a few kilometers away and refused to sell us any fresh produce. Or if they did consent to sell, it was at prices so outrageous it made everyone complain bitterly.

There were several distinct camps set up on shore. One consisted of the nobles and the king, one held the soldiers, one held the noble soldiers, and one was made up of the crusaders. The latter were the noisiest bunch and the least well prepared. Whole families had joined the crusade and children played around the docks, scrambled underfoot, fell into the water and generally got in the way.

One afternoon I sat on the docks and pulled three children out of the shallow water myself. Though it wasn't calm by any means, it was more orderly on the docks than in the camp or the village. Out on the docks it was easier to stay out of the way of archers practicing their archery, knights exercising their chargers and messengers running between the various parts of the encampment. Add to this the general hustle bustle of merchants hawking their exorbitant wares and natives come to gawk at the crusaders and you get a general idea of what the crusaders' encampment was like.

I was exhausted by the voyage and dreaded another week at sea. Jean, however, practiced fencing nearly every day with Jean-Tristan, and Charles slipped like a shadow everywhere, listening to every conversation he possibly could.

We set up our tent just on the outskirts of the king's camp. Charles was now our unofficial page and he gloried in his newfound prestige. He had a role to play and he puffed his chest out and followed Jean whenever he went to the court. I thought he would be no trouble, as he was a bright lad. Then I caught him playing dice with another page. Though playing cards and dice were tolerated, gambling wasn't, and the priests stalking about the camp were very strict. To most, the crusades were a holy endeavor and sin would certainly doom them. The priests punished anyone caught sinning in public in a terribly painful fashion. The Inquisition was starting to rear its ugly head.

"Charles, I would never, ever forgive you if you're caught gambling and the priests cut off one of your hands," I told him. He glared sullenly at the ground and rubbed his ear where I'd boxed it.

"You didn't have to swoop down on me like a madwoman. You scared me out of my wits," he said.

"I hope so. Imagine you'd been caught by one of the fanatics? You'd be in the infirmary right now, minus one hand. Don't be foolish, Charles. I won't have it. Either you promise never to play dice or cards again, or I'll sell you to the first slave dealer I find in Damiette."

"You wouldn't!" he gasped.

"Try and see," I hissed. "Now go outside and fetch me a bucket of hot water."

"You just took a bath yesterday!"

I eyed him. "And when did you last take one?"

He looked horrified. "Before we left Aigues-Mortes. Don't you remember?"

"Make that two buckets." I wrinkled my nose. "We'll have to wash your hose as well. It looks as if you sat in a pile of manure."

"It was the only place we thought we'd be left alone to gamble," he replied.

I shot him another angry glance and he left, dragging two buckets after him, his shoulders slumped and his head bowed. As soon as he thought he was out of sight he tossed the buckets into the air, caught them and trotted off toward the kitchens where huge caldrons of water were always heating.

"You were far too lenient," said Jean. His voice came from the shadows of our tent where he reclined out of the hot glare of the sun.

"You would have cut his hand off right away, I suppose," I said dryly.

"Come here." He patted the bed beside him. We'd been lying there all morning, except when I'd gone off in search of Charles.

"I want to bathe first," I said, stretching my arms above my head.

"I'll help you undress." His eyes gleamed in the darkness. The tent cloth was so thick only tiny pinpricks of light filtered through the roof.

I laughed softly. He was insatiable. With the normal, healthy appetite of a sixteen-year-old, he made love to me two or three times a day. Whenever he could and even some times when he ought not, he slid his hands beneath my shift to fondle me, his green eyes darkening.

He caught me by the hand and pulled me down on top of him. "I wonder why I never thought of getting married before. This is the best sport in the world."

I nibbled his earlobe. "If you get hit by an arrow or stabbed, you'll lose your health and your ability to make love. Wouldn't it be better simply to go back home?"

"Will you marry me then?" he asked. His voice grew husky as he pushed my dress up over my head.

I shook my head. "I'll never marry you, Jean, but I'll always be your lover." I sighed as he ran his hands over my rib cage, his fingers splayed, and caught my breasts in his palms.

"But why?" He bent his head to take a nipple in his mouth. He tugged it, sending delicious shocks of pleasure through my body.

I arched against him, unable to resist his ardent passion. He was so urgent, so eager. He hadn't learned to be subtle. With a fierce cry, he threw himself onto me, thrusting, holding me tightly to his chest. I wrapped my legs around his slim hips and drew him into me, as eager as he was. His body was finely drawn and made to give pleasure. We bucked against each other, shivering as the delight seized us. Our hearts hammered madly in our chests and our hands entwined. There was a moment when there was no sound, when there was sort of shock in the air. It crystallized around us, locking us together, and then it shook us apart.

When I regained my breath and opened my eyes, Jean was staring at the tent ceiling, his eyes cloudy. "Why won't you marry me?" he asked.

"I can't," I said softly. "It doesn't matter, anyway. We can stay together as long as you like, and when you fall in love with another girl you can get married."

"I'm in love with you," he said.

"No, you're not. You're in love with making love. It's normal." I tried to keep my voice light as I rolled over and groped for my robe. "Charles will be back any minute."

"I do love you, Isobel," Jean insisted. His voice wavered a little. "Please tell me why you won't marry me."

"Please don't ask me anymore," I said. "It tires me to repeat the same thing over and over. What difference does it make? We're together, and that's all that matters for now."

"Is it because of my father? I know you owe him a favor, but you kept your promise. You found me."

"I swore to bring you home," I said.

"I'll go back. I swear by all that's holy, and on King Louis' head, I swear to return."

"Shhh!" I sat up, furious. "Don't say that!"

"Don't say what?" He raised his eyebrows. "I made a pledge. That should make you happy."

I slumped back onto the bed, my head aching. "It's nothing. A premonition, I told you before. King Louis isn't going home. This whole crusade is doomed."

"You could be burned if anyone heard you saying that." Jean put his hand on my lips, then leaned over and kissed them. "Your lips are like rose petals, and your skin as soft as the finest silk." His voice caught in his throat. "You're an angel cast out of heaven for some misdeed, and I found you. You're my seraph. I will marry you, Isobel."

"I'm no angel, and there's no future for us," I said sadly.

# Chapter Six

🔊

In the evenings, after eating whatever we scrounged up, we'd sit just outside our tent, and I would tell a story. Charles would lie on his back, his head on his arms, and listen without a word. Jean interrupted the most. He had to know every detail about every character in the tale. When I told the story of Cinderella he wanted to know what the father had done for a living, how old the wicked stepmother was and how ugly, exactly, the stepsisters were. Then he listened skeptically to the part where the fairy godmother changed Cinderella into the belle of the ball.

"I don't see how she could do that," he said with a shake of his head.

"Do what?" I'd gotten to the part where Cinderella was admiring her glass slippers.

"Change a pumpkin into a coach. It wouldn't work at all. You could hollow it out—we do it all the time on All Hallow's Eve—but you couldn't affix wheels to it, and a woman could hardly sit in it." He snorted.

"It's a fairy tale," I said, exasperated. "Haven't you ever heard one before?"

"No, and I prefer the story of King Arthur."

"Let her finish." Charles plucked at my sleeve. "What happens next to Cinderella?"

"The prince sees her, falls in love and asks her why her robe is covered with pumpkin," said Jean.

I bit my lip to keep from laughing. "Well, more or less. Perhaps those stories are too childish for you, Jean. Didn't you study the Greek myths in school?"

"Only the Roman versions and even those our teachers told us were abridged. Mostly we recited Latin verbs and practiced rhetoric."

"That must have been interesting," I said.

"You're joking, of course." Jean pulled a sour face. "We also had to do math, and I hated math. We studied French poetry, Latin and some Greek. My favorite lessons were the natural sciences, studies of beetles and birds, and astronomy. Our tutor was only interesting when he spoke about the stars," he said, pointing upwards.

"I never leaned to read or write," said Charles suddenly.

We both left off admiring the sky and stared at Charles instead.

"I want to learn," he said.

Jean laughed. "A villain learning to read? Now I've heard everything. I suppose you'd like to study Latin and science as well?"

"And math and Greek." Charles nodded. "That would be wonderful. You have no idea how lucky you are, my lord."

I opened my mouth, and then shut it. Jean looked at Charles as if he'd suddenly sprouted horns. Charles' chin was propped on his knees and he gazed out over the camp, his eyes very big in his face, and very sad.

What would it hurt? I thought. Charles surely wouldn't change the timeline. "If you want, I can teach you a little," I said.

"You can read and write?" Now Jean stared at me instead.

"Of course." I frowned, and a thought crossed my mind. "Don't you know any women who can read or write?"

"Yes, of course I do. Noblewomen are educated, of course. You must be noble." He cocked his head, considering. "I wondered about that. Was your family in disgrace? Was that why you were forced out into the streets?"

"Noble? Me? Don't be absurd." I squinted out at the camp and changed the subject. "Tell me again what the council is discussing," I said to Charles.

He listened to every bit of gossip, and he loved to tell us about it. "They're trying to decide when to leave," he said. "The king waits for his brother, but most people think we'd better press on now. The natives are unhappy with our presence and would have us depart. The King of Tunis, so they say, is eager to become a Christian. He would welcome King Louis, in return for a baptism.

"From what I heard, I think we'll sail directly to Tunis. The king's counselors also say that if the King of Tunis proves to be obstinately heathen, there are treasures untold to plunder in his city. They say he's in the habit of furnishing the sultan of Egypt in his wars with the Christians."

"Oh," I said, looking askance at Jean. "That's not very fair, is it?"

"What?"

"Attacking someone if they don't prove to be as tractable as you thought."

Jean shrugged. "It's war."

"I don't approve of war," I said.

Charles gave a little laugh. "You don't approve of many things, Dame Isobel." He'd taken to calling me Dame, playing along with Jean's charade of our marriage.

"What do you mean?" I asked.

He cocked his head. "You don't realize it, but you're always criticizing everything. You complained about the boats, the crowds, the soldiers and their arms, the knights, the diplomats and even King Louis. What, if anything, pleases you? Will you tell us?"

I drew my knees up, imitating Charles, and put my chin on them. I suspect my eyes were sad as well, because suddenly I felt the crushing weight of the future upon me. "I like the king. I think he's a wonderful person. He's kind, and truly good. He has no business making war. His heart isn't in it, even I can tell."

"The Marmaluks have gained too much ground in the Holy Land. We must reclaim what's ours by holy right." Jean spoke with all the misguided fervor of a crusader.

I opened my mouth to say just that, but snapped it shut. Who was I, after all, to condemn? What was happening had already happened, and nothing could change the outcome. Fate had already decided who would win and who would perish. I only hoped that Jean would be spared, because of all the people on the crusade, only he, and I, of course, were out of place. Everything we did, no matter how unimportant, could have huge repercussions in the future. I was walking a razor-thin line, and it exhausted me.

I closed my eyes and leaned against Jean's arm. After a minute, he hugged me close. His body was warm, and I molded myself to him. In the distance, an argument rose over the murmur of the crowd. The bickering was soon hushed, and laughter took its place. I could also hear the steady slap of waves against the boat, thuds from the horses' hooves, muffled cursing and the whisper of a breeze in the rigging. Fatigue claimed me, and I fell asleep, the sounds of the night all around me.

\* \* \* \* \*

We left soon afterwards. The council had decided we'd sail directly to Tunis, and for once the winds were clement and blew us across the sea in two days.

Arriving at the coast, the king sent the admiral of his fleet with three ships to reconnoiter for a landing. We waited, hanging over the railing, watching the shoals of silver fish darting in and out of our ship's shadow.

"Look at that one," said Charles, pointing. "It's the biggest one yet."

"No, that one is," said Jean, pointing at another. The shifting water was making me giddy, so I lifted my head and peered toward land.

I noticed sails and shaded my eyes to see past the dazzle on the water. "The admiral is heading back," I said, "and he seems to have another boat in tow."

"Diplomats, do you think?" Jean squinted at the growing sail on the horizon.

We were anchored not far from the king's own boat, and I could clearly hear the voices carry across the water. When the admiral's ship approached, he hailed the king and presented his trophy. I heard this because my keen ears picked up the voices floating over the water.

I choked, and then giggled nervously when Jean asked me what I'd heard. "Is it a diplomat from Tunis, come to welcome us to land?"

"No," I said, trying to steady my voice. "The idiot's gone and captured a merchant ship. He's begging the king for reinforcements, as there are three other ships being held captive by his second ship in a cove nearby."

"He's rather exceeded his instructions for reconnoitering, hasn't he?" Charles gave me a wink.

I frowned. "Silly fool," I said. "No, not you. That's what Louis just said to his own admiral." I cupped my hands around my ears and leaned forward to pick up the king's comments to his son, Prince Philip, standing by his side. "He's telling Philip that he's going to anchor here while we wait to see what the Tunisians will do."

"What would you do if you were the King of Tunis?" asked Charles, his eyes wide.

"What I would do would be totally impossible at this time and age." I turned to look at Jean. "But I think you'll get your wish to fight. The king has arrived in Tunis and has declared war as surely as if he'd fired a crossbow."

Jean looked both pleased and worried and excused himself to go see to his armor.

Charles pursed his lips. "Silly fool, he said that?"

"That's just what he said," I replied. I sat in a patch of shade and scratched my head. "Damn lice."

We were anchored in the mouth of a wide harbor, out of reach of any crossbow shots. The weather was infernally hot, it was the twentieth of July, the year 1270, and half the sixty thousand people in the king's fleet would be dead in less than a month.

* * * * *

The next morning I woke to the sound of wailing trumpets.

The noise had insinuated itself into my sleep and taken over my dream, twisting it into a nightmare where a child screamed and screamed without drawing a single breath.

I sat bolt upright, my chest heaving in fright. The noise didn't abate with my awakening. Rather, it grew more insistent. I flung off my light covers, snatched my grubby dress from the peg on the wall and stepped over Charles' small form on the way out the door. The ceiling was so low I bent over double, and as I climbed the narrow ladder leading to the deck I felt like I was climbing out of a dark well. Below deck there were no lamps, no windows and no air. I was gasping when I made it to the top.

Jean was already perched on the railing, his feet drumming excitedly on the wood, his eyes glowing. "Look!" he cried, pointing toward shore. "The Saracens have arrived!"

In the indistinct light of dawn, I could make out a huge crowd of men and horses milling on the beach. I looked to the right. Another small army was now camped on the bluff overlooking the harbor. On the left, tents scattered across the land, and I could clearly see the glitter of light on the metal spearheads.

My head swam and I gripped the wooden railing until splinters dug into my palms. Unexpectedly, my stomach heaved, and I retched over the side of the boat.

"Are you all right?" Jean hopped off his perch and put his arm over my shoulders.

"It's just nerves." I wiped my mouth with a shaking hand. A shiver of fatigue washed through me, so I sat down on the deck.

"There's a whole shipload of sick people," said Jean conversationally. "They've all got swamp fever."

"Oh great," I said. "Malaria. That's just what we need. I suppose King Louis is going to attack the Saracens?"

"He's planning to do that, yes." Jean's face fell. "Our ship won't be fighting, though. We're going to retreat a ways back and keep the king's ship covered."

"That sounds like a sensible idea, don't you think?"

"The knights have been getting ready. I can hear the clanging of metal armor coming over the water. The sound carries well in the early morning. The horses have been kicking the sides of the boats, too."

The noise of iron-shod hooves striking the wooden planks was distinct. The knights must be the first ones off. The ship crews maneuvered the boats backwards, toward the beach, protected from arrows by large wooden panels. The boats carrying the mounted soldiers were simply hollow vessels, with two enormous gangplanks that the horses surged out of in a tight group. There were thirteen of these boats, one having sunk on the way to Sardinia.

Our fleet boasted ten of another boat designed for the archers, with towers and shields. These, including the king's own archers on their own special boat, would cover the flanks. The ships holding foot soldiers bobbed around the edges of the battle, searching for an opening.

The full force of the king's army landed that afternoon and drove the Saracens out of the harbor without much trouble. The knights galloped their heavy chargers out of the bowels of the ships onto dry land, the archers rained arrows on the hillside and the foot soldiers charged gamely up the beach.

The Saracens retreated toward Carthage, their fiery horses galloping with their tails held high in the air like flowing flags.

Jean, Charles and I cheered. "What happens next?" asked Charles, his face pink with excitement.

"We set up camp." Jean sounded morose, disappointed to have missed action.

"There will be other battles," I said, just as gloomily.

"We'd best get our things in order if we're leaving the ship," said Charles, ever practical.

I looked out over the water, toward the king's ship floating so close to ours. All the flags waved jauntily in the hot breeze, and the king sat under his awning and waved his thin, white hand at the soldiers on shore. His face was serene, joyful with the painless victory. However, it wasn't a victory, really. The Saracens had simply wanted to see exactly what kind of an army the French king had brought. Now they knew.

\* \* \* \* \*

Two days after we'd arrived in Tunis, we left the boats at last. Everyone set up camp on a swampy island just off the shore. There was no fresh water and no grazing land. We were miserable, the weather was hot, there were swarms of blood-sucking insects and an alarming number of people were falling ill with malaria and dysentery.

After three days of planning, the king's forces attacked the fortress of Carthage. They were aided by five hundred longbowmen and four battalions of foreign knights who sailed into the harbor from the kingdom of Naples. Even the sailors armed themselves and went to do battle.

I watched black smoke rise from behind the fortress and shook my head. "They shouldn't have burned the wheat fields. Now we'll have nothing to eat if we stay for a while."

"The king of Tunis will capitulate, and then we'll trade and have plenty," said Jean. "Does this seem too tight?"

I tugged at a string holding his breastplate in place and shook my head. "No, and don't forget your helmet."

"I won't." His green eyes glittered. "It's such an honor that Jean-Tristan asked me to accompany him."

My first misgivings overcome, I had to admit I preferred knowing he was with the king's own son, thus heavily guarded and on horseback, rather than on foot and surrounded by itchy-fingered archers. Jean-Tristan had sent him a shield, and to Jean's immense delight, some armor that fit him nearly perfectly.

I sighed. "Be careful, all the same."

"I will." He leaned forward and gave me a kiss.

I held him tightly, wincing at the contact of hard metal. Besides the breastplate, he wore a belt with flat, metal tongues hanging down from it, metal thigh guards, and a length of chain mail around his throat. I thought he looked very dashing, and told him so. He turned crimson with pleasure and adjusted his helmet on his head.

"What is that?" I pointed toward the top of the helmet where a scrap of familiar-looking cloth was tied.

His voice, coming from the depths of the helmet, was muffled. "It's your garter, my lady. I took it as my token."

I was speechless, but Charles uttered a stifled shriek of laughter before darting out of the tent and out of Jean's way.

A groom led his pony up. A stocky, bay animal with soft brown eyes and a black mane and tail, he wasn't as big as the warhorses, but Jean didn't have a full suit of armor on. The horse was a cob, actually, but Jean was too thrilled that he was actually going to battle to care.

He pointed toward the smoke. "Look over there. The crossbowmen have taken position!"

"Where will you be?" I asked, one hand on the pony's reins, the other on Jean's knee.

"Look for the flag belonging to the count of Nevers," Jean said. "Now let me go, woman, I'm off to war."

"You must have been waiting for weeks to say that, my lord," I teased, though my heart wasn't in it.

Jean grinned. "More than weeks. All my life, my lady." He nodded once, making my garter flap, and then cantered off to join his battalion.

Charles and I made our way to the group of noblewomen, children, ladies-in-waiting and pages. It was the first time I'd had contact with these women, our boat being one of the few with no family groups.

In the very center of the crowd was the young princess, Isabella of Aragon, wife of Prince Philip. She was dressed in fine robes, with a long gold chain wrapped around her slender neck. She couldn't have been more than twenty-five or so, with skin the color the French called bisque and very dark brown hair. Her eyebrows nearly met in the middle, which at that time was considered a sign of beauty.

I had yet to see Prince Philip closely. From a distance, he was of above average height with dark blond hair and his father's rangy build. He was hardly ever with his wife since he was in charge of his own cavalry and group of knights. I'm sure Jean would have given away everything he held dear to be a part of that group.

The crowd around the princess consisted of no less than twelve handmaidens, although most could be called matrons. She had a jester, three jugglers, a Spanish midget and five pages. Most of the pages and ladies-in-waiting lay on pallets. When I got closer, I saw they were drenched with sweat and flushed with fever, and several doctors hovered around, peering into eyes and whispering together. Malaria.

A large awning sheltered the princess and her retinue as well as the rest of the noblewomen and children. Though we too found space underneath, its shade was scant comfort from the sweltering heat. Charles and I watched some people playing cards or dice, although most just sat and bit fingernails or scratched lice.

We were on the outskirts of the crowd, as befitted my dubious rank. Jean might claim to be married to me, but to most people I was on the same level as a courtesan. In a sense, I suppose that's what I was.

Proof of that came when a page from the princess asked if I knew any songs or stories to while away the time. Many courtesans at that time were schooled in the art of entertainment and could play a lute or recite poetry in a pleasing voice. Noblewomen could as well, but they weren't expected to perform. As I didn't have a title and my family was unknown, it was normal I was thought a courtesan. It wasn't an insult, so I wasn't offended.

I stood up and curtsied. I had studied a bit of court etiquette, after all, and cleared my throat. "I shall recite a poem, if that pleases your majesty."

"It does." She inclined her head. "We adore verses."

I nodded and a bit nervously, I admit, began one of the many poems I'd learned in prison. It was by a poet called Rutebeuf, who had lived about fifty years before, and I expected that the company would have heard of him.

"*La Complainte par Rutebeuf.*
*Les maux ne savent seuls venir:*
*Tous ce qui m'était à venir*
*Est advenu.*
*Que sont mes amis devenus*
*Que j'avais de si près tenus*
*Et tant aimés?*
*Je crois qu'ils sont trop clair semés:*
*Ils ne furent pas bien fumés,*
*Si m'ont failli,*

*Ces amis-là m'ont bien trahi,*
*Car, tant que Dieu m'a assailli*
*En maint côté,*
*N'en vis un seul en mon logis:*
*Le vent, je crois, les m'es ôtés.*
*L'amour est morte:*
*Ce sont amis que vent emporte,*
*Et il ventait devant ma porte:*
*Les emporta."**

*\*Misfortune never comes alone:*
*And troubles of my own*
*Beset me, as they know how.*
*Where are all my friends now?*
*Those whom I thought mattered,*
*Have simply scattered.*
*I think they were too fey*
*And didn't want to stay,*
*If they have dismayed me,*
*They have betrayed me.*
*For as God has beset me with*
*Ills from every side,*
*None came to my aid:*
*The wind, I think, mislaid*
*Them. Love is gone:*
*My friends took it along,*
*The wind whistled at my door:*
*And called them away evermore.*
*By Rutebeuf 1225?-1285?*

When I was finished, there was an uneasy silence, made even heavier by the suffocating heat. The princess shifted on her chair, then smiled and said, "Had we known you were so melancholy by nature, we would have insisted upon a song! Nevertheless, it was a pretty piece, and well recited. In truth, I feel it quite apt for these circumstances, for aren't we all alone when misfortune befalls us? Let us hope that our friends have more courage than the poor poet's friends did. Thank you, Dame de Bourbon-Dampierre, for that is your name, is it not?"

Her voice musical, she spoke with the accent of her native Spain. She had a lovely smile, with one tooth charmingly crossed over the other in front.

"That is my name, yes, but my first name is Isobel."

"The same as my own!" she cried, and clapped her hands. "Come closer to me, so that I may see you better. My eyes are not strong and I fear you are rather a blur."

I was escorted to her chair, and I curtsied again. Charles' lessons on how to curtsy must have been more successful than I thought because the myopic princess complimented me upon my grace. Then she inquired after my young husband. Perhaps she didn't put much as emphasis on the word "young" as I thought, but I blushed. It was a source of embarrassment for me. I still couldn't believe Jean was my lover. He was thirteen years my junior and he exasperated me, especially at times like this, when I had to pretend he was my husband.

"He is fighting alongside the count of Nevers," I said.

"My dear brother-in-law, Jean-Tristan, speaks often of your husband," said the princess, squinting at me. "What a frightful scar you have. What happened to you?"

"I fell through a window when I was a child." I repeated the story I'd made up.

"Your face is as smooth as an angel's, otherwise," said the princess. She turned to the lady-in-waiting at her side. "Doesn't she look like one of the angels carved from marble in our palace chapel? The one with the crack right through its face. It's uncanny, the resemblance. I think you will bring us luck. I will call you Isobel, our melancholy angel. Will you stay by my side today and take my mind off the battle? The heat is so terrible, I can't imagine what our dear husbands must be suffering inside their armor."

"Of course, your majesty." I couldn't bear to think about it either. The sun reverberated off the water, scorching the boats docked behind us. I could smell the overheated wood, the linen sails and the bittersweet scent of tar and pitch. Underneath it all there was a heavy, cloying odor of sweat and feces that we'd never escape as long as we stayed grouped in such a small space.

I'd gone from the cold of spring to the heat of the African summer in the five short months I'd been in this time. Nowhere had I found the least bit of comfort except in the soft bed in the inn at Marseilles, in the arms of Maître Houdebert. I felt my cheeks turn scarlet and I looked down at my feet.

"Don't worry, my melancholy angel, I'm sure your young husband will come back tonight, victorious." The princess smiled at my distress, thankfully not divining its source.

I blinked back tears of self-pity and returned her kind smile. "I pray that the fortress will have more shade than this swampy island."

"If we win we will find out," she replied. "What games do you know?"

"Do you have any cards?" I asked. If we were going to be here all day, at least I knew how to play tarot, a card game popular at that time.

We played tarot all afternoon, though wilting with heat, our hands slipping with sweat on the cards. Stinging drops of perspiration ran down our temples and necks, and everyone's face was crimson.

Two ladies-in-waiting and one page played with us to make a game of five. Three other ladies-in-waiting tried to cool us with large fans made from hundreds of tiny blue feathers.

The air felt good, though it stirred up the odors, and twice I had to excuse myself and go be sick.

I leaned against the wooden planks set up to hide the septic fosse from sight of the court. Shivers ran up and down my back. The smells were making me ill, I was sure. Nothing could have prepared my nose for the rank scent of a thousand people who rarely bathed and all used the same toilet facilities—an open pit dug in the marshy ground. I leaned over it and retched again. Then I walked to the seashore and splashed water on my face. Overhead, gulls screamed, attracted by the offal and garbage. In the sea dark fins often surged out of the oily water, proving that sharks also appreciated the wastes that the sailors tossed overboard.

I didn't wade for long. Though the odor here was less intense and the water felt good on my feet, the sun beat mercilessly upon my head. As soon as I'd rinsed my mouth with saltwater and combed my hair with wet fingers, I made my way back to the awning.

Charles tugged at my sleeve. "Are you all right?"

"Yes," I sighed. "It's just so hot, don't you think?"

"I'm thirsty," he said, "but there's no more fresh water. I looked in the barrels, and their bottoms are all dry."

"Tonight we'll have some," I said, with more reassurance than I felt.

"The princess is waiting for you to finish the game." He looked up at me a bit shyly. "She seems to appreciate your company."

"Shall I introduce you?"

"No, I'll stay here." Charles had joined a group consisting of the pages of lesser noblewomen. In the middle of a grass mat, I caught sight of white bones, the knucklebones that they used to play dice.

"Don't get caught," I said.

Charles shrugged. "It's too hot for the priests to go walking around with their black cloaks, and the guards are all off fighting."

When I returned to my seat the princess leaned forward, touched my arm and asked me, "Is this your first pregnancy?"

I didn't think I'd heard her correctly, so I said, "Excuse me?"

"You're pregnant. I know the signs because I've had four children already."

I gaped at her, at a loss for words. Finally, I managed to choke out, "Pregnant?"

"Well, yes, of course. Don't you recognize the symptoms?"

"Symptoms?" I was too shocked to do anything but repeat what she was saying.

"You're nauseous, and I see you wince when your arm brushes against your breasts, as if they hurt. Your skin is very pale, yet you have that look pregnant women get, a sort of glow. How far gone are you? Not three months, I suppose, for you're still very slender."

My hands were shaking so badly I dropped my cards. The princess picked them up, clucking in pity. "Look at all these trumps, and the twenty-one as well! You could have bid a guard easily."

"I didn't have any kings." I stared at my hands. Sore breasts, I thought. They had been horribly tender lately, but that didn't mean anything. I wasn't pregnant. The TCF doctors had taken care of everything, or so they'd said. It was ludicrous.

"But you had four dames, three knights and one valet," said the princess, counting on her fingers. "That makes twenty-six points, plus the twenty-one that makes five more. Thirty-one points all together. What a splendid hand! Good thing you dropped it; I would have bid against you. I had the one, the excuse, and all the kings." Her voice was light.

"That would have been poor judgment," I said, mindless of the shocked looks I got from the ladies-in-waiting. "You had to pass. If you had all the kings, I would have called you and we would have played together. It only makes sense." I hardly knew what I was saying.

"Of course, how silly of me! Do you want my physician to look after your pregnancy? He's an Arab, and quite proficient. I'll tell you a secret as well." She leaned over and whispered loudly. "I'm pregnant too! Isn't that wonderful? Two months gone and terribly sick in the morning. My nausea gets better in the afternoon, though, unlike you. You're sick all day long, aren't you?"

I nodded. "I'm not pregnant," I said, my voice cracking a bit. "It's impossible, I assure you, it's quite impossible."

# Chapter Seven

**ɛ๑**

"Eight to ten weeks pregnant," said the physician. He sat back on his heels and smiled at me in satisfaction. "I'm never wrong."

I stared at him in shock. "It's impossible."

Jean poked his head into the tent and asked, "Well?"

"Two months pregnant," said the doctor, his narrow, dark face split in a large smile. He had perfect, white teeth. He patted my belly. The Church had yet to make it sinful for a woman to be touched by a man, so doctors were allowed to assist in childbirth. As many of the doctors in that time were Arab, and very well educated, medicine was practiced the way the ancients had practiced it. The dark ages had yet to make science obsolete, and medicine was still an art. The man in front of me had studied in Alexandria, had lived and worked in Paris, and had traveled to the Byzantine Empire to learn the different techniques of the Far East. If he said I was pregnant, chances were, he was right.

"Two months?" Jean grinned. "It must have been when we were in the cave, on the way to Montpellier." His face glowed so brightly it seemed to light up the entire tent. "How wonderful! I shall send a letter to my mother right away. She'll be so happy!"

He took the doctor by the arms and hugged him. "How wonderful!" he repeated. "We won the battle, we're moving into the fortress tonight and my wife is pregnant!"

I shifted on the bed, more than a little uncomfortable. I still couldn't believe I was pregnant. Didn't the doctors at TCF make me sterile? I'd assumed they'd cut my Fallopian tubes. Did those grow back? How had I gotten pregnant? The baby could have been conceived the night Maître Houdebert had shared my bed, or worse, when the man raped me in the prison.

I turned over on the bed and buried my head in the pillows with a sob. Agonizing over the paternity of the baby was the least of my worries. Now Jean would insist on making me his legal wife, and I had no business at all wedding him. According to the imbecile TCF historians, Jean had to marry and found a dynasty. I was only in the way! My sobbing redoubled. The only way out of the mess was to commit suicide, since I was likely to get erased anyway.

Jean sat down by my side and took me in his arms. He smelled good, he'd taken the time to wash. When he'd cantered up on his lathered cob after the battle he'd looked more dead than alive. His face had been covered with blood and his hair matted with sweat. The unaccustomed weight of his armor combined with exhaustion caused him to fall with a resounding crash when he'd dismounted.

I'd thought he was seriously wounded, uttered a frightened scream and fainted. That was why the doctor had been called.

The whole day had been too much. I shattered into a million, broken, sobbing pieces, and the doctor gave me a drink to calm my nerves.

Jean had to hold me until I fell asleep. He couldn't pry my fingers from his tunic.

* * * * *

That night the entire camp moved into the fortress the crusaders had wrenched from the infidels. There was none of the grain the crusaders had hoped we'd find or any sort of fresh food at all. Luckily, the valley was rich with grazing land and a stream ran through it, giving us fresh water. Women, children, the sick and the wounded were installed inside the fortress. Sentries were posted on the roof. Most of the nobles got rooms, and Jean managed to find a small room in a turret overlooking the sea. I was pathetically glad to get away from the smelly,

soggy island. The fortress had a large septic ditch du\
ways away, and the cooks soon had huge fires goin\
kitchens. The smell of roasting meat raised everyone's sp\   ...

Jean, Charles and I put our belongings in one corner, spread our pallets on the floor, and looked at each other.

"What shall we do now?" asked Charles.

I wrinkled my nose. "I want to bathe."

"Why don't you lie down," said Jean.

"No, I want to have a walk. I've been cramped on a boat or in a tent for far too long." I scratched my scalp and grimaced at the feel of my greasy hair. "Isn't there anything that kills lice?"

Charles looked sympathetic. "You can boil rosemary and thyme in oil, strain it, cool it and mix it with clay. You leave it on your head until it dries, and then you comb out all the nits."

"Does that work?" I asked, a spark of interest in my eyes.

"Not usually," said Charles. "Usually we wait until winter, and they die of the cold."

We went to fetch water, each of us carrying an empty goatskin slung over our shoulder. There was a long line of women in front of us, and the road was dusty. We were parched from walking. Charles looked at the line and sighed. "Why don't we cut across the fields?"

It was a good idea, except there was a marshy place and the mosquitoes there were ferocious.

Well, perhaps we would have gotten malaria anyway.

\* \* \* \* \*

"If I die, will you send this to my mother?" Jean asked me. His eyes were bright with fever, and his face was flushed.

I dipped the cloth into the water and wiped his forehead. "You're not going to die, it's just a touch of malaria."

"Take it anyway. I want you to have it." He pressed his locket into my hand.

"It's yours, and you're not dying." I smoothed a lock of hair off his face and smiled. I'd trimmed it to combat the intense heat and his fever. With it cut so short, he looked even younger than ever. My smile wavered. His forehead was burning hot, but he was young and strong. I didn't doubt he'd recover.

There were no complications, his breathing was clear, his urine normal and the white of his eyes stayed white. I kept the doctors, with their leeches and their endless bleeding, far away. They'd already killed one woman who hadn't even been that ill. She bled to death.

"I want to marry you, Isobel," Jean whispered.

"Don't think about that now." I stroked his brow, but he pushed my hand away.

"I promised my sister I'd marry someone wealthy, but I can't imagine life without you. Do you think she'll forgive me?" His voice wavered, and his eyes were so bright I doubted he knew what he was saying.

I dipped the cloth into the water and wrung it out. The water was tepid. In the heat nothing was ever cool, not even the breeze. "I don't think she'll hold it against you if you marry someone you love." I draped the damp cloth on his forehead and watched his eyes flutter closed as he fell asleep.

Charles was sick too, but less so. His youth and energy soon overcame the fever, and he was up and walking about now. I didn't get sick. The TCF doctors had vaccinated me. I was immune to the pest, cholera, malaria, dysentery and even the flu.

Apparently the only thing they hadn't done right was sterilize me. I was now three months pregnant, and my breasts hurt so much that even the lightest brush of cloth made me wince.

I sighed again and rubbed my face on my sleeve. Jean's short haircut looked very tempting to me in this heat. I thought of doing the same for my hair, although women were expected to have long hair. Coming into fashion now were tall, pointed caps with colored silk veils attached to the tops. The princess had one, and so did several of the richer noblewomen. Perhaps I could make one, then cut my hair short and hide it with the hat.

It wouldn't have pleased Jean, who loved my ash-blonde locks. I liked my hair well enough when it was clean and louse-free, which was a difficult thing to maintain. The week before, in desperation, I'd tried Charles' remedy for lice, followed by the princess' remedy. Then I'd asked the doctors and received several different recipes. The one with lye in it nearly burned my scalp. It did, however, kill the lice.

Now I dosed the chalk and vinegar more carefully and avoided putting too much lye into the mixture.

Once I'd gotten the potion down, I cut off Charles' hair and treated him for lice. Then I did the same for Jean even though he was ill. We were perhaps the three cleanest people in the camp. Even when Jean and Charles were sick, I insisted on washing them every day. Most people, including the doctors, were skeptical of my hygiene practices. The princess told me that I'd wash the skin right off my body if I continued to bathe so regularly.

"Furthermore, I never bathe while I am pregnant," she said, shaking her head emphatically. "It's very bad for the baby. He could drown."

I told her I'd be very careful.

Since we moved to the castle, Jean and Jean-Tristan had been nearly inseparable, and even while Jean was sick Jean-Tristan visited nearly every day. I liked the young prince. He was the youngest of King Louis' children and had been spoiled since he was a baby by everyone, but that hadn't made him capricious or demanding. Rather, it made him open and friendly to everyone, full of cheer, and affectionate toward his family. His blond hair was always carefully combed in the morning, but by midday, it was a riot of tangled curls. He was never at rest and always tried to make himself useful. The most menial jobs were done with a merry whistle when Jean-Tristan did them.

The fighting had all but stopped, and the crusaders were bored. To pass the time, we played cards and told stories, and I was invited to see Isabella at least once a day. I enjoyed her company, although I never stayed long. Her court was stuffy and crowded. In the heat, I preferred to stay in our tower room in the shade. At least we had a slight breeze. Then Jean and Charles fell ill.

They had been sick for two weeks when the first of August dawned hot and clear, the same weather we'd been having for a week now. Trumpets called the soldiers to their posts. The Saracens had been skirmishing with us for days now. So far, we hadn't lost any men. Well, except the man who'd had the misfortune to fall off the wall when he was drunk on too much ale, but you can't count that as a casualty of war.

The soldiers were entrenching the camp, and the Saracens seemed more interested in teasing us than actually attacking us. Diplomats rode in and out of camp constantly, to and from the King of Tunis. I wasn't privy to the messages, but I knew the king waited for his brother, the King of Sicily, to join the crusade. I also knew his brother would arrive too late but didn't say that, of course. Until reinforcements came, we'd stay put.

The outbreaks of malaria were fewer now, but dysentery had spread through the camp, and the king decided to confine his sons to their boats. Prince Philip insisted on staying with the king, which meant Isabella stayed as well. The other two princes, Pierre and Jean-Tristan, went to their ships.

Jean-Tristan had come this morning to ask if we would like to accompany him aboard his boat. I had no intention of getting on another ship. My seasickness would be worse now—even at anchor the boat's movement made me queasy. Down on the water, there was no wind at all, no shade and no respite from the heat. The ships' holds would be like ovens. I was therefore glad when Jean refused.

"I'm still not feeling well, your highness," Jean answered. His face was wan, but his fever had broken. "When I recover I'll join you, if you wish."

"I would like that very much," Jean-Tristan said. He leaned down and kissed his cousin, and then he bowed to me. I curtsied back and walked him to the doorway.

"Will he be all right?" he asked me in a low voice. "Shall I ask my father to lay his hands on him to cure him?"

I shook my head. "That won't be necessary, your highness." King Louis was reputed to have a healing touch, and soldiers were always asking him to touch their wounds. He regularly made the rounds with his physicians, to lay his hands on patients. So far in the encampment there were at least fourteen people who claimed he'd cured them with his touch.

Jean-Tristan nodded, and his face was somber for once.

"Don't worry," I said. "Jean is strong and the fever is broken. In two days he'll be as good as new, and we'll join you on your ship."

Jean propped himself up on one elbow. "Don't lose all your money before then, cousin. I intend to beat you at cards and win your allowance from you."

Jean-Tristan stuck his tongue out and laughed. "You're right. He's getting better."

I curtsied once more, Jean waved weakly and then I went to the window and watched the young prince ride off toward the bay.

* * * * *

Two days later, he was dead. He fell ill, along with the king's emissary, and both of them died within twenty-four hours of dysentery.

When the news of Jean-Tristan's death reached the encampment, the silence was as oppressive as the heat. Then low moans sounded, women started to wail and men pounded their chests in grief. Jean, still in bed, sat up and cupped his face in his hands. Tears seeped through his fingers, and his shoulders shook. He made no noise as he wept.

I thought of the poor king and went to the window again. From our room we could see the royal tent and beneath the awning. The king sat in his habitual place in the shade, but his face was hidden in his hands and he wouldn't speak to anyone, not even his priests.

I had known, of course, what was to happen. But knowing something and living through it are very different things. I'd let myself get close to Jean-Tristan. In the back of my mind his death had always been a fact in a history book, and when I'd met the living man, the specter of his demise vanished. Was it because these people had been dead for centuries when I studied them? I didn't know, but I couldn't associate these vibrant, living people with the shadowy figures in my history books, all long dead. I refused to think of who was next to perish.

I gazed over the encampment. Black flags unfurled and sagged in the dead air. Sobs rose from the king's tent and the guards wept uncontrollably.

I went to Jean and put my arms around him. "I'm so sorry," I whispered.

"I should have gone with him," he choked.

"Thank goodness you didn't. You would have died, too," I said with a shudder. My arms tightened around him. I closed my eyes, too frightened of the future to think. Jean was safe, that's all that counted for the time being.

Jean-Tristan's body was embalmed and placed in a wooden casket in the hold of the king's ship. The August sun blazed overhead, the crusaders buried their dead and the Saracens watched and plotted.

# Chapter Eight

**ൊ**

The weeks passed. The horror of Jean-Tristan's death hung over the encampment like a dark shroud. Blistering heat tormented us, and there seemed to be no end to the misery we endured.

The twenty-fifth of August dawned, a sweltering day, and news was shouted from the battlements that the King of Sicily's ship had been spotted a half a day's sail away. The camp's spirits rose, and the smell of smoke tickled our nostrils as the cooks lit the fires to roast meat for the celebration feast. The camp needed to be cheered—the king had been ailing for some time now. Some said it was sorrow over losing his son, and a few thought that it was fear for Prince Philip, though he was out of danger now. Some even said he was pining for his wife. In this day and age, it was considered important to have sex nearly every day, and the king had been celibate for nearly six months now.

Jean's illness was not fatal, but I wanted him to regain his strength. Used to having sex two or three times a day, Jean had chafed at being ill and celibate. He'd insisted that a bout of lovemaking would set things right and wanted to get a physician's opinion to sway me, but when Jean-Tristan died the shock brought his fever back.

Jean grieved to the point where he was nearly prostrate. I tried to raise Jean's spirits with card games and stories, even offers to make love, but he simply turned his head to the wall.

"Leave me alone, Isobel."

"Jean, look at me, please." My voice was gentle. I took his chin in my hands and turned his face to mine. His eyes were red-rimmed and swollen from crying.

"I am wretched. My prince is dead, and I'll never see him again. I was to have gone to Nevers with him to stay in his court. We would have hunted with his falcons, and…and…" He choked and new tears spilled down his cheeks.

I brushed them away and shook my head. "Jean, you're a man now. You have to understand that fate has other plans for you."

"I'm not a man," he said.

"You are." I stroked his cheek again and laughed softly. "Have you felt your beard coming in? It's so dark it looks as if your face is sooty. You'll have to shave now. Look, I got you a razor. Do you want me to do it for you?"

He dashed the tears out of his eyes with his fists and rubbed his cheek. "It is a beard!"

I nodded. "Shall I ask Charles to fetch some hot water?"

"Knowing you, you've already done so, and he'll be here in a minute with a bucket."

"I guess you know me too well," I said, relieved.

"Have you been crying too?" He looked closer at my face and frowned. "You have, haven't you? What is it?"

I sighed. I had to warn him, but it depressed me more than I'd thought it would. I truly admired the frail king. "Prince Philip and his wife are both ill with the fever, but they'll recover. The doctors aren't afraid for their lives."

"But?" Jean sat up straighter now and took my hands in his. "You look so melancholy. I heard what the princess called you, and I think it suits you well. The melancholy angel. She thought you'd bring good luck. She hasn't asked for you again, has she?"

"When misfortune strikes, friends tend to evaporate like smoke. She's right not to call for me, though. I will not bring any luck to this crusade. I told you before, Jean. It's doomed."

His face softened. "You're prey to your pessimism. The doctors told me pregnant women often get that way. Did you know that I wrote a letter to my mother?" He sat back, a satisfied look upon his face. "I managed to send it with the king's own courier. She will receive it, God willing, in three months."

"Fast mail," I said, almost teasingly. Then my disquiet grew. "What did you say to her, Jean?"

"I told her I'd married an angel," he said, kissing me softly. "And I said you were having my babe. I told her that Jean-Tristan was dead of the flux. Then I wrote that the King of Tunis lost Carthage to King Louis. I explained that we were camped here waiting for Charles of Sicily, which was why we hadn't pushed on the Holy City of Jerusalem. As soon as I get there I'll buy her several souvenirs and try to find a piece of the true cross, although I think it will be hard. Did you know that King Louis bought the crown of thorns from the king of Jerusalem for three hundred and fifty thousand pounds?"

I looked suitably impressed. Then I frowned. "We are not married," I said. "And I don't think there's the slightest splinter left of the true cross. It's been a thousand years, my lord."

"We will get married as soon as I shave." Jean winked at me as Charles came into the room carrying a basin of hot water. "See? You didn't even have to call him."

Charles set the bowl down. "There's bad news in the camp," he said without preamble.

"What is it?" Jean splashed water on his face and leaned back. "Will you shave me now, Isobel?"

Charles frowned. "The king's illness has taken a turn for the worse."

Jean uttered a cry and stood up so suddenly, he nearly overturned the basin. I righted it just in time. He went to peer out our window. "I see him. He's lying on a pallet under his awning."

I stood next to Jean, a strange, tingling feeling growing between my shoulder blades. I was watching history unfold.

A crowd gathered around the royal tent, but there was hardly any noise. Soldiers stood in straight lines, guarding the fortress and the king's tent, but most of the crusaders milled about aimlessly, and silently.

"What's going on?" Jean asked. "Why is that girl being led over?"

Charles pushed his head between us and squinted. "It's the virgin," he said.

"I beg your pardon?" Jean stood on tiptoes to get a better look.

Charles made a face. "The doctors say the king needs to make love in order to get rid of the sickness inside of his body. They've fetched a virgin. She will lay with the king, and he'll get better."

"Why don't they just bleed him?" Jean asked.

"They have, but nothing has helped. He's been in agony since last night, and every hour he grows worse." Charles pursed his lips. "She's very young."

"I'd say she was about twelve. What on earth...why, they're taking her clothes off!" I was shocked. "Jean, that's not..."

"She doesn't mind," said Jean haughtily. "It's an honor for her."

"I don't think so!" I said. The girl dropped her shift and stood naked in the bright sun. Her small face puckered worriedly, and her hands were cupped in front of her sex. Her breasts were simply tiny rosebuds. After she was escorted to the pallet, the king propped himself up on one elbow and motioned to his head physician.

The sound of their voices traveled upwards. I cocked my head and listened unabashedly.

"What's he saying?" Jean hissed.

"Shh, his voice is so weak." I cupped my hands behind my ears and strained to hear. "He says he won't sully the vows of marriage he took with his wife. He will lie with no one but her. The virgin will have to go."

"No!" cried Jean, incredulous.

"He says thank you." I nodded, impressed. "He's very ill, I can hear it in his voice. Poor Louis." I was suddenly very sad. He'd been one of the kindest persons I'd ever met. Below us, in the tent, the doctors pushed the girl forward, all begging the king to reconsider. They went so far as to put her right into the bed with him. One held her down, and the others begged the king to have sex with her.

"No," said King Louis, and he turned his back to the naked virgin and refused to speak again.

"Wow." I was impressed. "I don't know many men who could have resisted." I looked sideways at Jean.

He snorted. "When you're ill with the flux the last thing you want to do is make love."

"I prefer to believe King Louis is a saint," I said, then clapped my hand over my mouth.

"What is it?" Charles asked.

"Nothing." I straightened up. "Come, Jean, let me shave you. You must go pay your respects to the king before he dies."

Jean whirled around, his face very white. "He's not dying!"

Now was the time to tell him. "I'm afraid he is." I took his hand and led him to a stool. "I want you to be prepared for the worst. Your king will die before his brother can come."

"But, but the scouts said his sail was spotted not six hours away!"

"We'd better get you ready quickly then."

The king of Sicily stepped ashore almost exactly one hour after his brother drew his last breath. The king's body was still warm when Charles of Sicily kissed his forehead and then turned and knelt at Philip's feet.

"My nephew, you are now King of France," he said in a choked voice.

Philip blanched. I don't think he'd quite realized what his father's death meant for him.

Charles' troops pitched their tents a few kilometers away from the king's camp. I thought it a prudent move to avoid the illnesses running rampant through the ranks of the crusaders. There were other reasons — the Sicilians and the French didn't get along very well, as we were soon to discover.

That night, Jean and I were both leaning out our window, as usual, so we spotted the quarrel right after the sentries did. "Fight! Fight!" the sentry screamed and motioned with his spear toward the seashore.

A man in crusader's garb pushed a soldier and shouted. They scuffled and bumped into a local merchant, causing him to drop his basket of dates. Losing his temper, the merchant smashed the basket on the soldier's head. At his cries, more soldiers came running. The shouting grew louder.

"You'd think that they could let the king's body repose in peace," Jean said bitterly. He pulled away from the window and paced in the room. "I hate it here. Why did I come? This place is cursed. You were right, Isobel. How could I have been so blind? War! Ha! It's nothing but pest and dysentery, plague and flux."

I glanced over my shoulder at him and raised my eyebrows, but he was too busy kicking at our bedcovers to notice. The fight on the beach had reached epic proportions. At least fifty soldiers, half as many crusaders and a handful of what looked like native merchants were all involved in the brawl. "Come look at this," I said. "War is also a melee."

I looked upwards to swat at a mosquito and frowned as something caught my eye. There was a shadow on the horizon. "Uh oh. I think trouble's coming."

Jean stopped kicking the covers and rushed back to the window. His youthful enthusiasm for fights sparked his interest. He gazed at the crowd and winced. "I don't think that man will walk again," he said.

"Yes, but look, over there on the hill!" I said, pointing.

Jean followed my finger and his face suddenly paled. "It was a diversion," he whispered.

He leaned as far out the window as he could. "Sentries, sentries!" he screamed. "We're being attacked! Look up on the hillside! You fools, can't you see we're being attacked?" He pounded the stone window casing with both fists. Then he turned and kissed me hard on the mouth. "Idiots," he said. "I have to go."

"Be careful!" I felt his forehead out of habit, but he was fine. A little wan, but done with his malaria.

He shot me a half-amused, half-annoyed glance. "I'll do my best to stay out of trouble." Then he clattered down the spiral staircase, shouting as he went. "To arms, to arms! We're being attacked!"

He was right, actually. The Saracens had sensed the tensions between the two camps and sent spies while they readied for a surprise attack. Luckily, the sentries hadn't left their posts, and the soldiers were ready. The horses were saddled and the soldiers armed in less than a quarter hour. The foot soldiers took their places in the trenches and, as the Saracens rode up, engaged them while the cavalry took their places. The longbowmen clambered up onto the roof of the fortress and started raining arrows down upon the attackers. In no time, the real battle was engaged.

The King of Tunis, hearing that King Louis was dead, thought to profit from the tragedy and strike while the French army was leaderless. He hadn't counted on Charles of Sicily and Philip uniting their forces so quickly, or on Philip's leadership qualities. The new king was a natural commander and an excellent tactician. He quickly rallied his troops and riposted with fury.

Perhaps part of it was grief—he was mad with it, some said. He rode at the head of his army, waving his great Damascus steel broadsword and bellowing "*Chargez! A mort les infidèles!*"

The army swept in behind him like a wide, prickly curtain. After three hours of hard fighting, the crusaders won. A huge cheer shook the soldiers when the Saracens turned and fled. The

King of Tunis, seeing the battle lost, pulled all his soldiers out of range of the crossbows and sent his emissaries immediately to sue for peace.

I could see most of the first part of the battle from my window, but it was too far away, really, to see individuals. When Philip's forces pushed their opponents over the crest of a hill, the fighting was lost from sight.

Afterwards the soldiers trickled back into the fortress, many clutching scraps of the flag that they'd wrenched from the infidels. I looked for Jean among the crowd, but he was nowhere to be seen.

I wasn't worried. There was already raucous singing coming from the soldiers' quarters. Flags were hoisted, flapping in the dusty wind. The sun started to set, and the whole world looked as if it had been dipped in gold.

Men continued to pour into the gates, many limping now or being held up by friends. A horse cantered in, saddle empty, scattering people in his way. A soldier made a grab at his bridle and missed, and the horse veered off toward the stables. He knew where his oats were. I started to smile but froze when I recognized the horse as Jean's brown cob.

"Charles!"

"What is it?" He leapt to his feet and strewed chess pieces all over the floor.

"We have to go find Jean. His horse has come back without him."

"That says a lot for his horse," said Charles. However, his face furrowed with worry. "We'll go the back way, there will be less of a crowd."

I grabbed a shawl and flung it over my head. Charles asked me what I needed it for. "It's hot as an oven outside."

"In case Jean has wounds that need binding."

Charles led me out of the fortress through a back door, but even that was blocked by milling soldiers. We finally wormed our way through and set off down the dusty road at a quick trot.

The road wound past the coast before dipping into a low valley. As we jogged, we dodged horses, soldiers and civilians like us, going back to the fort. Several times we had to leap off the road to avoid being run over by a galloping steed.

"Can't you go any faster?" I begged Charles, tugging at his arm.

"I'm hurrying!" Charles puffed. "I'm still feeling a bit weak, if you really want to know."

"I'rn sorry!" I stopped so suddenly he nearly crashed into me. "You're barely over your fever. You shouldn't be rushing around like this. Go back if you wish."

He shook his head. "No, my lady. Jean needs us both. Come, the battlefield isn't very far."

"How can you tell?" I craned my neck, but we were in the bottom of the valley, and I couldn't see over the hill.

"Can't you smell it?"

I stood still and sniffed. My nose was assailed by a sharp, coppery scent. "What is it?"

"Blood," said Charles, his face still. "The battle must have been harder than I thought."

Besides the straggling soldiers, the doctors hurried along, carrying their medicines, while men trotted to and from the fort with stretchers. I peered at each one going by me, to see if I recognized Jean, but I saw no one I knew. Other women hastened toward the battlefield as well, their faces drawn with anxiety.

I pulled my shawl tighter around my shoulders. Despite the evening's heat, I was shivering. As we topped the last rise, below us was a plain, and upon it were hundreds, no, thousands of bodies.

Charles yanked me off the road in time to avoid being hit by a wagon pulled by a team of four mules. In it, I saw with a sinking heart, were men with spades over their shoulders. They weren't wasting time digging graves. In this heat the bodies would decompose and spread all sorts of diseases.

Charles crossed himself, speechless at the sight of the battlefield.

"Come on," I whispered. "Jean must be down there somewhere."

"I hope we get to him before the gravediggers do," said Charles.

"Oh God, don't say that. He's not dead," I cried.

"They bury living men, too," said Charles wryly. "That's what I meant. Shall we separate? I'll go to the left, you to the right. We'll stay within shouting distance."

"It sounds as if you've done this before," I said. "All right. Let's go." Dread prickled over my body.

\* \* \* \* \*

Some of the dead men looked so much like Jean that once or twice I cried out, and Charles came running. Each time he found me on my knees, trembling, but from relief. Each time he pulled me to my feet and shook me hard.

"Isobel! Get a hold of yourself. He's out here somewhere, and we'll find him."

Night fell but offered no respite from the heat. Torches flickered in the navy blue air as women searched for husbands or lovers and doctors searched for survivors. There were sporadic shouts when doctors yelled for the stretchers or women screamed as they found what they had feared. Overlying everything was the constant thunk of spades hitting the earth, the steady swish of dirt flung over shoulders, and the occasional sharp clang of iron hitting rocks.

I staggered on. The battlefield stank. It was soaked in blood, and once I tangled my feet in someone's intestines and nearly tripped. I uttered a strangled scream, managed not to vomit and stepped out of the slippery mess. It took me a good three minutes to get myself together and moving once more.

In the dark the still, dead horses became huge, threatening shapes. Wounded horses neighed plaintively, their whinnies blending in with the cries and moans of the wounded. There was less crying than you would think. Most men lay in shock and watched their last stars, their minds already somewhere else.

One or two men called to me, begging for water. I had no waterskin with me. Each time I shook my head and they nodded, slumping back onto the grass, staring off once more into the sky.

I walked, calling Jean's name softly, like a litany, over and over. "Jean, where are you? You can't be dead—the sky would already be cracking open to swallow me." In my mind, the erasure would start like a huge rip in the heavens, a gaping hole that would suck me into nothingness. Lightning would flash, and clouds would roil and churn as they met the vacuum the TCF would use to erase all the damaged parts of history.

I stumbled on someone's outstretched hand and stopped, head bowed, chest heaving, willing everything to be a dream.

Charles called me. His voice rose over the sound of the graves being dug and the cries of a wounded man being pulled from under his horse.

"Over here. Isobel, hurry!"

I dashed across the field, leaping over a fallen soldier, a sword, a spear. There was a horse in my path—I swerved around it and nearly fell upon Charles, kneeling just on the other side. He cradled Jean's head on his lap.

"He's dead," he said softly.

I dropped to my knees at his side. In the feeble light, I could see that he was right. Jean was dead. His face was peaceful but devoid of all color. I stuffed my fists into my mouth. Horror iced my spine. Jean was dead, my green-eyed boy, my dark-haired lover, dead on the battlefield with an arrow in his side.

"No," I managed to whisper.

Charles looked at me. His face was dreadfully pale. "I'm so sorry."

"No." I repeated stubbornly.

"Shall we take his armor off?" he asked me gently. "His mother will want to have it."

"No!" I couldn't stop. My head shook, and my entire body trembled. My teeth started to chatter.

"I'll do it. You should go back now." Charles stood, and Jean's head slid off his lap.

"No!" I lunged forward and caught it, let it down gently. Then I crouched over him, my tears falling on his face. "How could you die?" I whispered to the still body. "How could you leave me here alone? What will become of me? You can't die, you have to go back to Paris. What about your descendents? Who will rule France now?" My voice shook. "My God, Jean, what have you done?" My voice rose in a thin wail. I was rocking back and forth now.

"Isobel, please!" Charles took my arm and tugged, but I ignored him.

"Jean, wake up now, please," I begged. I couldn't see anymore. Tears obscured my vision. Sobs were torn from my throat—I couldn't stop them any longer. I lay over Jean's body and sobbed, wailed and keened all of my fear and despair. The night was split with the sounds of crying, but my wails soared over the rest, drowning them, drowning me.

Charles sat by my side, his hand on my arm, and murmured quietly. I have no recollection of what he said. I have no memory of returning to the fortress, of lying on the pallet or falling asleep. I was caught in black glue that held my mind prisoner. My eyes were open, but all I could see was Jean's white face.

# Chapter Nine

## ❧

Charles was curled up at my side. When I stirred, he sat and looked down at my face intently. "Isobel?" he whispered.

"Tell me it was all a dream," I begged.

"I'm sorry." He bowed his head, and tears dripped off his nose. He looked so thin and pale, almost as sickly as he'd looked that evening in France when I'd first set eyes on him.

"How long have I been sleeping?" I asked. I felt so drained it was an effort just to speak. Why hadn't I been erased? Had the TCF forgotten about me? No, that was impossible. I tried to clear my head, shaking it weakly.

"It's been five days," whispered Charles.

"What?" I froze, my voice cracking.

"Don't cry, my lady, please don't cry." Charles patted my arm, an expression of desolation on his peaked face.

"I'll be all right," I said as I hitched myself up on one elbow then sat up painfully. "Where is everyone? Why is it so quiet?" For a strange second, I thought we were all dead. The morning sunlight streamed in the window, making the colors in my cloak and on Jean's armor, propped in the corner, glow. The rays glittered off his helmet and set the scarlet plume afire.

"They have left for the hills. The pest is upon us and already three hundred people have died. Can you hear the chanting? The priests think to keep it away with religious fervor." Charles closed his eyes. "I never thought I'd see so many people die." He scrubbed at his eyelids with his fists. "We'll die too, won't we?"

I slumped against the wall, my head bowed to my chest. A great lassitude took hold of me. In a haggard voice I said,

"Listen to me, Charles. The pest is caused by fleas. The rats carry them. When the fleas bite you, their saliva deposits the pest in your bloodstream and you fall ill. It isn't always fatal—some people resist better than others do. If you can avoid fleas or rats, it's better."

Charles looked at me through narrowed eyes. "When you were sick, after Jean died, you lay in your bed and raved. You spoke of things I'd never heard of, of kings and princes and travels through time. You said that Jean couldn't die. That it was impossible because he had to start a dynasty of kings and now your mission was a failure. You kept begging the time magicians to let you try again. 'Take me back and let me try once more', you cried."

I gaped at him. He was speaking of things that he never should have heard. Now I was sure to be erased, Charles along with me. "Shh! You mustn't say those things! If anyone hears you, we'll both be…killed," I said. "They'll think we're sorcerers."

"Yes, but what about the magicians who sent you back in time?"

"I can't tell you about them," I said, horrified that he'd overheard. "It will be the ruin of both of us. Forget you ever heard anything, I beg you!"

"I'd never breathe a word to anyone," he said, looking offended. "You can tell me the truth, Isobel. Besides, I have no wish to be branded a sorcerer and turned over to the Inquisition."

I rubbed my face. What had I done? Rule Number One was drilled into our heads from day one—never, ever let on to anyone that you're from another time. Better to die than admit you're from the future because it could create a ripple in the time continuum and would practically ensure the erasure procedure had to be used. The historians had insisted.

I sighed. They'd also insisted Jean would be easy to manage, that my mission was a simple one and that I'd been sterilized. What else had they gotten wrong? What harm could it do now? I trusted Charles, and he deserved to know the truth.

"I'll tell you, but not today. Right now I have to think of what to do. I failed, don't you see?" My voice cracked. "I've failed, and when those time senders…I mean magicians will find out, they will destroy me and everyone around me."

He pursed his lips and gave me a doubtful look. "If you say so. At any rate, the mission you dreamed of hasn't failed. You carry Jean's babe. Have you forgotten that?"

I raised my head to stare at him. He looked at me with his wise eyes, his weary face pale and tearstained but set with a determination I'd rarely encountered. "Oh my lord," I whispered.

"You had forgotten, hadn't you?"

"It may not be his." My chest shook with each heartbeat and my whole body vibrated like a guitar string.

Charles thought about that, his head to one side. "Who else knows that?"

"No one," I said. It was true. Even the TCF with their vacuum-sealed book would not know. People's movements and actions aren't recorded, only their impact on the future. Now that Jean was dead, I had to give this child his name. Perhaps it wasn't such a fiasco after all. I licked my dry lips, thinking hard. Jean had never done anything of note—his birth and death had been unrecorded. Only his bloodline was important. Dizzying relief swept over me.

"Then you'll have to go back to Paris and bear the babe in his family home. You will have to raise him as Jean's son. Will that be too difficult?"

"That's what I'll do." I rose halfway, and then sat down when my head spun. "Charles, will you help me?" I begged. "Will you stay with me, please?"

"On one condition."

"Name it."

"That you tell me all your secrets. I want to know by what sorcery you voyaged through time and what you were speaking about when you were delirious."

I stared at him, undecided. If Charles was right, maybe I wouldn't be erased after all. However, if he knew, or suspected, I'd come from the future, it would unbalance everything—according to the TCF historian. The same historian who assured me that I was sterile. A hysterical giggle bubbled out of my lips and I clamped them shut.

He waited patiently, his chin on his knees. Then I said, "We'll speak of this later, and only in private. First, can you show me where Jean was buried? I need to see his grave."

\* \* \* \* \*

We stood in front of a small monticule of dirt. There was a cairn of stones at its head, and for the first time I noticed Charles' hands were scraped and reddened. He caught my glance. "I made them bury him by himself, not in the ditch with the others."

"Thank you."

"He was my friend too," Charles said.

We stood shoulder to shoulder while the sun rose high into the heavens. The heat made us retreat, finally, to the shade of a cypress. Charles opened his pouch and took out two pieces of stale cheese, some flatbread and a flask of wine. We ate while the flies buzzed noisily around us. In the distance, the waves crashed upon the beach. Faintly from the north came the sounds of the crusaders' encampment. They were all grouped in the caverns. Charles told me that the King of Sicily was discussing a truce with the King of Tunis while Philip made plans to leave the Holy Land. He would bear the bodies of his father and brother to France.

"Poor Jean-Tristan," I said softly. "Poor King Louis and poor Jean." Tears spilled down my face. I didn't try to stop them. My pain was still too raw. Perhaps I never loved Jean as he'd loved me, but he had been my lover, and already my body missed his soft caresses. He'd been so handsome, so insouciant and so enthusiastic. I would never know if I'd truly loved him, unless you could measure love by the empty space it leaves when it is lost. If you could, then my love had been immense, for I felt as if my entire body was nothing but an empty shell now.

Charles patted my shoulder and swatted at a fly. "Isobel, we had better make plans for leaving."

"I thought I would send a message to the princess. I mean, to the queen. She is the queen now, isn't she?" I asked.

"Queen Isabella of France," said Charles.

"I hope she won't hold all this against me," I muttered.

Charles shot me a startled look, and I shrugged. "She thought I'd bring her good luck."

"Then I hope she is the forgiving sort," he said.

\* \* \* \* \*

She was. "My melancholy angel!" she cried, as we boarded the ship. She swooped toward me. Her arms were held wide, her pointed cap was askew, and her yellow veil floated behind her like a swarm of bees.

She hugged me tightly, and I felt her body tremble.

"My poor angel," she repeated. "Your husband was so young and handsome. Jean-Tristan adored him and told us before his death that he wanted him to accompany him to Nevers. You will have to honor his wishes. After we land in France, you must visit his court. I'll make sure that you're welcome." She pulled back suddenly, her eyes glazed. "Oh look, they're raising the sails. Are we sailing then? Where are you going?"

"I am going to Paris to take Jean's armor to his parents," I replied. "Your majesty, perhaps you'd like to sit down for a while. The boat is pulling anchor, and we'll soon be leaving.

Shall we sit here? It looks rough out there. I fear the swells will make you fall."

"Of course, of course you must go to Paris. What was I thinking?" She laughed and put her hands on her stomach, where a tiny bulge belied her pregnancy. "I mustn't fall down, either, it would be bad for the baby. Oh, where is my nurse, Carolina? I hope she isn't sick with the plague. I lost all my handmaidens but these two, and my midget died." She waved toward two sickly-looking women huddled behind her. "My juggler is dead, as is my confessor. I shall have to find another one right away — I can't use Philip's confessor. No, I shall have to find another one. How lucky you were that the plague didn't affect you." Her voice was high and shaky. She talked as fast as she could, I suspected to keep whatever demons lurked inside her head at bay. Her hands tightened convulsively on her belly.

I led her to a cushion and waited until she sat down, then I looked around for Charles. He stood near the tiller, his face turned toward land. I followed his gaze, toward the hills, where Jean lay forever sleeping. My eyes filled with tears and I blinked them away. It would do no good to cry, especially now.

I put on a brittle smile and turned toward the queen. "It will be good to go back to France," I said.

"Yes." She smiled tremulously. "The oriflammes are black. Our ship is decked in mourning. We're less an army of crusaders than a funeral cortège now."

The long, black pennants at the top of the masts flapped in the wind and I couldn't repress a shudder. I sat next to the queen and hugged my skirt tighter around my legs as the ship moved toward the open sea and the breeze grew stronger. It filled the sails and they swelled out above our heads, heavy, gray curves of linen. Sails on other ships billowed like storm clouds all around us as they caught the wind. The masts creaked and the sailors cheered. The boats moved out of the harbor.

Charles didn't budge from his post. As everyone else looked forward over the vast water toward France he stayed perfectly still, staring at the place where so many had died.

The queen tried to remain gay. She chatted brightly about the weather, the birds, the sailors and the ships. However, her voice often cracked and her hands were white on her skirt, the fabric bunching as she clutched at it. Her two remaining handmaidens sat like drooping lilies nearby, not speaking.

Her husband, the new King of France, was on the ship with us. He sat on his father's throne beneath an awning, surrounded by men in black robes and long faces. Deep lines of sorrow dove from his nose to his chin and marred his forehead. His skin was fair, though burnt by the fierce African sun. The same sun burnished his hair bright gold and his eyes were chips of blue sapphires beneath pale brows. He sat still and seemed to take no heed of anyone around him.

Later I heard rumors that he'd run from the fortress out of fear after the battle that had taken Jean's life, rumors that he'd fled from cowardice. I can tell you now that I don't believe that is true. Although I wasn't in my right mind afterwards, I was there. During the battle, while fighting the infidel, he was valiant. He fought in the thick of it.

Then, when his soldiers and the crusaders started dying of the pest, he did what he thought best. Should his country lose two kings, or more? He left the miasma of the marshy lands around the forest and headed to the caves. Unfortunately, the dusty caves didn't stave off the rats, which followed the grain, and on the rats were the deadly fleas. After less than a week, the death toll was stupendous. Weakened by malaria and lack of proper food, the crusaders were decimated by the plague. It was a miracle that the queen and king survived.

The queen clutched at her skirt, raised her pale, thin face to the sky, and asked me if I knew how long it would take to sail to France.

"I wish I knew," I answered.

She sighed and got to her feet. "I shall see you soon, angel," she said, in her high, quavering voice.

"Where are you going?"

"To my quarters to pray. I'll stay there until we get out of sight of land. The sight of the Holy Land makes me weep." She gave a little, choking sob and motioned at her ladies-in-waiting to accompany her below deck.

I looked for Charles, but he was gone. He must have put our belongings away, for I no longer saw the bundles we'd carried on board the ship. I peered down the trap door where a ladder disappeared into the darkness. Sighing, I wrapped my robe tightly around my legs and climbed down.

The wood was rough, and I got two splinters before I reached our level. I couldn't walk upright as the ceiling was too low, so I had to hunch over as I searched for Charles and our room. The rooms were separated by planks knotted together with hemp rope, so the word "wall" didn't quite describe them, and they had no doors. I looked into each one, trying to find mine.

In one room was a flock of priests, crowded together and arguing about who was to sleep on the only bunk. In another were the two ladies-in-waiting and nurse Carolina, their pale faces glowing like moons in the penumbra. I bade them good evening, but they were petrified with fear. Their only reaction was a sort of shiver that ran over their bodies and set their pointed caps knocking together like branches on a tree in a high wind.

Our room was in between those and quite cramped, especially as we'd bought our tent, our rug and all our belongings with us. A narrow wooden plank fastened to the wall boasted a peg upon which to hang our cloaks. We rolled everything into tight sausages and wedged them wherever there was space. Fortunately, our donkey had been loaded onto a ship carrying livestock.

Our tiny cabin was just behind the main mast, two stories below deck. It was perhaps six feet square and damp. After sailing for months then being docked in a bay where it had baked in the sun, the tar and pitch that sealed the planks of the boat had begun to give. The ship was still seaworthy, but repairs were in order. I touched the rough wood that separated me from the deep water and my hand felt the damp.

"It's better than nothing," said Charles stoically.

"And it could be worse," I said. "Most of the crusaders are bedded on dirty straw in the hold of ships carrying livestock."

He didn't answer, too occupied with shoving the rug as far as it could go beneath the wooden shelf that was the bed.

"Let me help," I said.

"No, you have to take care of yourself," he said.

I smiled. He had appointed himself my guardian angel, and there was nothing I could do to dissuade him that I didn't need one. He was sure I was as fragile as porcelain, now that I was "*enceinte*" as he put it.

Above us came the sounds of footsteps walking across the wooden floor. A thump was heard, and loud voices started arguing about who was going to sleep where and on which bunk. "The nobles," Charles said succinctly. "They're all on the first level."

"Where is the king's room and where do the sailors sleep?" I knew Charles had likely explored the entire ship. He was always curious.

"The sailors share a room at the bow — they take turns sleeping in hammocks. The supplies are in their room, and one floor below us are the water kegs. They're heavy enough to use as ballast, I suppose. King Philip and Queen Isabella have the biggest room, at the stern. The nobles are all packed in small cabins to the left and right of a narrow corridor, and there is a steep staircase leading to their quarters." He grinned. "The stairs are always jammed with nobility trying to go above deck for fresh air or back to their cabins to fetch something."

"We have a ladder to get to our deck," I said. "It will be crowded too, I imagine."

"Yes, full of maids, priests, sailors and uncertainties, such as us."

"Uncertainties?" I raised my eyebrows. "Well, that would describe us. Shall we go eat? I just heard the dinner bell."

\* \* \* \* \*

That evening, after we'd eaten a few bites of the cold lentil stew the cooks offered to everyone, we huddled into the small space left by our baggage and braced ourselves against the rise and fall of the waves. Since we'd left sight of land, the waves had grown steadily bigger. The wind picked up, whipping the tops of the waves into white foam, and the mast creaked with the strain. The ship bobbed like a cork, rising to the top of the swell and then sliding down into a trough with a sickening lurch. From neighboring rooms came sharp cries, thuds and moans as people were tossed about. Through the wide cracks in the walls I saw the four priests huddled together like a murder of crows in their black cloaks as they raised their arms to the sky and chanted in prayer. The maidens on the other side of our room squealed and shrieked each time the boat shuddered with the onslaught of the waves.

The swells deepened. The boat pointed her nose at the sky, climbed up another wave, her timbers groaning and masts creaking, before plunging downwards again. I huddled closer to Charles and hoped my poor little donkey wasn't suffering too much.

"Stop worrying about the donkey and pray for us," Charles said.

"Oh Lord…I think my stomach is somewhere in my throat," I moaned.

"That's not a prayer."

"Then I pray I don't throw up on you. Pass me the bowl, quick!"

"Oh no! Not again!"

I retched miserably into the tin bowl clutched in my hands. The sour smell of vomit filled the stuffy cabin, and Charles wrenched the bowl out of my hands and bent over it, his sides heaving.

When he had nothing left in his stomach, he raised his pale, crumpled face and looked at me. "The waves are getting bigger," he said. "I hope there's not a storm coming."

"Don't be silly," I said weakly. Just then there came the sound of trapdoors slamming shut and darkness enveloped us.

We looked at each other, but all I saw of Charles were the whites of his eyes. We clutched at the walls as the boat heeled once more. I heard the rush of water on deck and imagined the sailors, what they must be suffering as they attempted to hold the tiller straight.

I heard shouting. "Lower the sails! Quick!"

Another gust of wind came and the sound of tearing cloth silenced our cabin, as well as those around us. After a moment, the maidens screamed in unison. The scent of urine was now mixed with that of vomit. I buried my face in my sleeve and wished for perhaps the thousandth time I was still in my own century.

The boat struggled gamely up another wave, tottered for a moment, then swooped downwards. I gave a strangled cry and gasped as the sound of the wind and waves rose above the sailors' shouts and the handmaidens' cries. The priests started chanting again, but it sounded more like crying.

"Our Father, who art in heaven," said Charles feverishly. "Are you there, Isobel?"

"I am. Lord, it's dark. I wish we had some light," I said. There was no light. Some filtered in through cracks usually, but the sky had darkened and the only thing coming though the cracks were sprays of seawater. I couldn't see them, but I could feel them, sometimes on my back or face. The waves forced water through the boat's sides, and the timber moaned like a living beast.

A bolt of lightning showed for a split second through one of the seams, and a clap of thunder followed soon after. Charles prayed under his breath, but I was too terrified to remember any of the words. The only thing I could keep thinking of was Philip, King of France.

"He doesn't die," I muttered. "He doesn't die, he doesn't die, he doesn't die."

"Who?" shouted Charles, raising his voice above the wind.

"King Philip. He reigns for many years," I cried.

"How do you…" His voice was lost in a huge roar of thunder and the boat pitched with renewed violence.

"I just know." I clutched his arm to keep from rolling across the floor. The tin bowl clattered across the ground, and the reek of vomit added to our discomfort, but at that moment it was the least of our worries.

We held each other as the storm mounted in fury and the thunder deafened us. Rain battered the ship and hit the water with a sound like an avalanche. The mast cracked so loudly I figured it had split in two, and I screamed, my voice joining the chorus of screams from neighboring cabins.

"Does it hurt when we drown?" Charles asked, his whole body shaking.

"I don't know." I bit my lip as the boat slid into another trough. We were jarred as it plowed bow first into the waves. It righted itself, shuddering like a wounded hound, and staggered back up while the wind howled all around us and the thunder cracked the sky in two.

For a while I wondered if Charles had been wrong about the babe in my womb, if this was the erasure starting. I kept waiting to vanish, even though I suspected that I had succeeded in my mission in a very hands-on fashion. My head spun, and I felt faint prickles all over my body. But it was just the static electricity from the storm, raising our hair and sparking whenever we touched something woolen.

Charles propped himself against the rug, and he shrieked when the greenish light ran up and down his arms. He leapt up to flee but lost his footing and fell. In the eerie light his face was a mask of terror.

The thunder boomed, the ship plunged and I grabbed Charles and tried to calm him the best I could, although I was half mad with fright myself. "It's nothing, just St. Elmo's fire. Don't worry, it can't burn!" I pointed, but the ethereal light had already vanished and we were once more in inky darkness. We tried to clamber onto the tiny bunk, but the tossing ship made that impossible. Clutched together, we rolled about on the floor.

Gradually, the storm blew itself out, thunder fading into the night. Above deck, the sailors shouted to each other as they rushed to repair the damage the sails and masts sustained. The sea calmed, the waves subsiding to choppy swells. The storm had lasted for many hours and we were exhausted. In the ensuing silence, Charles and I fell asleep, tangled in a heap on the soggy floor.

I woke first. My mouth was dry and filled with a bitter, acrid taste. My head ached, and my eyelids stuck together when I tried to open them. Charles was curled up, wedged beneath the rug. Faint snores came out of his open mouth. His little face looked battered, and great, lavender circles around his eyes made him look nearly dead. But he'd always looked pale, thin and ill. I hoped to remedy that once we reached Paris and I could feed him some decent food.

A gray light filtered in through the doorway, which meant the trap door was open. I hauled myself stiffly to my feet and stood, whacking my head on the ceiling. Stars danced in front of my eyes and tears of pain ran down my cheeks. I used them to clean my face. Then I rubbed my poor head, trying not to mind how greasy and lank my hair was. With shaking hands, I braided it the best I could, smoothed my stained dress over my hips, and made my way up on deck.

Watery sunlight blinded me and I stood for a moment just blinking. When I could see through the dazzle, I went toward the bow where the cooks had set up a large cast-iron pot.

"Ah, lentils," I said.

I wasn't a noble, so I was given a small bowl but otherwise ignored. The smiles and fawning were for those with power and prestige. I knew from both my studies and my observations that the hierarchy of French courtly politics was merciless and rigid. Well, at least I was being fed.

I said thank you with my best finishing school courtesy and got a flicker of a glance from the assistant cook. I wandered over to a clear space on deck. Most of the passengers had come out of the bowels of the ship to get some air. Coils of ropes and great lengths of sail were spread out everywhere, and the sailors were busy painting cracked planks with pitch, tarring weakened joints and checking the masts and rigging.

Charles appeared, a bowl of lentils in hand, and sat next to me. We found a place out of the way of the sailors and nibbled our breakfast.

The air was perfectly clear, scrubbed clean by the storm. I wished I felt the same. My robe was stiff with grime and smelled atrocious. I finished my tasteless, overcooked lentils and waited a few minutes to see if I was going to be sick. Happily, my stomach seemed to have quieted.

My next concern was using the bathroom, always an adventure on board the ship. Toilet facilities were buckets standing near the sides. One used them, emptied them over the side and set them back in place. Stuffed into a crack, usually, was a piece of indescribably filthy cloth, the use of which can be surmised. I carried my own rags, which I used once and tossed over the side or washed, if I was running low. I had gotten more or less used to availing myself of the toilets in plain sight of everyone, though I preferred the out-of-the-way buckets. No one else gave it a second's thought. Nudity bothered no one, though a woman's modesty was considered a virtue. In this time, bodies and their functions were considered natural and healthy. Puritan notions of propriety hadn't been dreamed up yet.

King Philip clambered onto the deck, was greeted by deep bows by everyone, and went to the closest bucket and sat down. As he was sitting there, others who hadn't bowed to him a first time came and greeted him. He inclined his head graciously to everyone.

Then he stood up, adjusted his royal robes and ate lentil stew for breakfast. A servant emptied his bucket over the side. Afterwards the priests led us in prayer, and we gave hearty thanks to God for sparing us from a watery grave.

After the meal, King Philip gave orders to his sailors to search for the other ships, for we were alone on the shimmering sea that morning. We had been scattered like chaff by the storm, and the other ships could be anywhere by now.

All day long, we searched. People climbed the rigging, strained their eyes toward the horizon and peered through spy-tubes for a glimpse of white sails. When someone spotted one, he'd give a hoarse cry and we'd all pile onto the railing and wave frantically, our voices shrill in the vast sea.

Slowly, the other boats drifted toward us. Some limped badly, their masts splintered, sails tattered, and half the crew vanished in the tempest. Some were nearly intact, as our boat was. That evening there were fifteen boats bobbing alongside of us. Fifteen out of a hundred. At night, sailors lit lanterns and hung them on the tops of the masts so that the remaining ships would see us. Sails were reefed, anchors lowered and we waited, water slapping against the wooden hulls, for the rest of the fleet to arrive.

That night was strangely silent, almost soothing. Perhaps we all knew where the other ships were, but nobody would say it aloud. The priests chanted from sunset to sunrise while King Philip sat immobile on his throne. At his side, like a dark shadow, huddled his wife. She'd fallen during the storm and injured her face. Purple bruises bloomed on nearly everyone. We were all battered and worn out, beaten by the storm. Charles and I elected to sleep on deck. I couldn't bear to go down into our stuffy, stinking cabin. Urine, feces and vomit made below deck a sort of preview to hell, especially since there were no windows and water had leaked in to soak everything. I salvaged an almost dry robe and wrapped myself in it, propping my back against Charles'. We both dropped immediately into a deep slumber.

Because of my exhaustion, compounded by the pregnancy, neither footsteps nor waves woke me the next morning, not even the sun shining brightly on my face. Quiet, shocked whispers stirred me out of my slumber. I raised my head and groped for Charles. He hunkered next to me, but his back was stiff, and when he took my hand, his own hand was icy.

"What is it?" I asked, my voice coming out raspy with thirst.

"Another ship has been spotted."

"That's good, isn't it?" I struggled to arrange my clothing into some sort of order.

"The ship was upside down." There was a silence as we stared at each other. "One hundred ships are lost," he said. His blue eyes were bleak in his face. "More than four thousand people died in that storm. Some are saying that the infidels put a curse on us with their black magic."

I licked my dry lips. "What happens now?"

"We raise anchor and go back to France." Charles wrapped his arms around his knees and hugged them to his chest. "We'll be there in another week, if the wind holds."

I looked over at the pavilion, beneath which was Philip's throne. He still sat upon it, motionless. How could he not turn into stone? To lose his brother, his father, and now over half of his followers, in the space of a couple weeks. Isabella, on the other hand, wrung her hands continuously, her face a white mask of terror. When the anchor was hoisted, she crossed herself, and with each pull of the ropes to raise the sails she flinched.

With black oriflammes cracking in the wind and the mainsail billowing, the boat heeled slowly around and headed toward France.

# Chapter Ten

ဆာ

In November, we landed in Italy. The sky mocked us, blue and limpid as if the world was fair and just. A soft breeze blew the ships to the docks, where hundreds of people were gathered to hear the news. Because the ships wore the black of mourning, they must have known something terrible had happened. The crowd stood, silent, shifting, watching the boats carefully. Perhaps they counted them too. As one ship, then another cast anchor their bewilderment grew. When all the ships were anchored, there was a stir in the crowd. Banners were raised, a bit timidly, and a man stepped onto the docks.

I stood at the rail, Charles at my side. "Do you recognize that man?" I asked.

"From the banner his page holds, I would say it is the King of Sardinia, come to welcome the King of France back home."

"He doesn't know?"

"I don't believe so." Charles sighed. "Shall we prepare to leave the ship? We need to buy another donkey — ours drowned in the storm."

I gave him some coins. I still had some left, and I'd taken Jean's purse, though it had been nearly empty. "You take the money and go buy one. I'll wait here."

Charles nodded and tucked the money I handed him into his belt. "I'll be back as soon as possible." Then he surprised me with a quick peck on the cheek. "Don't worry, I'll take care of you."

I blinked several times, rapidly, as I watched him make his way down the crowded gangplank and into the crowd. In a moment, he disappeared. He was still small for his age, but his eyes were ancient.

The king held his wife's elbow as they made their way down the main gangplank. Isabella leaned heavily on her husband, and even from my perch I could see her hands trembling. Her belly was a round mound now, accentuated by the dress she wore. The style was close to the body, with a tight belt just below the breasts and a narrow skirt. Her clothes were filthy, her hair, tightly braided, was greasy, and her face was pallid. King Philip wasn't in much better shape. We were all filthy, lousy and smelly. The King of Sardinia wrinkled his nose as he stepped forward to greet Philip.

A low wailing grew in the crowd, and I guessed that news of King Louis' death had been announced. Soon everyone was beating their breasts, crying and sobbing his name like a chant. The dirge followed us as we made our way to the campgrounds, where the Italians had built fires and the smell of roasting meat tickled our nostrils. This was our welcoming feast.

As we watched, the meats cooking on the fires were heaped upon platters and carted around to individual tents. Two men held the poles that supported the platters while a third man handed out pieces of meat. Other men passed huge pitchers of mead around as well, and there was even wine for the nobles. We were all famished, but there was no jostling, shouting or reaching, even from the peasant crusaders. We stood, apathetic, while the food was passed around, and then we simply ate where we were.

During the days that followed, the crowds dispersed as crusaders made their way back to their homes. Silently, banners drooping, groups of tattered pilgrims took to the road once more. Their progress was hurried — winter nipped at their heels.

After a week's rest and recuperation Charles and I followed the court, headed for France. The king wanted to head immediately for Paris, but his advisors considered it prudent to wait until spring. The season was unusually cold. Ice fell in showers, breaking tree branches and making roads impossible to travel. Then cold winds swept down from the north along with deep snow, even as far south as Venice. In Italy, the court made a temporary home while the snowflakes whirled and ice glittered on every branch.

So it was decided we would wait until winter eased its grip. Time went by slowly. My stomach swelled, as did the queen's, and we often stood side by side and compared bumps. She hadn't forgotten me, and an invitation had arrived as soon as we left the campground for us to come to the queen's quarters.

We were staying in a castle near the coast, and the room Charles and I shared was spacious. It overlooked the courtyard and the front gate, and there was always something to see from my window. I spent hours leaning against the stone casement, a warm shawl over my shoulders, watching the comings and goings of diplomats, peasants and merchants. Dinners were eaten in the great hall, where everyone sat according to a strict hierarchy. Only I was somehow exempt. I was the widow of Prince Jean-Tristan's dearest friend, said the queen to anyone who asked.

"You must miss your husband dreadfully," she said to me one evening, patting my hand gently.

"Yes, I do," I was surprised, as always, by the stab of sorrow I felt when I thought of Jean.

"We will try and find you another husband as soon as you birth your babe," she said.

"I think I'll wait a while. Perhaps Jean's father will let me stay with them." Actually, I had no idea what would happen to me. I'd received a letter saying that Jean's mother had died. But Jean's father didn't know yet that his son was dead. The letter I'd written telling the family about Jean's death, and the one Jean's father had sent must have crossed each other en route. A message had arrived from Jean's father nearly two months after we arrived in Italy. It was brief, but explicit.

"From the Count de Bourbon-Dampierre,

"My son, a misfortune has befallen us. Your mother is dead. Your departure left her grieving while the messages you sent from the Holy Land only hurt her more. That the king wants you near him is flattering. King Louis is a brave man and I am sure you will learn much from him. It is too bad you couldn't have waited for another crusade before running away like a villain. The news of Prince Jean-Tristan's death reached me only yesterday, along with your latest letter. Alas for your mother, that she wasn't alive to read it. She suffered a cold that went to her chest. Never very strong, she succumbed as so many others did in the palace. I have decided to take your sister to Tours.

"Now I arrive at the heart of the matter. You said that you have married and that your wife, Isobel, is carrying your child. I shall look forward to meeting you both in Tours. Make haste.

"On this day of October, 1270, your father, the Count."

I knew Jean hadn't been an only child. Sometimes he talked about his younger sister, the one he promised he'd marry a wealthy woman. He hadn't known that his mother had died soon after he'd left. He would have been crushed. The reason was given as a chest cold, but the allusion was from a broken heart. Now I had to write for Jean's father to come and fetch me.

Perhaps, I thought wryly, I'd break the news of Jean's death to him gently, along the lines of "A misfortune has befallen us". It took me three days to compose a suitable message telling him of Jean's demise. Charles helped me, looking over my shoulder, and trying to sound out the letters as I wrote.

"That's an 'F', not a 'T'," I said to Charles. "I've written, 'Sire de Bourbon-Dampierre, it grieves me to write this letter, but I see no other way to break the terrible news. Your son Jean died in battle. His body rests in Tunis, beneath an olive tree. He died bravely, fighting alongside Prince Philip."

"King Philip," corrected Charles. "Is that how you spell Tunis?"

"Yes. Lord, where was I? 'I hope to reach Paris in the spring, as I will travel with Queen Isabella. I am now her lady-in-waiting. I await your reply. Sincerely yours, Isobel, wife of Jean de Bourbon-Dampierre'."

"No, that sounds terribly awkward."

"What does?"

"That you're the queen's lady-in-waiting, awaiting his reply."

"You're right. Oh Charles..." And here my voice broke. "I hate writing letters. Especially this one. But I can't start another one. I haven't any vellum left, and the ink is nearly gone. Take this to the queen's messenger and have him put it in the bag with the rest of the mail. I only hope Jean's father receives this letter before he gets here."

Thus November passed. In December, we celebrated a sad Christmas, and I received another curt message from Jean's father addressed to Jean. He'd received word that the king was dead. He was on his way to Italy and would arrive as soon as possible. There was no mention of my letter.

In January, the weather was bitter, and I huddled in a multitude of cloaks, my feet practically inside the fireplace.

When the warm winds of spring finally broke winter's grip, we made plans to leave. Isabella was eight months pregnant, and I was seven months along. When we stood side by side, my stomach stuck out much further than hers did, and she teased me.

"Look, you're fatter than I am," she said. The months we'd passed resting had put weight on both of us. Her cheeks were smooth and the wings of hair peeping from beneath her pointed hat were sleek and shiny.

"It only means my baby is bigger than yours." I ran my hand over my dress, thankful each time I did that the cloth was warm and clean. "Perhaps you're to have a girl and I'm to have a boy."

"No, you're carrying him higher than I am. Look, your belly is still pointing straight out. Mine has dropped. It means the child is getting into the birthing position."

"Aren't you afraid of traveling now?" I asked. "Won't it be better to wait until the baby is born?"

Isobel shook her head. "I want to leave when my husband does. I've stayed with him since we were married, and I'll leave him only when death separates us." She crossed herself. "That reminds me. Would you please send my confessor to me? I need to speak with him before vespers."

"Very well." I curtsied and left her room to seek her priest, Père Sebastian. Since nearly all her ladies-in-waiting had perished, I did many of her errands. Mostly I fetched her shawl, recited a poem or a story, or looked for her confessor. She confessed at least three times a day, sometimes more if any impure thoughts flitted through her head.

As I'd discovered, being pregnant makes a woman's hormones go rather mad. Impure thoughts were easy to come by in a castle filled with males. I even found myself eyeing Charles one day as he took off his shift for his bath. The shock of my thoughts was so great I nearly rushed off in search of Père Sebastian that minute.

If Charles, twelve years old and scrawny, could spark an interest, you can imagine what a handsome knight in a short tunic and tights could do. There were a few around. They spent their days polishing their armor, riding or fixing their helmets, which always seemed to break. Several of the queen's younger ladies-in-waiting found many excuses to go to the blacksmith, stop by the armory or stroll through the courtyard as the knights supervised their grooms. If, through my open window, I heard a chorus of giggles, I knew there was a knight in sight. I'll admit, it usually gave me an excuse to put down my lamentable embroidery and lean out the window.

I made no effort to go beyond that. It was nothing but the tug of war of hormones in my body. My breasts swelled, I grew languorous, my appetite was ferocious and Charles remarked that I had grown as big as a warhorse, which was the largest animal he'd ever seen.

I tucked the last of my tunics into the leather bag on my bed and tossed a lock of hair out of my eyes. "I am not enormous," I said, fingering my braid. My hair was nearly to my waist now, and I wondered when it would stop growing.

"You are bigger than Sire Quentin's horse, and his is the biggest in the stables," said Charles.

I was no horse, but I was huge and ungainly. A thought crossed my mind. "I hope I won't be a nuisance. We're leaving tomorrow, and the trip will last nearly a month."

"Luckily we're not going all the way to Paris," said Charles.

"Where is Jean's father? What if we leave before he gets here?"

"We'll meet him en route," Charles said with a shrug. "We can't miss him. There's only one road."

"That right. I forgot." I sighed and put a hand behind my back to support it. "How lucky that I'll be riding in a litter. I couldn't imagine how I was going to sit on that poor little donkey that you bought."

"She'll carry our belongings." Charles held a pair of stockings up to the window. "Did you really mend these?"

I blushed. "I tried. Didn't the hole disappear?"

"The hole is gone, but now one leg is shorter than the other."

"Perhaps your tunic will hide that." I'd quickly discovered that the mending I'd taught myself in prison was limited, but I persevered because women of my supposed class would have known how to sew.

Charles shrugged. "It's of no importance, Isobel."

When everything was packed, he shouldered the bag and made his way to the stables to load the donkey. I waited at the window and watched the bustle as everyone prepared to leave.

Despite the effervescence, the caravan that left Italy was not gay. Jean-Tristan had been buried in Tunis, but King Louis' body accompanied us to Paris. Mourning flags hung low on the standards, and voices were muted. Even after two full months' rest, we were still shaky. The tragic crusade had weakened everyone who'd managed to escape the war, the plague or the shipwrecks. Mostly we were silent, the only sounds the snorts of the horses and the steady clop, clop, clop of their hooves. The weather was dismal, wet and foggy. Winter left the roads gutted and muddy, and progress was slow.

Two weeks after we left, five horsemen were spotted galloping toward us.

The guards rode out to intercept them, and then standards were raised and Charles grabbed my leg. "It's Jean's father," he said. "I recognize the flag. Jean had the same insignia on his cloak." His eyes sparkled. "When he sees you and recognizes you, he's going to have a royal fit."

I swallowed as I realized I was going to have to level with Charles. He never plagued me again about my ravings in the dark time after Jean's death, but I often caught him watching me with a speculative look in his eye. I lowered my voice so only he could hear. "Charles, he won't recognize me. He's never seen me before." I spoke in a very low voice. My throat was so tight I could hardly breathe.

"Of course he will! Why, you told us he chased you through the streets of…" he stopped chattering and stared at me. "He never saw you? But you said that, that…"

"I know what I said. It was all a lie, to try to convince Jean to go home. I've never met Jean's father."

Charles stopped smiling. "There is some mysterious force at work here," he whispered. "You told me you knew the king would die and that Philip would not die. But you lied to Jean about his father. You swore you weren't a witch, so what are you, Isobel? Are you a seraph, as Jean said? I'm starting to believe he was right. You're one of the fallen ones, condemned to suffer on Earth for the sins you committed in time." He crossed himself.

"I'm not a witch."

"You promised you'd tell me of your mission and the time magicians. Can you tell me about it now?"

"I don't know. I have to think about it. If anyone else finds out, they will have us killed as surely as the Inquisition."

Charles looked undecided. "I hope someday you'll tell me everything."

I watched as the rider trotted nearer. As he passed, people turned and pointed toward my litter. I arranged my robes the best I could with hands that shook. In a quiet voice I said, "Charles, I need you. Don't fail me now."

He gave a little start and said, aggrieved, "I will never fail you, my lady, no matter what you are." He reached for my hand and helped me out of the litter. Shoulder pressing against shoulder, we waited together for Jean's father.

He clattered up on a great warhorse. He didn't dismount. His head was bare, his face an older, harder copy of Jean's with deep-set green eyes. A long scar dove from his cheek to his throat. Seeing it, my hand strayed toward my own scar. I checked myself and managed a clumsy curtsy.

"My lord," I said.

"Are you Jean's wife, Isobel?" He leaned down and frowned at me.

"I am." I turned away from his piercing gaze, too tired, too frightened to confront anyone. Head bowed, I waited for his verdict.

"I received your letter, telling me about my son's death, two weeks ago." His voice was dry, with barely any inflection.

"I'm very sorry," I said. I waited for some sign of emotion, but he simply shrugged.

"You will accompany me to Tours." He never dismounted. He tugged on his horse's reins, turned him around, and kicked him into a heavy gallop. He positioned himself right behind King Philip.

"There goes a man who knows his place in the world and isn't afraid to show it," Charles said to me.

I climbed into my litter and Charles took the donkey's bridle. Since our route would be the same for several weeks at least, we didn't leave the king's company. Then the king and his court would go north to Paris, and we would cut across the great swamp and lake region toward Tours.

That night Jean's father sent one of his guards to help set up our tent. Charles, who had been doing everything by himself, was relieved. The guard was a tall, sturdy red-haired man called Lucien. He bowed to me and said that his services had been offered to me by the Lord de Bourbon-Dampierre. I nodded and thanked him.

We all gathered for dinner. Traveling was a slow business with the court. We left after the morning prayers, stopped for lunch at noon, had a short nap and more prayers, traveled until the shadows grew long, then stopped for vespers. After the prayers were done, we set up tents and the cooks started dinner. Servants set up the long benches and trellis tables and covered them with thick cloth. The table was set with pewter plates and jugs of wine and water. After the king and queen said a short prayer, we all sat. They ate while we watched. Then we ate. Servants cleared the table and everything was put away again.

After dinner, I usually tried to find a stream to wash in or, failing that, begged a basin of warm water from the cooks. The grooms cared for the horses and donkeys, although Charles himself took care of our donkey and my litter, which was carried by two docile ponies the queen had given me.

That evening was no different. We ate dinner while a troubadour sang a mournful song, as befitting our state as a funeral cortege. Afterwards the women were excused and readied themselves for bed. Charles obtained a basin of water for me, and I bathed in the privacy of my tent after lighting a small brazier for warmth. I put on my sleeping gown and lay on my hard pallet. The tent flap was open, and I could see the stars and hear the faint sounds of men talking.

Charles unrolled his pallet next to mine and we huddled together for warmth. He rested his hand on my belly, as he did so often. He loved to feel the baby moving, bumps sliding under the skin like a dolphin, he said.

"A dolphin?" I was amused.

"He has a pointy head," said Charles in a whisper.

"Perhaps that's his elbow." The night grew deeper and my eyes slid shut.

"Tell me how you knew," Charles said.

I sighed. "We need to go to sleep."

"You can't sleep anyway when the baby is moving so much. Oh, he just turned over! Did you feel that?"

I gave a tired chuckle. "Of course. Now let me sleep."

"You promised. When you were ill you raved about the world ending." His voice was a mere whisper, but it was tense. "Will the world truly end? I'm frightened."

I sighed and propped my head on my arms. The time had come. I could trust Charles, and perhaps it would ease my burden to speak to someone. "No, it goes on and on. I come from a time in the future so far away I can't even begin to describe it. I was sent back to save Jean's life, and I failed. I should have been punished, but I think the baby gave me a second chance. He must take Jean's place as the founder of a dynasty. One day, his descendants will inherit the crown of France."

"How will he do that?"

"I don't know. Or rather, I know who founded the dynasty, but I don't know how my baby and that person are related. In two hundred years, there will be a bloody war in France. Two religions will confront each other, the Catholics and the Protestants. The war will also involve two families, one headed by the Catholic king of France and the other by the king of Navarre, a Protestant called Henry."

"Go on!"

"Henry will marry the king's daughter in a vain attempt to pacify the kingdom. Right after his wedding, on the night of St. Bartholomew, the people of Paris massacre the Protestants, killing more than six thousand men, women and children."

"Six thousand!" Charles gagged. "That's horrible!"

"More horrible than you can imagine. Rivers of blood will run in Paris that night. Henry manages to flee to Navarre and hide in a fortress. After several years when the king dies and his sons die with no heirs, Henry, by right of marriage and blood, becomes King of France. He is obliged to give up his religion and becomes Catholic. He is the first of the Bourbons to rule France."

Charles digested all this. "So your child must somehow rule Navarre," he said.

"No, I don't think so. Perhaps he will marry a princess of Navarre. Who knows?"

Charles swallowed. His hand tightened on my belly, then relaxed. "What a terrifying story," he whispered.

"Hush, I need to sleep now."

"I can't sleep. I'll have nightmares for sure. Can't you tell me anything cheerful? Do the time magicians send people back in time every day? How does it work? Will time run amok if you make a mistake?" His voice trembled.

"Don't be frightened," I said. "Time is like a river. It flows in one direction. We're but tiny minnows in that river. We can swim upstream a ways, and it won't change anything. You and me, our actions won't change the flow of the river. It takes something terribly drastic to change the course of time. With Jean, a small portion of the river was diverted. I was the minnow sent back to put a twig in place and dam it up. The time magicians are there to make sure the river flows on and on. But that doesn't mean we can tell anybody they exist or where I'm from."

"We're just little minnows then," murmured Charles, his words ending in a huge yawn. "I'm glad you're the one they chose, Isobel. Otherwise, I'd never have gotten to meet you."

I was strangely touched and smiled in the darkness. "I didn't have much of a choice," I said. "But thank you, Charles."

His only reply was a soft snore.

I was left staring at the glowing brazier, wondering what sort of man Jean's father was. For some reason, when I closed my eyes, I saw his face. His green eyes seemed to mock me, and the cruel scar on his cheek made my own scar ache.

# Chapter Eleven

❦

Each morning, the encampment woke and stretched its myriad arms and legs. Cooks hurried to fetch water. Grooms led the horses to drink and harnessed them. Priests intoned their morning prayers. Smoke rose in lazy spirals as fires were lit and meat was grilled for breakfast. The king and queen were greeted by the court. Chamber pots were filled and emptied. I wrinkled my nose and dressed while Charles folded our tent. Lucien, the guard assigned to us, rode up and offered to help.

Charles showed him where my ponies and litter were, and soon I sat more or less comfortably in my narrow, curtained litter as we moved off. The whole procession was lengthy, clumsy and slow, but we were advancing, even if it was sometimes no more than ten kilometers a day.

That day, a white mist covered the sun. Fog lay in soft swaths in the road, and sound was muted. Water droplets sparkled on spiderwebs and decorated the manes and tails of the horses. It was colder than usual. At noon, we stopped and the cooks built a huge fire to warm everyone.

I stood on the periphery of the fire and searched for Jean's father. Except for demanding if I was, indeed, Isobel, he hadn't made the slightest attempt to speak to me. I didn't catch more than a glimpse of him.

The queen was by herself, so I went to see her. She stood hip-deep in the mist, wrapped in a thick, blue cloak. Her face was very pale.

"Are you feeling well?" I asked.

"My travail will start soon. I lost a bit of blood this morning. That's a sure sign. You will need to look for it yourself soon, my angel." She smiled at me. "I'm always anxious before it starts. Then, when it finally gets underway, I put myself in the hands of God and pray. It's easier to accept."

I shifted my feet. An ache had begun low in my back that morning. "Should you journey today? Would it be better to stay here?"

"It could be days before it gets underway. The full moon isn't for another two days. Usually it happens then. The pull of the moon works on birthing, as well as the tides," she said, glancing at the sky. "It's lovely when the fog covers the ground like a silver cloud. Philip says I suffer from flights of fancy, but he says it so kindly. I truly believe he loves me."

Her comment surprised me. "Of course he does. Do you doubt it?"

"After what happened in the Holy Land, I've begun to doubt everything." She raised her eyes to mine. "Some nights I can't sleep. I lie awake and remember."

I nodded awkwardly. "I'm sure time will erase those memories."

Her eyes glittered and her mouth trembled. I thought she would cry, but instead, she darted off onto another subject. "The trees are starting to bud already, did you notice? The willows are always first, then the hazel." Her voice was high, nerves making her laughter brittle.

I patted her shoulder gently. "I'm sure everything will be all right now." The look in her eyes frightened me. In prison, sometimes, I'd seen looks like that. Usually the woman was taken to the infirmary and given a strong dose of tranquilizers. Here, I wasn't sure what to do besides keep her talking. "Tell me about your childhood," I said.

She gave me a startled look and her dark eyes softened a bit. "It was nearly always sunny, and orange trees grew in our garden. Sometimes I dream I'm back home, and when I wake up the scent of orange blossoms is in my nostrils. My mother was a very small woman, only reaching my chest." She held her hand up to show me. "So very tiny, yet she ruled the entire palace, and even my father jumped when she called his name. Her black hair reached her heels when she let it down."

The queen laughed, and I was relieved to hear her sound almost normal. She took a deep breath and smiled at me. "When I was twelve my marriage was announced, and the whole kingdom had a fête in my honor. For three days the people feasted, and we invited musicians from all over the country. When I saw Philip, I fell in love. He'd sent me a miniature, but the painting did him no justice. Don't you think he's handsome? His hair is so golden, and his eyes so blue. I love the way he…"

"Your highness!" One of the priests stepped up behind us.

We jumped, and the queen blushed. "Père Denis, you frightened me!"

"Your litter waits." He eyed me frostily. Perhaps he thought I'd started the conversation about his king's physical attributes.

"I want to ride my mare next to my husband this afternoon. Have her saddled," said the queen.

The priest looked as if he wanted to refuse. He was a priest, not a messenger or a groom. Nevertheless, after a second's hesitation, he bowed very low and trotted away, his black robes flapping in the mist. To avoid tripping, he held them high and displayed his muddy shoes and thin, white shanks.

"Will you ride with me?" asked the queen.

I shook my head. "I'm a poor rider, and in my condition I'd roll off my pony's back like a ball."

The queen, who was proud of her equestrian prowess, smiled kindly. "I'll teach you how to ride once your baby is born." She cocked her head. "The trumpets blow. We're off now. 'Til tonight, my melancholy angel." She pecked me on the cheek and waded through the soft mist.

Although the air had warmed, the fog had grown even thicker. It took me awhile to locate Charles. He held my lead pony with a look of worry on his face. When I appeared, he crossed himself and helped me into my litter.

"You mustn't fret about me," I said, parting the curtains and leaning out to see him.

"Hush, it's not that. Jean's father came while you were gone and asked me many questions. I don't know what to make of the man."

The blanket of fog made it seem we were alone, though I knew we weren't. I could just barely see the rump of the pack mule in front of me, and behind us, the head of a white horse poked out of the mist like a phantom.

"What did he want to know?"

"How long I'd been in your service. Where you'd come from, who your people were and when Jean married you."

"What did you say?" I wasn't worried. That day, for some reason, a strange, relaxed glow enveloped me.

"I told him I was born in your family's palace and that you were from a village just north of Marseilles. I said we met Jean en route, and he fell in love with you. Your parents were in the Holy Land with us, by the way, and they both perished."

"Charles!" I clapped my hand over my mouth, then took it off. "What if he asks someone else?"

"Who can he ask? Your family is dead, and the only other person who knows you is the queen. Sire Dampierre would never even think of verifying such a story, believe me. The bigger the lie, the better it sounds." Charles shrugged. "Perhaps I should have added a few more family members who died in the storm."

"Stop killing off all my family," I snapped, then giggled. "What else did he ask?"

"He wanted to know if you had lands or any money. I replied that your family had sold everything to pay for the crusade and that your father, a merchant, had been buried with his armor in Tunis."

"A merchant? Go on." I was smiling broadly now. I hadn't felt so good in ages. Charles and I grinned at each other, enjoying our joke.

"Well..."

At that moment the pack mule in front of us skidded to a halt and threw its head up, braying loudly. The man holding its reins cursed, and we heard more shouting. Whatever was causing the ruckus was muffled by the fog, and we couldn't see what had happened.

"What is it?" I peered into the thick mist. "Is the trouble in front of us, or behind?"

Charles pulled the ponies to the side of the road, for the sounds of clattering hooves could clearly be heard now. My ponies tossed their heads and whickered as Charles swatted their sides, urging them into the tall grass. The litter swayed alarmingly as the ponies edged away from the road.

The sound of galloping hoofbeats grew louder, although with the dense fog it was hard to pinpoint where they came from. Louder and louder they grew, and as they got closer, yells and shouts accompanied them. Hoarse cries of fright echoed through the fog, and shrill screams as well. All around us, we could barely make out people and horses moving out of the way. Fear made my heart pound, and my hands clutched the drapery as I peered into the grayness. The curtain of fog hid everything.

Suddenly a horse surged into sight. It was a runaway, careening out of the mist, its head thrown high and eyes rolling. At first I thought it had broken free from a cart and that part of its load dragged behind it.

When the horse slalomed by, I realized otherwise. A human body hung by the foot from the ornate harness. I caught a glimpse of the horse's white-rimmed eyes, and then it was gone. I froze, shock washing over me like an icy, prickly shower. I'd recognized the person trapped by the stirrup. It had been the queen.

We drew further back as more horses galloped out of the mist — the king and his guards racing after the queen. I saw Jean's father among the white-faced men.

I heard the sound of a heavy crash, then voices shouting they'd caught the horse and to get help, quickly.

I threw my furs off my lap and struggled out of my litter. Sharp sobs escaped my throat as I hastened down the road, Charles at my heels. Other people joined us, all hurrying toward the sound of heart-wrenching screams that had no trouble penetrating the muffling fog.

The mist clogged my nostrils as I ran, pearled on my hair and made the stones underfoot slick as glass. Charles grabbed my elbow when I staggered, and we hurried through the grayness. Dark shadows slowly revealed themselves as a crowd huddled in a circle around the queen.

I elbowed my way to the middle. My pregnancy made most people move out of my way. No one stopped me. If only someone had.

The queen, freed from the harness, lay crumpled in the road. She screamed as she writhed on the stony ground, wet with a dark stain I realized was her blood. Her cries horrified me, chilled me and raised the hair on my head. I clenched my teeth together.

"She's giving birth," cried someone. "Hurry! Get the priest! Fetch a midwife! Hurry, man!"

I stood at her side, frozen in horror. There was nothing anyone could do except put her out of her misery, but she wasn't a dog. She was a woman, and she was dying.

Slowly, heavily, I knelt by her side. I wanted to touch her, but where could I place my hand? She was broken, shattered, everywhere I looked there was the scarlet of blood or the white of bone. As I watched, her body convulsed and steam rose from between her legs.

She gave birth to her baby in the middle of the road. The pain must have been indescribable. Her legs and arms were broken and folded in impossible angles. Her scalp flapped back with the skull bared, and her nose was torn clear off her face.

Her robes had been shredded by the horse's hooves and the stones.

She gave another gurgling scream and arched her back. There was the sound of something ripping, and the baby surged out of its mother's womb into the waiting hands of a priest. The child was dead, its head limp, and the king, kneeling just behind the priest, toppled over in a faint. Other people swooned as well, hitting the ground with loud thumps, but I knelt at the queen's head and touched her cheek.

She opened one eye. The other was gone. I saw the pain, the question, and the white veil of death slowly obscuring her view, like the fog. Little shrieks were torn out of her throat with each breath she drew. Her hand scrabbled on the rocks, digging into the bloody ground.

I leaned over until my mouth was near her ear. "The baby is well. It's a perfect little girl. She is tiny, with jet-black hair, just like your mother's."

She closed her eye again. Her teeth were bared in pain, ribbons of blood seeping between them, and a rattle sounded deep in her throat. Her hand scraped madly in the mud. A strange quivering seized her body, and a priest took a hold of the back of my robe and pulled me up. It was time for the Last Rites.

Someone took my arm and led me away. I followed blindly, not seeing where I was going.

Bile welled in my throat. "Charles, stop, I'm going to vomit," I gasped.

The man holding my elbow tightened his grip. "Go ahead," he said. It was Jean's father.

Startled, I whirled around. I clapped a hand over my mouth, but it was too late. I threw up on his feet.

With an oath, he leapt backwards. I lost my balance and would have fallen, but he was quick, I'll grant him that. He caught me neatly under the arms and set me onto a nearby boulder.

"I'm sorry," I said. The shock caught up with me and I shook uncontrollably. I screwed my eyes shut to block out the image I still saw in my mind, but it didn't work. "I can't," I gasped. "I just can't."

"Can't what?" His voice was neither harsh nor gentle, but it was strong. As was his hand. I winced as his fingers dug into my arm.

"I can't bear to see any more," I said, and then I was sick again. I retched miserably while he held my head and shoulders. Afterwards he hefted me into his arms and walked back to my litter, where he tossed me none too gently inside.

"We go now," he said.

"Where?"

"Tours. We're leaving. A dead king, a dead queen and a stillborn child. A funeral cortege is what Philip is bringing to Paris. I won't accompany him any longer."

He slapped my pony on the rump and we started to move.

"Charles!" I cried, but Jean's father only grunted and took my pony's bridle. "Charles!" I sobbed, leaning precariously out the litter.

Jean's father glared at me, his green eyes uncannily resembling Jean's. "Get back inside and close the drapes. I'll send Lucien after your page and your pack mule."

I dared protest no longer. All the strength drained out of my trembling limbs and I sank back onto the furs. I was suddenly grateful for them, and I snuggled into their warmth like a child. The day had been too much for me. My mind switched itself off and I fell asleep.

* * * * *

I awoke the next day after dozing on and off for twenty hours. Devastation had clenched my teeth so tightly together I could hardly breathe. The muscles in my neck and back ached, and my chest hurt. Stabbing pains made me wonder if I was having a heart attack, but it was just stress.

The worst part was, I'd known. I'd known that Isabella died young, but I'd forgotten, and I'd never known how or exactly when she was to die. Life and friendship had gotten in the way of history lessons, and the two lines I'd read in prison had escaped me. Only two lines were written in a history book about a lovely, fanciful Spanish princess with a fondness for oranges. Two lines that I'd chosen deliberately to forget. I pounded my litter in impotent fury. What good would it have done? Would I have changed time, changed the future, if I'd been able to, or would I have let events take their course to save myself from erasure?

I was suddenly glad I'd forgotten.

We camped near a dirt track, a path really, which Lucien assured us led right to Tours through the charcoal maker's forest.

"The forest is a tricky place, and many have gotten lost there," Lucien said. He took a piece of rabbit from the carcass and chewed it carefully.

Charles and I looked at each other. My throat was still locked too tightly to speak, eat or even drink. The sight of food made me shudder. Charles nibbled on a crust of bread, but I could tell his heart wasn't in it.

"How long will it be until we arrive?" he asked.

"That depends on the weather, our speed and the lady here," said Lucien, nodding at me.

Jean's father ate his meal as far away from us as possible and never spoke a single word to us. He never looked my way, either, and I found it most troubling. Did he doubt the fact I was married to his son? He was right to do so, as there had been no ceremony. If my lies were found out, I'd be cast into the streets, or worse, in prison.

Stiffly, I made my way to the ditch to relieve myself. The fog hadn't lifted, and the day was as gray and cheerless as could be. Memories of yesterday's drama kept flitting through my mind, and every time I closed my eyes the sight of Isabella's ruined face intruded.

I finished my business and stood up slowly. If only that ache in my back would disappear! I put my hands behind me and winced. At that moment a queer feeling swept over me. It was like something tearing painlessly inside of me. Sweat sprang out on my forehead and upper lip. I hurried to lift my skirt again and squatted over the ditch. Hot liquid splashed onto the ground, and a strange odor assailed me. It was soon finished, and I actually felt a bit better afterwards.

I wondered what had happened. I counted backwards, frowning. Was it my waters breaking? Isabella, poor Isabella, had mentioned that although she hadn't said what it was like. Damn the TCF! Since I was supposed to be sterile, I'd never given a single thought to childbirth. In my time, it was all done by machines. Test tubes and incubators were so much more reliable than human bodies. What was natural childbirth like? I tried to dredge up memories of history books, but nothing occurred to me.

I lay down on my pallet, Charles at my side, and prepared to sleep. Instead, strange cramps in my abdomen kept me awake. They grew stronger and stronger, and my whole belly shuddered and tightened with them. It felt almost like food poisoning. Around midnight, after three or four hours of this, I woke Charles.

"Something is wrong," I whispered, then groaned as another pain swept over me. If only I'd questioned Isabella more!

"I'll get Lucien." In the short time Charles had known the worldly guard, he'd grown to think of him as the answer to all questions. While Lucien was handy with setting up tents and skinning rabbits, I had no idea what good he could do as a midwife, for by now I'd realized this must be childbirth. Before I could protest, Charles had gone, the tent flap fluttered and I was alone and gasping with another pain.

Within minutes, the tent flap opened again, but it was Jean's father, a peculiar look on his face. "Is it starting already?" he asked.

"I don't know," I moaned. "I've never done this before."

He almost smiled. "Neither have I, but I've seen it done."

"You have?" I gasped.

He shrugged. "When my wife gave birth to her children I helped. Don't worry. You'll be fine."

"No, I won't," I said stubbornly.

Lucien and Charles came in with their arms loaded with sticks. Soon the brazier glowed brightly and a pot of water boiled on it. Charles fetched clean linens from my trunk, and Lucien disappeared into the night. I heard the sound of galloping hooves, and Charles said, "He's gone to the charcoal makers to fetch a midwife. Don't worry, Isobel, we'll take care of you."

His small hand found mine, and I took it for comfort.

While Jean's father tended the fire and fashioned a makeshift cradle with supple willow branches, Charles sat at my side. I was fascinated to watch the tiny cradle grow before my eyes.

"How lovely," I breathed, then grunted as a cramp shook me.

Charles whimpered as well, for I'd crushed his hand in my grip.

"Sorry," I gasped. "I'll hold a stick. Oh Lord." Another pain came, this time nearly submerging me. I didn't understand them. Sometimes they were painless, and only the muscles across my huge belly tightened, and sometimes they wrenched me from the inside out. The pain of the forceful ones left me panting and bewildered. To add to my discomfort, the aching feeling was back, and heaviness seemed to grow between my legs.

I felt the baby then, moving downwards. It surprised me, and more than that, it frightened me. I hauled myself to my elbows and stared at the mound that was my stomach. My knees parted by themselves. I had only one urge, to push as hard as I could. I gave a sharp scream.

Charles echoed my cry, and Jean's father dropped the cradle and sat down at my side. He placed a hand on my shoulder. "The child comes. I shall have to catch him. Don't look. Close your eyes and push."

I thought that it was an odd command, but I was used to taking orders. I gritted my teeth, closed my eyes and bore down. Two strong hands pushed my thighs apart and lifted my robe to my waist, but I kept my eyes shut. While I shuddered and strained, the iron hands stilled my trembling legs. After one huge push, a sharp, tearing sensation made me squeal.

It was the baby crowning. Someone—not me—uttered an excited gasp. Pain flowered and subsided as soon as a slippery, heavy weight left my body. It happened so quickly I thought my insides had come undone, and I fainted.

The next time I opened my eyes, a warm glow bathed the tent and a tiny baby nestled in my arms. I peered at the crumpled face, a dusky, dark red color, and felt absurdly proud of myself. Tears pricked my eyes and I laughed softly. The infant stirred, opened the tiniest mouth imaginable, and yawned with the same mewing sound a kitten makes.

"What a precious little boy," I whispered.

Charles cleared his throat. "It's a girl, actually."

I stared at him. "Wh-what?"

"A girl. A fine, healthy girl." His tone was apologetic. He knew, as well as I did, that I had to have a boy, or my mission was a failure. At least, that's what I'd thought.

I held my breath and listened for thunder. All I heard was the sound of branches crackling in the fire and the wind in the trees. "A girl," I said dully.

"She's a fine, healthy g—"

"I know, you said that." Exhaustion kept my voice level. Otherwise, I think I would have screamed. Would I be erased now? What of my child? Panic, pain and exhaustion warred within me. The result was a curious numbness and buzzing in my head.

Jean's father stood from his corner and held up a small cradle made of woven willow branches. He eyed it critically and set it down by the fire. He stretched and lifted the tent flap to peer at the sky. "It's dawn," he said.

"Dawn," I echoed. I looked at the peaceful creature in my arms and sighed. "We'll call her Aurore," I said, the French word for dawn.

"That's a nice name. Lucien's coming back. I hope he's found someone decent." Jean's father spoke absently, still looking outside.

"Found someone for what?" I heard hoofbeats now, quite clearly, but I was amazed that Jean's father had heard them before I did. My ears were usually the keenest.

"For the babe. She'll need a nurse." He still didn't look at me when he spoke. Instead he drew on his cloak and went into the gray dawn without a backward glance at me or his new grandchild. I think I clutched the baby to my breast. I vaguely remember someone taking her from my arms, and I tried to protest, but nothing I could do kept me from falling deeply asleep.

I met the woman Lucien had fetched the next morning when I awoke. The nurse was a stout peasant woman with a thatch of black hair so dense it looked at first like a felt hat. Her round face was small, her mouth constantly pursed, and for a very long time she never uttered a single word. She was nimble and did everything with an efficiency of movement that was almost poetical to see.

No one told me her name—she was called "Nurse". When I asked her what her name was, she ducked her head and turned beet red. Perhaps she was mute and couldn't speak, although she crooned in a rough voice to the child as she nursed her or held her on her shoulder to burp.

I noticed almost immediately Nurse was only as clean as peasants went in that time and thought to myself I might have to do something about that, if she were to tend my baby. She did wash her hands and face, and the rest of her body stayed unwashed until spring thaws. I was slowly getting used to odors, thankfully, for she was to share the litter with me as we traveled.

The first two days we spent at the campsite and I learned how to hold my baby and how to nurse her. I wanted to feed my own baby, but my breasts were sore and I couldn't sit up without wincing. Mothers in my time didn't nurse and didn't give birth, so I had no idea if anything I was doing was correct. I had to put my entire trust in an uneducated peasant woman. It was both frustrating and frightening.

As for my other ills, I knew that salt was an antiseptic, so I sat in a shallow tub filled with hot salt water for a few hours. To my relief, this seemed to help and I started to feel better.

Nurse assisted me a great deal and I was quickly grateful. She cleaned my bed linens and clothes and took care of Aurore. She approved of my salt baths and produced a cream for my sore breasts. The cream was in a wooden vial and smelled like herbs, garlic, and lanolin.

After three days, I felt almost human again, except for my sore breasts, my sorer nipples, and having to change the thick pad between my legs every hour or so. Nurse was a wonder in efficiency, and I never went without a clean pad of cloth.

Jean's father spoke to Charles and even to the nurse, but not to directly me. I'd wondered if Aurore's birth would make him friendlier to me, but I was the vessel into which Jean had poured his seed. I'd carried the progeny, and now I was simply an extra mouth to feed at dinnertime. Nothing was asked of me, nor was I supposed to take any initiative. Women of my supposed class were expected to follow meekly whatever orders were given to her, to raise their children, and to sew, mind the house and hearth, and dabble in the stewpot or gardens every now and then.

The only change came one day as I lay in my bed contemplating the tiny infant in my arms. He entered the tent, ducking through the heavy tent flap, and looked down at the baby with sharp eyes. His expression was so bleak I felt a quick stab of pity. It welled up out of my own emotional state, and my exhaustion made me weak.

"She's a lovely baby, sir," I ventured. "Sir. It seems odd to name my husband's father so. Is there nothing I may call you except sir?"

"You may call me François," he said. Then he closed his mouth, turned on his heel and left the tent, as if he'd already said too much.

François? I turned the name over in my mouth, but it seemed too soft for him. I'd have thought that he'd have a harder name, something with more bite. "François." But the name didn't soften his attitude toward me. He hardly addressed a word to me, except to say, "We're off now," or, "No, we can't stop here. You'll have to wait to relieve yourself later".

I rode in the litter, I ate, I nursed and I sewed three little vests for my baby out of an old skirt I'd torn apart. My strength slowly returned, and my breasts grew less sensitive, but Nurse had more milk than I did and nursed Aurore more often. It didn't bother me. I was content to hold my baby and cuddle with her. She hardly slept anywhere but in my arms, and I was completely besotted with the tiny creature. Since she had two women nursing her, Aurore was never hungry and she thrived, growing rosy with good health.

The voyage was slow. I was weaker than I thought and couldn't sit for any length of time. The litter was uncomfortable as it rose and dropped with each of the two ponies' footsteps. Once the lead pony shied and jumped sideways. The litter rocked violently, and I nearly fell out of it.

Nurse grabbed my dress and hauled me back inside. Her other arm was firmly locked around Aurore, and the baby didn't even stir.

I thanked her for saving me from a nasty fall, but she only flushed again, the blood rushing to her cheeks and staining them violet. She shook her head, wordlessly, but a timid smile darted across her face. She was strong, silent and smelled like ripe cheese, but she'd acted swiftly to save me and my daughter. Any reservations about trusting her with Aurore faded that moment.

# Chapter Twelve

இ

We arrived in Tours at dusk on the ninth day. Valets and grooms crowded the narrow, cobblestone courtyard, some taking hold of baggage, others grabbing the ponies and leading them away.

The bustle made me feel faint, though more likely it was fatigue. I was so stiff I could hardly move as Lucien helped me out of the litter. He turned to take Aurore from Nurse while she clambered down and I stretched, rubbed my back and neck, and sought Charles with my eyes. He was just disappearing around the corner, taking our donkey to the stables.

François' voice rose over the chatter and clattering hooves. "Elaine! Come and meet Jean's wife Isobel and your new niece."

I turned to see a hooded figure move gracefully forward and stand beside her father, not far from me. He pointed toward me, and I smiled, intending to greet her.

Without throwing back her hood, she curtsied abruptly, like a puppet whose strings have suddenly been jerked. Then she whirled and left, her cape swooping outwards like huge, dark wings. Soon thereafter, Nurse and I were installed in a small room in the north tower, reserved for unwanted guests, I'm sure.

That night at dinner, I finally saw Elaine's face and her clear, emerald-green eyes. The meal was informal, and Charles ate with us. I was thankful François had suggested Charles sit next to me. Perhaps he wasn't so bad after all.

Elaine was a pale girl with dark hair. Her resemblance to Jean troubled me. It seemed that François had placed his stamp upon his children, and I suddenly wondered what his wife had looked like.

"Pass the water, Elaine," her father said.

She reached her arm toward the pitcher and dragged her velvet sleeve in her dinner plate. "*Merde*," she swore, which caused her nurse to drop her spoon with a clatter and her father to thump his tankard on the wooden table.

"I'll not have that word at the table," said François.

"And I'll not have a whore at the table," Elaine snapped right back at him. "That woman can't be Jean's wife. She's nothing but a whore he met on the crusade."

I raised my eyes, shocked. Nothing had prepared me for that onslaught. Elaine had been quiet, but polite. She had inquired as to the voyage, speaking more to her father than to me, but I thought that normal. She hadn't seen him in nearly three months.

Perhaps she was troubled because of her mother's recent death, so I gave a tiny shrug and continued to eat. Besides, wasn't she right, in a very small way? Jean had indeed met me on the crusade, though I wasn't a prostitute.

Silence caused me to raise my head again. Everyone, I suddenly realized, was staring at me. Elaine with spite, Charles with something like terror and François with the first spark of interest I'd seen in his eyes.

"I'm not a whore," I commented mildly. Keeping my temper under control was easy when I was as numb with exhaustion as I was. "Pass the salt, please, François."

He did, and Elaine rose suddenly, nearly overturning her chair. Before she left, she turned and stared hard at me. She opened her mouth, then shut it. I watched her go and realized that my hand gripped my spoon so tight that my knuckles cracked. Otherwise, a blanket of fatigue had anesthetized my feelings. I tried to dredge up some emotions, but it was too much of an effort. Besides, I had no idea how to react.

"Elaine is usually very friendly," said her nurse, Dame Blanche. She was from Paris and had white, soft hands that fluttered at her breast when she spoke. When we were introduced, I learned that she was François' aunt and had been Jean and Elaine's nurse. Dame Blanche leaned toward me over the table and smiled, showing a wide gap between her two front teeth.

Not knowing what to say, I shrugged again. She sank back in her chair with a loud sigh. "It's a pity, Sir François, that your daughter accuses her own sister-in-law of being a whore. Perhaps you should reprimand her."

"Why? She's just speaking her mind." François sounded amused.

I choked on my watery soup. "Excuse me?" I raised my head and met his eyes. "And what, pray tell, can your mind be on the matter?" I was surprised to hear my voice come out of my throat in such an even tone. It sounded almost light, as if I was bantering. His words had shocked me out of my apathy, though. What would happen if he found out I'd never married Jean? What would happen to my new baby? Panic made my heart thump painfully—I couldn't let him know.

He matched my tone, although his eyes were icy. "I have no thoughts at all on the matter. Jean wrote, then you wrote and Queen Isabella, God rest her soul, wrote as well. What would you have me do? Berate my daughter for being rude? I'm sure she realizes it by now, or she'd never have left the table. Shall I call her back?"

"No!" I lowered my eyes. I was so tired. My shoulders slumped and the energy I'd mustered for the dinner left me in a rush. The news that Queen Isabella had written Jean's father bewildered me. Why had she written? What had she said? I wanted to ask, but I didn't dare.

"Will you excuse me? I want to go to bed now." I stood up without waiting for a reply and made my way to my room. The narrow, wooden corridors seemed endless, poorly lit with sputtering torches. It was bitterly cold, and I was glad to reach my room. Heavy tapestries hung on the walls, and the fire was lit, although it burned low. Nurse sat on a cushioned stool by the chimney, Aurore in her arms. The coals turned her sallow skin orange. I shut the door and leaned on it.

"I'm so tired," I said to Nurse. "I hate it here. I wish I could go home." The enormity of my words sank in, and I dug my nails into the wooden door at my back. I felt depression settle over me like heavy water. I could hardly breathe. My melancholy was coming back, and I was too weak to resist.

"You can't go home." The voice came from behind the door, muffled by thick wood. "Let me enter."

It was an order, and I backed away. The door swung open and let in a gust of cold air. Jean's father stepped in, which made me realize just how tiny the room was. I shivered. His body filled the whole room. In two strides, he was at the chimney. He tossed another three logs on the fire and stirred the flames with a poker.

"Put the child to bed," he said to Nurse and she complied, placing the sleeping infant in her willow crib. She curtsied and left the room, shutting the door behind her.

"What do you want?" I sat heavily on my bed and started to unbraid my hair, but my hands slid down the tress and landed on my lap. It was an effort to sit upright. I drew a deep breath and raised my eyes, expecting to see François staring into the fire, or anywhere else than my own face. But he was looking at me with a queer expression.

"You can't go home," he repeated. "Your family is dead, and I'm all you have left."

"I have Charles and Aurore." I smiled thinly. "I don't have you at all. You don't care for me or for your granddaughter. According to Jean, you didn't care for him either." I spoke rashly, but exhaustion and hopelessness made me short-tempered.

"My son and I never got along. It was my wife's fault—she spoiled him." He spoke absently, his eyes still locked with mine. Before I realized it he'd come to my side and lifted my heavy braid. "Here, let me." He deftly unplaited it and smoothed it on my shoulders. Jean had sometimes done that at night.

"You have lovely hair, Isobel," he said. "It looks like wheat just before the harvest."

"Thank you," I said dully. Tears seeped from my eyes and trickled down my cheeks. Why did he have to look so much like his son? In the firelight, in the darkness, I could imagine it was Jean. "Go away, please."

"No." His hand found my cheek and wiped the tears away with his thumb. "You may think I don't care, but I do. Jean was my only son. I loved him, although I never told him. It's not my way to speak of such things as love or hate. I prefer to speak of hunting. Perhaps you know something of stag hunting?" His voice was low, almost teasing.

I jerked back. "No. I never hunted."

"Tell me, Isobel, about your family." He sat down beside me. His arm, next to mine, felt as strong as steel. Behind his words was a hidden threat and I trembled.

"My family?" My mouth dried with nervousness and I licked my lips. I knew what Charles had said about my history and what we had agreed upon should anyone question us, a mixture of fact and fancy that none could, hopefully, disprove.

I thought of my parents. How could I describe them? I saw my mother's face clearly. She sat on a folding chair in the hospital when I awoke from the coma after the accident, so straight and stiff it looked painful. Her white face stared at the screen in the corner of my room. When the judge on the portable television screen pronounced me guilty, she swallowed once, very hard. Then her shoulders slumped and she leaned against my father.

My father never looked at me again. As soon as the verdict was given, I'd ceased to be his daughter. They'd left the room before the television had been turned off. The door locked behind them with a sharp click. I was alone in the prison hospital, alone and without family. The letters I wrote to them came back unanswered, and with the mention, "Addressee unknown, no forwarding address".

I didn't tell these things to François, of course. Instead I said, "They were kindly people, and I was their only daughter."

"Did you sail with them to Tunis? Where, exactly, did you meet Jean?"

"I met him in a shelter, with the other crusaders. He was so different from anyone else around him. He glowed. I saw him…" My voice trailed off.

"You met him before you sailed then? Is that it?"

"Yes. My family left on one boat, and I sailed with Jean on another boat. Charles came with me because he's been in my service since he was a lad."

"He's not much older than a lad." His voice was dry.

"He's devoted to me." The fire cast tall shadows on the walls, and Aurore whimpered in her sleep.

"You've told me nothing." Jean's father took my chin in his hand and tipped my face to his. "You have a fearsome scar."

"Stop. Stop, please," I begged. The voice, the eyes, it was all too much. Even the words were the same. My composure was breaking, and I could feel the cracks like sharp pains in my chest.

"What happened?" His fingers traced it, ignoring my feeble attempts to turn my face away.

"I fell through a window." I stopped struggling. He was too strong, and I was too exhausted.

"Glass cut your face?"

"Yes. And your scar?" I spoke without looking at him, but I could still picture his scar, a jagged silver stripe on one cheek.

"A sword cut me." His voice was soft. "Did your parents leave you any money?"

"No. They sold everything to pay for the crusade. My father wanted to buy goods in the Holy Land and bring them back to sell, so he had a large sum of money with him. But it disappeared when their boat sank."

"I thought they perished of the plague."

I gave a small start and remembered Charles' words. The bigger the lie, the better it sounds. "They were rescued from the water, but their money was gone. All that remained was my father's armor. When he died in battle, my mother buried him with his horse and his armor. Then she died of the plague within the week."

"It must have been terrible for you."

"Jean was there. He gave me comfort."

"How did he die?" Suddenly I realized why he was with me. The anguish in his voice couldn't be hidden.

I faltered as the painful memories flashed before my eyes. But François deserved to know. "The battle was short, but terrible. So many died. I walked across the battlefield, looking for him. I called and called..." My voice cracked. "He was dead, and he couldn't answer. There was an arrow in his side." There was no stopping my tears now. I leaned against him, and I sobbed.

He held me until I fell asleep, although I have no recollection. I woke the next morning still dressed, but my hair was carefully arranged on my pillow. Nurse sat at the fireplace rocking Aurore in her arms, and weak sunlight made the tapestries hanging on the walls glow with jewel-like colors.

My head was clear, my depression had passed, or more likely it had simply been stress and fatigue. A good sleep often put things right and my bed had been comfortable for the first time in weeks.

I wondered if François would be different with me now, but when I made my way downstairs I learned that he had gone to Paris and wouldn't be back until late spring.

"He's gone to see about business matters," said Elaine. She'd decided to like me, or at least to act as if she did. Sometimes I caught glimpses of anger, but I was beginning to understand why. Jean had spoken to me of his sister, and sometimes he'd mention the fact that she hadn't wanted to marry. I thought I knew what angered her now. She'd been expecting a rich, titled heiress. I was a penniless commoner, and the family's fortune, which I quickly realized was dilapidated, was now hers to save.

\* \* \* \* \*

"It's hopeless." I set a linen square down on my lap and tried vainly to smooth the stitches.

"If you tug on them like that, you'll tear the cloth," said Elaine. With impatient hands, she plucked it away from me. "Look, you must try and make all the stitches go in the same direction. If you cross over this way, it will make the fabric pull. It's very fine linen, and you're ruining it. Didn't anyone teach you to sew?" Her tone was scornful.

"I'm sorry." I rubbed a weary hand over my eyes. "I can hardly see anymore. The sun is dipping below the battlements. Do you think we could light a lamp?"

"Heavens, no! Do you think we're rich?" She laughed, but it was a brittle sound. "What a pity that Jean didn't marry a wealthy woman so we could afford to light lamps all day and all night. We also wouldn't be obliged to live in this dreary castle, in the middle of the swamps and forest. We could return to Paris where there are fêtes every night and lights on every street. I'd be able to see my friends, instead of being shut up like a nun in this horrid, cold, damp ruin." She finished her tirade and poked her needle savagely through the linen.

"I was wealthy once, I suppose, although not by your high standards." I thought back on all my conversations with Jean about his sister. "Is your father going to bargain for your husband in Paris? Is that why he left so suddenly? Did you beg him to leave?"

The white spots around her nostrils showed how close I'd come to the target. "I am engaged to be married, if that's what you insinuate."

"I insinuate nothing. Who is it? Do you know him well?"

"He's Robert, Count of Artois." She sounded almost smug.

I peered closely at her face. She turned away quickly to look out the window. It was an unfortunate choice if she wanted to hide her fear, because the remaining daylight only emphasized the sudden pallor of her cheeks and the twitch of compressed lips.

"Who is he?" I asked.

Now surprise lifted her eyebrows. "You don't know Robert of Artois?"

"Not unless he was on the crusade, then I would have seen him in the court. Perhaps my memory fails me. Was he there?"

"No." Her silent fingers plucked restlessly at the stitches. I was afraid she'd undo all my work, so I tapped her gently on the arm. She jumped, startled. "What?"

"Do you love him?" I asked.

"It doesn't matter whether I love him or not. He's wealthy, and he asked for me in marriage. He saw me in Paris, just before Jean left."

I nodded slowly. My suspicions had been right, and there was something else as well. "Your brother didn't leave because he hated your father. He left to gain fortune and spare you marriage," I said. "You helped him get away, didn't you?"

She bowed her head and tears sparkled on her lashes. "You're not rich, so I don't believe Jean should ever have married you. Anyway, mother always loved Jean the best."

I thought about what she said and then spoke slowly. "You and Jean must have been very close to each other. You know, he didn't betray you. I was rich at the time he met me." I stuck to the story Charles had woven. "My father's fortune sank with the ship."

"So he did try." She spoke quietly. "Before I saw you, I hoped you'd be rich. But when you came and I saw how poor your valet looked, and the state of your thin ponies and wretched donkey…"

"The ponies were a gift from her majesty, Isabella. Is your betrothed so dreadful?"

"He's rich," she said sullenly. The needle flashed.

"Is he nice?"

"He's been married three times before. I'll be his fourth wife."

With that admission it was as if the floodgates on Elaine's fears burst, and words tumbled out in a rush. She took my hands, her embroidery sliding to a heap on the floor. Tears sparkled on her long lashes.

"I do wish you had money left! His first wife was unfaithful, and he sent her to a tower, where some say she was strangled and others say she starved to death." She said this in a matter-of-fact voice. In those times, an adulterous woman was usually punished by her husband, so Elaine probably thought she'd deserved her fate. "His second wife died in childbirth, and the third one died in a fall. She tumbled off the battlements while walking with her baby son in her arms. They both perished. Some say she was the only woman he ever loved, and now his heart is as cold as stone."

His heart had probably never been very warm, especially hearing how he'd had his first wife punished, but I held my tongue. Elaine was very young, only sixteen, and, if I knew anything about her family, impetuous. "Do you want to marry him?" I asked.

"I don't know," she said. "If only Father would find a wealthy wife so I wouldn't have to marry d'Artois. I could wait awhile. I'm afraid to marry and have children."

I nodded, suddenly understanding. That was probably the real reason behind her fear. Childbirth was the main cause of death among women at that time, with one-third of the deaths of women due to child birthing complications. Thankfully, that statistic had slipped my mind when I was in the middle of birthing Aurore. "Does your father search for a new wife?"

"I believe so." She sat back, sniffed and wiped her cheeks. "He wants to see me married and secure, but I'd never feel safe if I had to bear a child every year. Robert only wants an heir, I'm sure. Then Father said we were nearly ruined, and the lands are fallow. There are no more serfs to work for us — they've all left, gone to the crusades or into the forest to be freemen. We've no money to pay the dime, so Father has gone to speak to King Philip and beg for an extension. I don't know how long we'll be able to hold on to the castle. Already Father has sold his horses and gold cups that belonged to our grandfather."

"I'm sorry." I thought of the gold coins still sewn in the hem of my robe. I'd save them for an emergency — there was no use telling Elaine about them. They'd only buy a few months' respite for the people living here, and for me, they were my only insurance. If I were cast adrift and if, of course, Aurore's presence managed to get history back on track and we weren't erased by the TCF. "How will we feed everyone?"

"Lucien and Father hunt nearly every week. Luckily, we have hunting rights to the forest around us. Some vegetables grow in the kitchen courtyard, and the chestnuts were abundant this year. We dry them and grind chestnut flour. Without those, we'd starve."

"Don't you have any chickens?" I asked.

"No, a fox got into the coop and killed them all. We haven't had any for months and we'll have to wait for spring to buy some pullets. The rabbits died of fright during a lighting storm, and the milk goat died of old age." She ticked off the dead animals on her fingers.

"Can't we get a chicken and use the eggs?" I asked. "Some farmer must have one or two for sale."

"Chickens don't lay in the winter. You city folk know nothing at all."

I stood and pulled Elaine to her feet. "Show me the larder. I might not be rich, and I may not know anything about farming, but maybe I can make myself useful."

I hadn't studied those history books for nothing. I hoped I could use my knowledge to find something to do to help. One of my books claimed that dandelions, among other common plants, were rich in vitamins and that peasants of the times often used them for food. I imagined myself bringing baskets of fresh greens to the kitchen to go with venison steaks.

We left the sitting room and crossed the courtyard to the kitchen, which was a separate building made of stone with a thick, thatched roof. There were two small doors and large casement windows covered in dust. Though it was nearly empty now, I saw traces of the kitchen's past splendor in the rusting spit, the long chains that could hold a whole ox over the fire, and in the fireplace itself, big enough to hold the ox with room to spare. A black kettle in which I could have bathed sat useless off to the side, and a functioning well, just a hole in the stone floor, was in the corner of the room. I peered down its mossy sides but could see only blackness. A bucket on a long rope and a dipper hung from a nail on the wall above.

Turning, I surveyed the room. The main fireplace was no longer used as such. Instead, a small brick oven had been built in its center. The servants baked bread there, and meat, when it was available, was cooked on a grill on the top, the drippings falling onto the bread beneath. Beside the fireplace was a three-legged pot for cooking vegetables and a flat, iron stovetop for the chestnut-flour pancakes. The reed torches were burnt to stubs, and small beeswax candles lit the room, though not the dark corners, where cobwebs covered massive wooden plates and platters, a legacy from the castle's prosperous era.

The cook stood, hands on narrow hips, and stared at me. He was an old man, by those times, toothless and gaunt. Elaine introduced me.

"Sad thing that young master Jean didn't come home," he muttered in a gummy voice.

"Yes," I agreed.

He scratched his head, examined his nails for signs of lice, and motioned us toward the pantry. "There's not much left," he said. "We'll have to make do with that until Lucien gets back from the forest." He opened a creaking door and took a lit candle from its place on the table.

"Each time he must go further afield," said Elaine.

"Game is getting scarce." The old man shrugged. "But Lucien can scent a hind as well as any hound."

I peered into the darkness, then took a candle and held it above my head. A set of spiral stairs was dug out of the bedrock. I sneezed, lifted my skirts and descended into the cellar pantry. Cook and Elaine followed, chatting together about Lucien, whom I gathered was Cook's grandson.

There were more spiders in that room than food. A wooden crate held some old cabbages, a half-full bag of carrots hung on a nail and the bin of chestnuts was nearly empty.

I pointed to the chestnuts. "Shouldn't we get more of these?"

"It's not their season any longer," said the cook. "But there's bound to be mushrooms in the forest. I'm not as spry as I used to be. Perhaps you could ask your valet, the little chap, Charles, to get some."

"I'll ask him." I continued with the inventory. "Is there any dried meat?"

"No, and no salt left either. No honey, no nuts, no buckwheat..." The cook ticked off the absent food on his fingers.

"What is there besides shriveled carrots and chestnuts?" Elaine asked, worry in her voice.

"Mushrooms if we're lucky, fresh water, some shriveled parsnips, two ponies in the stable and a donkey." He didn't lack humor. His eyes sparkled though the tone was serious.

Elaine didn't smile. "Don't be frivolous." Then she sighed. "I'm sure Lucian will be back soon. Shall we go look for Charles? If we all go, perhaps we'll find thrice as many mushrooms."

\* \* \* \* \*

"Thrice nothing is nothing," I said, wiping my muddy hands on my skirt. "There isn't a mushroom within a hundred leagues of here." My books had shown loads of pictures of edible mushrooms, but had given no indication of where to find them. Elaine didn't know much more about mushrooms than I did, and even Charles had had no luck.

Charles stood from picking around the base of an oak tree and nodded. "I think you're right. I looked for field roses, oyster mushrooms, death trumpets and spring porcini. There are none around. The wild boars must have gotten to them sooner than we did."

"Death trumpets?" I asked. "Are they poisonous?"

"No, they're quite good. They're also called horns of plenty, and they're pitch black, thus the name 'death trumpet'. I find them in the fall, but sometimes you can get some in the spring." Charles, as I'd noticed on the crusade, knew all the edible plants, more than my books could ever have taught me. He'd already dug up handfuls of dog-tooth violet roots and stuffed them in his pockets. I'd found a few miserable dandelion leaves, but there were hardly enough. My élan of helpfulness was rapidly turning into the familiar feeling of uselessness.

"Who lives in the castle now?" I asked Elaine. "Besides you and your father, the cook, Lucien and Dame Blanche?"

"There are three farmhands with their families in the stable wing. Over the gatehouse lives old Marthe who used to be Father's nurse. She can hardly walk and we take food to her in the evenings." Elaine scratched her head and frowned. "Father still has his groom, Richard, who has three sons. They do odd jobs around the castle. Last month they drained the moat and we had fish for a week."

"Any fish left?" Charles asked.

"The last ones were buried in the vegetable plot just before you arrived. They'd started stinking."

"What about ducks?"

"We ate the last duck a year ago, it seems. The canny birds used to come to the moat every evening, but they stopped when we started snaring them. Father wanted to net the whole lot of them, but they got away. A pity — we could have smoked some." Elaine grimaced. "We would have starved if Lucien hadn't caught the deer at Christmas. Mother was already dead then. I think her heart simply gave up."

"I'm sorry about your mother," I said.

She glanced at me sideways. "She loved Jean the best. I was used to it, but when he left, it was as if he'd betrayed her. I thought she'd go mad. For three days and nights she didn't do anything but scream."

"It seems a bit much. After all, he planned to come back." Charles made a face.

"She knew he wouldn't. She always said she had fairy blood and could see the future. When Jean left, she mourned him as if he'd died. She knew it, you see, just as she knew about her own death. She told me she'd die of a broken heart."

"Elaine!" I exclaimed.

"It's true. She was proud of her fairy blood. She said her family came from Brocilande forest, and Morgaine la Fée was her ancestor."

"What does your father think?"

"He hated when she spoke of things he couldn't understand. When she died, I heard him talking to her body." She clamped her mouth shut.

"What did he say?" Charles asked.

Elaine thought for a minute then admitted, "I'm not sure — I was crossing the hall and I heard him murmuring. The words were indistinct, but I think he was talking about Jean. He'd just gotten the letter telling about Prince Jean-Tristan's death and Jean's marriage to you."

"Oh." I looked askance at Charles, who shrugged. "I suppose it was a great disappointment to your father that Jean ran away and married someone like me."

"Yes." Elaine was no diplomat.

Charles bristled, but a sharp look from me shut his mouth. I looked down at my dirty nails and wondered what was going to happen. The TCF hadn't erased me yet and there had to be a reason.

I doubted it was Elaine's news about her forthcoming marriage to Robert d'Artois, whom she said was one of the most powerful men in France. Even with all her frightened tears, she was unable to move me. However, the mention that her father looked for a wife made me wonder. Would he remarry and perhaps have a son named Jean, in memory of his first son? Could the TCF and the Tempus Reporting Program both be wrong about the name? Who could help me?

I looked at my two companions and my mouth twitched. Charles was brushing the dirt off the roots he'd gathered. His peaked face was a study in concentration. Elaine stood quite still, her face turned toward the castle, just visible in the distance. The setting sun cast a coppery light over the fallow fields. Shadows grew long, and the trees, just beginning to bud, were tipped with ruby light.

We gave up any notion of having mushrooms for dinner and made our way home. My breasts were leaking milk by the time we arrived. It was past nursing hour.

Aurore wasn't hungry. Her wet nurse had plenty of milk, and I was simply a between meal snack for the tiny girl. My milk was slowly drying up, and soon I'd have none left. Even now, the pale drops were fewer on the tips of my nipples. I squeezed the rest out as the nurse had shown me. Aurore slept peacefully in her crib. It seemed that all she did was sleep, but when I worried the nurse assured me it was normal.

I bent over the infant. In sleep, her little face was as pure as an angel's. I touched my scar, running my fingers down it, my heart aching so I could hardly breathe. A mother had loved her child as fiercely as I loved mine, and I had killed him. Tears trickled down my cheeks as I breathed in the sweet, milky scent of my baby and watched her sleep.

Dinner was frugal again that evening. The staple meal for those times was soup, and when there was no meat, they made soup with wild herbs. Sorrel, onion, my dandelion and what looked like grass floated in the broth along with a thin layer of grease. Lucien hadn't returned. At the table, Elaine sat at her father's place, and I was at her right. Also with us was the priest, whom Elaine had neglected to count in her tally of castle residents.

Père Martin was a short, swarthy man with whiskers so dark his face looked navy blue even when closely shaved. His eyes were black and very sharp, his fingers were fat sausages and his face was as round as the full moon. He was unused to fasting, and when he said the blessing for our meal, he could hardly hide his disdain. Apparently, he too missed the luxury of Paris life.

The cook shuffled around the table, serving us. The first course was boiled herb soup with no salt. Afterwards we had chestnut flatbread, and I was grateful for the violet roots that Charles had found. Cook had mashed them and added cloves of garlic to cover the insipid, starchy taste.

We spoke little until the end of dinner. Then Père Martin leaned back, fixed me with his obsidian stare and asked, "How long has it been since you confessed, my lady?"

I gaped at him, but as usual, Charles came to my rescue. "My lady confessed with the queen's own confessor, the Père Denis." He blinked, looking as innocent as a choirboy.

"Oh." The priest looked decidedly put out. "You'll have to choose another confessor, my lady, as that good man has gone to Paris to accompany his queen's body."

"I'm sure I will," I said.

Elaine said, "Père Martin is the only priest within ten leagues, but I'm sure he'll be able to find time for you, Isobel. Don't forget the new edict about confessing every day."

I looked at her sharply, but she could look as bland as Charles when she wanted to. I wished I knew what mischief she was brewing. I had gotten the impression that the only things that interested her were money and going to Paris to escape this "dreadful countryside", and here she was, suddenly concerned with my immortal soul.

"Thank you," I said, and left it at that. If Père Martin wanted to hear my confession, he'd have to come and get it. I was certainly not going to trot after him.

After dinner, we all went to our rooms. Candles were scarce, and there were only rush torches to burn. They burned so quickly that by dinner's end we were practically in pitch darkness.

Nurse had eaten with the farmhands in the kitchen. There was no difference in the food between the kitchen table and the dining room table except that in the kitchen the food was served still hot. After being carried through chilly hallways by the shuffling cook, our food was stone-cold when it arrived.

I undressed and crawled hastily into bed. Aurore nursed with little suckling sounds, her little hand opening and closing in the air. I watched it for a while. Nurse sat in her usual spot by the fireplace on her low, cushioned stool. When Aurore finished eating, Nurse burped her, changed her diaper, wrapped her up in cloth so tightly she couldn't move and lay her in her cradle. I winced, but babies at that time were swaddled like little mummies, their arms pinned to their sides.

I supposed it was all right because it didn't bother Aurore, who cooed for a moment before falling asleep. Nurse rocked the little cradle with her foot as she stared at the flames. I had no idea what she was thinking. Any attempt at conversation was met with silence and flushed cheeks. I'd given up trying to pose questions, but it didn't stop me from talking. After so many years in prison, with no one to speak to and no one around, I tended toward silence myself. But when someone was in the same room as I, it was hard to ignore them.

"It's getting warmer," I began, propping myself up on one elbow and leaning down so I could watch Aurore. "Soon spring will be here, and we'll be able to take the baby for walks in the fields. I hope that Lucien comes back with some meat. I'm sick of cabbage soup, cabbage salad and cabbage sauté. It gives us all gas, and we smell badly enough as it is. Thank goodness we don't have any cabbages left now."

This elicited a tiny grin from Nurse. Encouraged, I went on. "I don't know about you, but I think this castle is dreary. Not that I've seen many others, but the one in Italy was nicer. We stayed there two months. Our room was warm." I sighed. "The food was better too. Queen Isabella had oranges brought by courier from Sardinia. I used to think oranges were of no importance, but now I find myself longing for them."

"I n'ere seen un," said Nurse, in an almost inaudible mutter.

I gaped at her, then closed my mouth and nodded. "I'll have to find one for you, somehow. They are as orange as the sun when it sets and full of sweet juice. You peel the skin off, and it's so oily and fragrant your hands are scented for hours afterwards. The flesh is divided into sections, not like an apple with a core. Each section has its own seeds. They're white and round. Charles made a game of spitting the seeds out the window, trying for the knights' helmets. When his aim was good, the knight would think it was a bird shitting on his helmet."

I laughed, and Nurse joined me. "In the Holy Land, oranges were sold by the basket. The crusaders used to eat them all day long. Even during mass there would be the sound of people spitting orange seeds into their hands; and it almost covered the smell of garlic."

"Soundzgud," she said, her voice rusty and creaking. "Was z'Holy Lan' gud?"

"There were good things in the Holy Land," I said. "The people, although you call them infidels, are very kind and love life and God as much as any human being. They would come to sell their goods at the fort, and I used to buy oranges and dates from them. It's funny. They call us the infidels and wonder why we come to kill and plunder. The forts that the crusaders built are marvelous to see, but so are the cities and the countryside. It's so warm that figs grow all year 'round, and there are dates too, much sweeter than honey."

"Ztop talkin' fud," said Nurse, shaking her head.

"I'm sorry." I laughed again. "I wasn't thinking. You must be hungry all the time, like I am. The queen, God rest her soul, warned me that nursing a baby does that to you."

"Mine died," she said, quite clearly.

I felt as if I'd been hit very hard. The woman's expression didn't alter. She sat as still as stone next to the fire. "How?" I asked, after the silence had stretched to its limit.

She shrugged. "Dunno. Fever."

"Was it a girl or a boy? What was its name?"

"Girl, Jan."

"Where is your husband?"

"Works forest making charcoal." As she spoke, her voice limbered as if she'd not spoken in years. After each phrase she'd snap her mouth shut and frown, embarrassed by her speech. Yet each phrase was clearer than the last.

"Whenever you want, I'll send you home," I said to her.

"No, prefer here." She nodded once, emphatically, then turned her back to me to stir the fire. The conversation was finished.

# Chapter Thirteen

ഇ

The next day and for days after, rain fell in sheets. The countryside was soon flooded as we were in lowlands, and shining ponds grew all around the castle and covered the fields. The swamps left their boundaries and encircled us, and a warm spell brought forth a burst of creation from plants and trees. Buds popped open and each tree laced itself with pale green. Primroses bloomed on each patch of dry ground, along with wild cabbage and purple crocus.

With the rains, frogs emerged. Cook was so excited he could hardly wait until the rain stopped to go catch them, and we ate them grilled, boiled or stewed for weeks. Along with the frogs, the ducks came back, and we snared four. We held a feast in honor of Lucien, who returned from the hunt one rainy day with two wet stags slung over his tired pony's back.

The rest of the meat was smoked to preserve it. Elaine and I took great satisfaction one day in cleaning out the meat pantry and whitewashing the walls. The lye we used stung my nose for days and my hands turned gray, but after the cleansing three haunches of smoked meat replaced the millions of cobwebs in the room.

I stood in the pantry, hands on hips, and laughed in delight. The walls were still damp and the lye fumes still brought tears to our eyes, but the sight of so much meat was like a gift. Elaine had a sneezing fit, and Charles counted her sneezes to see if they came to an even or an odd number.

"Five! That's good luck," he crowed.

"I hope so. I hate to think it's a cold coming on. Quick, tell me, do I have a fever?" She turned to me and stuck her wrist out.

I took her wrist and frowned. "How can I tell from your wrist? I need to touch your forehead."

"You feel my wrist to see if my humors are balanced. Everyone knows that." She rolled her eyes. "Honestly, Isobel, sometimes I think you're so strange."

Charles came to my rescue. "In the south we feel the forehead to check humors," he said loftily. "You can tell by the heat it gives off if you have a fever or not. If it's damp, you must be careful, as the humors are out of balance."

Elaine raised her eyebrows. "What shall I learn next from you, Charles? For one so young, you're certainly erudite!"

Charles bristled, unsure about the word "erudite", but I heard the faint sound of hoofbeats and shushed him. "Someone is coming," I said.

"It's Father!" Elaine shrieked and bolted toward the steps.

"How do you know?" I gathered my skirts and trotted after her. "Slow down, you'll trip on these blasted stairs." We climbed the spiral stairs out of the basement pantry and dashed through the kitchen, now brightly lit by spring sunlight streaming through the casement windows. Cook was at the stone sink, muttering at a plate, and didn't turn as we rushed by.

"He's deaf as a post," said Charles with a laugh.

Our pace increased as we reached the long main hallway and turned into an impromptu race. Charles, unhampered by skirts, was in the lead with Elaine bounding at his heels. I was unused to running, but my legs were longer than theirs, and I soon caught up.

The end of the hallway was in sight, and we were gasping with pent-up laughter when the door flew open. A dark shadow blocked the sunlight, and a knight in full armor stepped through the door. Elaine was going too fast to stop—she crashed into Charles and sent him headlong into the man's legs.

There was a huge clang, a crash as the man fell and a cry from Elaine as she tripped over the uneven flagstones. She landed on top of Charles, and the three of them lay in a heap on the floor.

"Get off of me!" came the muffled command from the bottom of the pile.

Elaine scrambled to her feet, and Charles stood up slowly, his hands pressed to his forehead where a bruise bloomed like a purple flower. The knight, face down, rolled over with the sound of falling pots and pans, and I started to laugh. It began as a snort, but it bubbled out of my throat and ended in a roar. I held my stomach, doubled over with mirth, tears pouring down my cheeks. Elaine started to giggle, then laugh, and the sound bounced around the hallway as gay as spring sunlight.

The knight lifted his visor, and François stared at us. His green eyes were at first angry, then a spark of humor lit their emerald depths and he chuckled warmly. "That was some welcome," he said. He got to his feet and examined the armor. The breastplate, which he unbuckled, had a fresh dent.

"Let me help," said Elaine. She leapt forward and tackled the stiff leather straps. "I'm so glad you're back. We've been terribly worried about you." This was news to me, but I hastened to nod when Elaine said, "Haven't we worried?"

"Yes, terribly. How is everything in Paris?" I tried to smooth my hair. My cheeks were hot, and I couldn't seem to get my breath back from the run. My dress was laced too tightly — it hurt to breathe.

Charles rubbed his fingers across his bruise, looked at his hands, saw there was no blood and sighed. "You have fine armor, sir, but why are you wearing it? Are there brigands in the area?"

François gave him a sharp glance. "As a matter of fact, yes. I met them three days ago, and they've been following me ever since. I hardly dared sleep, and if I hadn't taken Richard with me, I probably would have been robbed, or worse. Don't worry now. I sent Richard and his sons to the village to warn the mayor."

Elaine gave a cry and threw her arms around ⊦
metal-plated shoulders. "I'm so glad you're all right
come and sit down and tell us all the news of Paris. vvere tnere
any parties? Has it changed much since we left? Did you see any
of my friends?"

"Don't you want to hear about the Count of Artois?"
François asked, his voice stern.

"I suppose you'll tell me of him anyway." Elaine shrugged
sulkily. Her eyes lost their sparkle.

"He's dead."

Elaine's hands slid off the buckle she was unfastening.
"How?"

"Hunting accident." François sounded weary. "The stupid
man went chasing wolves in the middle of winter and fell off his
horse while fording a frozen stream. The ice broke and he
drowned."

"Wolves?" I gasped.

"Wolves." He shook his head and grimaced. "You can't
even eat the beasts, so what's the use chasing them? Poor sport,
if you ask me."

"Wolves." I rubbed my face and looked at Elaine. She was
trying very hard to find a suitable expression.

"Well, I won't have to be in such a rush to finish my
trousseau," she said. She didn't seem sure whether to be upset
or relieved. She wrung her hands together. "Now what shall we
do?"

"We're going to Navarre," said François. He shrugged out
of his thigh guards and tossed his gloves to the floor. "Damn it, I
broke a lace."

"What about the castle?" Elaine asked.

"Sold. We're free of this pile of sticks and stones. My niece
is marrying the Count of Tours, and she wants a place of her
own. I reminded her about our grandfather's glorious castle, the

rich, outlying farmland, and the lovely chapel, and she bought it." He shrugged.

"Did you include Père Martin in the deal?" I whispered, forgetting how sharp François's ears were.

He chuckled again. "No, he's coming with us. We can't travel without a priest, especially now. The Church's Inquisition has declared it a sin not to confess, and now even the priests outside of Paris have started selling pardons." He snorted. "As if you could buy God's pardon."

"The Inquisition?" Charles asked, still rubbing his head.

"That's what I said. Let me see that." François bent down and peered at the egg-sized bruise. "You'd better go see Cook and ask him to put some arnica on that." He swatted the boy on the shoulder and sent him scurrying down the hall.

He and Elaine grinned, but I shivered. Père Martin had been sniffing around me like a hunting hound scenting its prey. I had refused to confess, and lately he'd taken to pointing his fat finger at me during mass and saying, "Beware the sinners among us, who refuse God's pardon and even His word!". He didn't dare say my name, but I assumed that he was simply biding his time. I had no idea what he wanted of me—I'd made it clear from the beginning that I wasn't wealthy and wouldn't buy the pardons he sold to the valets and farmhands. As the family had recently dwelled in Paris, Père Martin had known about this new trend and taken it up, especially with François gone these months. I hoped François would put a stop to it now that he was back.

Père Martin had asked me, of course, as he asked everyone in the castle and outlying villages. Nurse had given him a part of her wages, and I'd scolded her roundly. Even Dame Blanche paid him. I saw her slip him a coin after mass one day. Of course, Père Martin made a great show of pardoning all her sins right there, on the chapel steps. Impressed, some of the poorer peasants asked if he'd accept fresh eggs or cream as payment.

I was of two minds about that. The wages of sin ended up in our kitchen since Père Martin lived with us, and it was hard to fault him when he gave a clutch of eggs to Cook. On the other hand, the peasants needed food just as badly as we did, and I hated the thought of taking a dinner away from a hungry child.

The day was too lovely to waste worrying about the priest, though. While Elaine and François gossiped about the court, I slipped away for some fresh air, first fetching Aurore to take her outside. The sun warmed the grass, and the flowers scented the air. Honeybees droned in the apple blossoms, and Aurore opened her slate blue eyes wide and looked at the vast world. Actually, it was simply the walled orchard. We sat on a thick rug that Nurse carried outside for us. She darned stockings while I taught Aurore a little song about puppets.

"*Ainsi font, font, font, les petites marionnettes!*
*Ainsi font, font font, trois petits tours et puis sont vont!*"

The baby gave a wide, toothless smile, and I clapped delightedly. "She's smiling, did you see?"

Nurse nodded, intent on her knitting. Her mouth moved silently as she counted the stitches.

We were perfectly content, with the soft grass waving gently in the spring breeze and the white apple blossoms drifting like snowflakes through the balmy air. Aurore yawned and fell asleep as suddenly as only babies can do. Her pale eyelashes rested gently on her round cheeks. I lay down beside her and watched her. She was still brand-new, a miracle to me. Her little nose was so tiny, the wings of her nostrils translucent in the light. Her cheeks were rosy, her mouth a perfect, tiny replica of my own. Her hands were small yet strong when she grasped my fingers. As she slept she dreamed, and her mouth worked softly. Her breath was as sweet as honey, and her hair as fine as gossamer, shining in the bright sun.

I hadn't realized how strongly a baby affects emotions. Whenever I looked at Aurore, I felt a joy so sharp it was painful, and I knew that if I had to, I'd defend her with my life. My own self faded to nothing when I was near her. I was simply a link in the chain, and the newest link was all that mattered. It was strange and powerful. I leaned over and kissed her perfect cheek. She uttered a faint snore, and I laughed.

Footsteps sounded, and I turned to see who intruded in our haven of tranquility. To my astonishment, it was François. I shut my gaping mouth and scrambled to my feet, brushing strands of grass from my skirt. I gave a little curtsey, my eyes fastened on his tall form.

He hardly glanced at me. He was looking at Aurore. He tilted his head, a faint smile on his lips. "She's grown," he said.

I let my breath out. "Won't you sit down a while?" I motioned with my hand.

He settled in the grass near Aurore. Nurse had fallen asleep as well, slumped against an apple tree, her chin on her ample chest, and now and then a faint snore escaped her. François glanced her way. "She's a good woman."

"I can't thank you enough for getting her," I said.

"Thank Lucien, not me." His voice was mellow.

"Will you be sad to leave this place?"

"Perhaps. It's been my home for all my life, yet I can't honestly say I love it. There are other places that are grander, or smaller and more comfortable."

"Often places are loved for the memories they shelter."

"My children were born here…" His voice trailed off. He looked at me with a strange expression in his eyes. I turned away. "Do I make you so uncomfortable?" he asked.

"No!" Surprise made me face him again. "No, that's not it. You were staring at me, that's all."

"I was just thinking that Aurore was born in a tent. I wondered what sort of memories you would have." His hand was close to mine, and when he shifted in the grass, we touched.

I drew a quick breath. "You were there. I'll always remember how you wove the cradle and how strong you were when you brought Aurore into the world. I didn't know what to do."

He laughed. "You don't have to know anything. Nature takes care of itself."

His hand crept over mine, and my heart pounded. There was a sort of tingling sensation where our skin met. Flower blossoms floated in the air between us, along with motes of golden pollen and the silver thread of a spider's web. All that I saw clearly, but what most impressed me was the steady regard of the man in front of me. He sat in silence, his hand covering mine, and both the silence and the touch were more intimate than any moment I'd shared with Jean.

We held hands, watching as Aurore slept. François asked no questions of me, and every now and then, he reached over and gently touched my cheek, as if to reassure himself I was real, and sitting next to him.

I didn't want to talk. To speak would break the spell cast by the sun, the fragrant apple blossoms and the sweetly sleeping baby. Instead I leaned against François' shoulder and let myself relax into a tranquil bliss that lasted all that afternoon.

The day went by too quickly. It was the last peaceful day I'd have in a very long time. How fortunate we cannot see ahead in time, and how ironic it is that I should be the one to say those words. But I believe that if we could see the future, most of us would decide it wouldn't be worth living.

\* \* \* \* \*

We packed the contents of the castle into crates, cramming as much as we could into wooden chests and rolling tapestries into long sausages. There was bustle everywhere as wall hangings were unhooked and shrieks as huge spiders and mice skittered out of every nook and cranny. The plates were packed in sawdust. Whatever torches could be salvaged were laid in rows in the hallway. The rushes that had cushioned our feet all winter and insulated the stone floor from the bitter cold were raked out of the dining room and burned.

Elaine and Dame Blanche oversaw the chambers while Charles and I were appointed Cook's aids. We carried the huge, iron spit outside — after dropping it twice on the stairs — only to be told crossly to take it back to the kitchen.

"Iron doesn't travel," said Cook, narrowing his rheumy eyes at us. "Do you want us all to drown the first time we cross a river?"

We didn't know that. All the iron stayed in the castle.

The gardener dug up the rose bushes and packed them in jute sacks. Roses traveled, then, and it amused me to see them wrapped so carefully in preparation for their journey.

The beehives were carefully emptied and the honey added to our baggage. The bees themselves were left behind, to Lucien's regret, as he doubled as beekeeper.

The moat was emptied one last time and scoured with rush brooms. The fish we hoped to find were not forthcoming, except for three skinny minnows that were quickly snapped up by a tall, gray heron stalking the banks.

"Shoo! Shoo! Damn him!" screeched Cook. "He's taken a frog too!"

I hid my relief. We'd had frog's legs so often I was beginning to think I'd turn green.

I held my hands to the light and examined them critically. They weren't green — they were red, my knuckles raw from scrubbing. There were two new cuts on my thumb from the sharp copper kettle. My wrists stuck out like white twigs from my work dress, and my nails were broken to the quick. I'd bunched my hair into a snarly braid and shoved it under a worn cap that tied under my chin. The linen was rough and chafed my throat. My legs ached, my back hurt and I hadn't taken a decent bath since François had gotten back from Paris, one week ago.

I was glad that the packing was nearly done. The few people working for us had performed a titan's job. Stacked beneath the eaves of the hay barn were twenty numbered crates and chests. Elaine had a list somewhere of every item packed away and its exact location. We expected the muleteer to come any day now. Lucien had gone into the forest to hire one away from the charcoal makers, as it was no longer the season for them to sell. We were ready to leave.

I let my weary shoulders sag. Soon the bells for vespers would ring from the chapel then dinner would be served in the stableyard. We'd have to set up a makeshift table with hay bales to sit upon. I could hear arguing from the stables, Richard's sons, no doubt, squabbling about who would lead the livestock to drink that evening. They could never decide whose turn it was. Water trickled into the moat from the stream and its gurgle was hypnotizing.

I let myself slide down into the long grass beneath the gate I leaned on. The water bubbled merrily, the argument quieted as Richard came around the corner and I fell into a deep sleep.

The bells for vespers failed to awaken me, so Charles was sent to look for me and found me sleeping soundly. He shook me awake and made a face.

"Père Martin ranted hellfire and brimstone this evening. You were right to miss mass."

I yawned. "I'm sorry, I was watching the brook one moment and the next I was having the most marvelous dream."

"Dinner is ready." For Charles, dreams and food were closely linked. "Richard's sons caught some pigeons."

"I'll wash up here and join you in a minute." This was a polite euphemism for "I'd like to pee in the stream, could you leave me alone?".

Charles disappeared and I hitched up my skirts and waded into a sheltered spot beneath the willow branches. In the castle, the bathrooms consisted of metal buckets or porcelain bowls, which were emptied into the stream or into the fertilizer heap, depending on the nature of the contents. I was just skipping a step.

Afterwards I walked upstream and washed my face and hands at the spring. I tried to smooth some semblance of order into my hair. It didn't work. I stuffed my cap back on, tied it beneath my chin, wincing at the rough cloth, and strode off to the stables. I was starving.

We ate dinner beneath a calico sky. The sun was setting, and the clouds were gilded with deep orange and rose. In the east, the night sky was indigo, and the first stars twinkled in it. Lucien lit smudge torches, supposedly to keep the mosquitoes away, although it never seemed to work. Luckily, there weren't too many insects in France. All the birds, bats, frogs and spiders kept the horseflies and mosquitoes in check. As we ate, bats swooped into the flickering torchlight, so close that their wings glowed transparently red. Huge, pale moths blundered about, landing in our hair and food. Their soft wings shed powder when we touched them. Two half-wild cats slunk around the edges of the light, waiting to pounce on any bit of food that fell upon the ground.

François had a dog, the last of his once-mighty hunting pack. The dog was old now and stiff jointed. His muzzle was white and his eyes opaque. He sat with his bony head resting on François' knee. François slipped him tender morsels when he thought no one was looking. Once or twice, beneath the table, our knees or hands collided. Each time we both froze, as if trying to make the most of the brief contacts. When our hands strayed apart, his eyes twinkled, although he said nothing.

Elaine, with her bird-sharp eyes, sometimes caught these glances, and each time she did, her lips pinched tight and the skin around her nose whitened.

Did she suspect something of the growing emotion between François and myself? We were never alone, and with the bustle of packing, François was so busy he sometimes literally fell asleep standing up. He hadn't courted me, except that one day in the apple orchard. All that happened was, if we met, he found an excuse to touch me. Sometimes the touch was fleeting, sometimes it was almost a caress. Each time I felt a shock, as if electricity flowed from his hands to my skin. Each time, his face reflected a little of what I felt. His mouth grew softer, and his eyes deepened. I started to dream about him at night, and I would wake up, prey to a longing so sharp that nothing but holding my baby close to my breast could assuage it.

During dinner, I propped Aurore in a little cradle right on the table. Her little face glowed in the candlelight. Her wide eyes followed everyone's movements avidly. She was beginning to take interest in the world around her, and I was absurdly proud whenever someone leaned over and chucked her under the chin or addressed kind words to her.

Richard's sons carried Old Marthe down. She had the only chair while the rest of us sat on prickly hay bales. Her supper was a bowl of broth, and she sucked noisily on boiled onions. Her teeth were gone, but her mind was sharp, and she loved reminiscing.

"Jean was a good baby, never fussy or difficult. He ate everything you put in his mouth. Just like this little sweetheart." Marthe leaned over to peer at Aurore. "I can't believe I'm seeing Jean's baby, and him cold in his grave."

A silence fell over us, and then Elaine said in a mournful voice, "I wish he'd never left." She'd admitted to me that she'd felt pangs of guilt ever since she discovered Robert d'Artois had drowned. All her planning to send Jean on the crusade had gone for naught, her brother was dead, and she didn't have to marry anyone. Before she could speak further, one of the cats leapt on the table and snatched a whole pigeon. The resulting hue and cry as two of Richard's sons jumped to their feet, overturning the ale jug, distracted everyone from the gloom that had threatened to overwhelm us at the mention of Jean.

I felt my shoulders relax, and I took a rather shaky breath. Any talk about Jean made me uneasy. I darted a glance at François. He sat perfectly still, his hand resting on his dog's head. His face was halfway in shadow, but the bones seemed to show right through the skin. He gazed unseeingly at the table and his mouth drew into a thin line.

Gently, I reached under the table and took his hand. It was the first time I dared do so. He jumped a bit, and the look he gave me was sharp, but I hung on, tightening my fingers when he made to pull away. His mouth curved in a smile, a real smile that lit up his eyes. He gave my hand a squeeze and nodded. "Thank you," he said softly.

"I don't understand," I said, puzzled.

The smile stayed, though his eyes grew bleak. "I hope to God you never have to," he said. He took a deep breath, as if he'd been holding it, and nodded toward Aurore. "I think she takes after you, more than Jean. She has your pure features." With his free hand, he traced the line of my scar. "If it wasn't for this, you'd look like an angel."

There was a loud crack as Elaine set her knife down hard enough to break the bone handle.

I hastily pulled away from François. He bent over to pat his dog, but I could see a smile dancing at the corners of his mouth, and so I didn't pay the slightest attention to Elaine's venomous looks.

Dinner finished soon after that. Light bantering punctuated with guffaws gave way to yawns and remarks about rising early in the morning. The torches were doused, the food gathered up and taken into the kitchen, and we all made our way to our rooms to collapse fully dressed on fresh rushes covered with linen sheets, having packed the beds and bedding already.

# Chapter Fourteen

🔊

"HEEEhaawww…HEEEEhawwww!" The cry woke us all before dawn. The sky was steely gray, a light frost covered the ground, and the muleteer trotted into the courtyard with thirty mules and called out in a huge, bellowing voice.

"Is anyone here? I say, is anyone about?" He brayed as loudly as his charges. The mules milled about, hooves clattering on stone, and hee-hawed shrilly. Steam rose from their backs in white clouds, and sparks flew when their iron-shod hooves hit the cobblestones. The muleteer stood in the middle of the small herd, his huge fists on his hips and a long whip wrapped around his broad shoulders.

We stumbled to the windows and leaned out. We must have made a comical sight, our sleep-crumpled faces peering out of nearly every window on the courtyard side of the castle.

"Richard!" François cried. "Get the man settled in the stables!"

There were more cries as Richard woke his sons, and then a flurry of shrieks and more yells as he apparently found one of them in the hay with a peasant girl.

"Damn your rutting, boy! I've told you to stay away from that wench!" A figure scurried from the barn clutching a dress and cap. She halted in front of Richard and waggled her naked buttocks saucily in his direction. Then she stuck her tongue at him, adroitly dodged his foot as he kicked at her, and ran down the path into the darkness, crying at the top of her lungs, "I'm tellin' my dadda, an' he'll make ye pay, ye ol' fool!"

"You stupid clod!" Richard yanked his naked son into the courtyard by his hair. He swung his fist at the boy but missed as his son darted away.

We all stayed at the windows to watch, of course. Charles and the cook erupted in gales of laughter while the women — Elaine, Dame Blanche, Nurse and I — watched with wide eyes. The young man ran around the dark courtyard, trying to escape his father's flailing fists and the mules' hooves.

"What's this? What's this?" The hoarse cry came from the priest's window. Père Martin held a lantern outside, which cast a yellow glow on the commotion below. Immediately the priest uttered an outraged shriek. "*Par tous les saints!*" he cried. "A naked Saracen in our midst!"

The young man quickly hid his privates with a handful of hay, but it was soon scattered as he ran about. Finally the muleteer collared him, booted him in the rear and sent him sprawling.

"Listen to yer father next time, boy!" he bellowed. "Now help me with these mules!"

The spectacle finished, we withdrew into our rooms to gather the last of our belongings and leave the castle for the last time.

The castle disappeared as if it was sinking into the ground. As we rode further and further away, the stone buttresses shrank, the walls were swallowed by the fields and, last, the pointed tops of the wooden turrets vanished.

I heard a sigh and turned toward my traveling companion, the Lady Elaine, late of castle Touraine, soon to be resident in the court of Navarre.

"Are you sad to be leaving?" I asked.

She shrugged, and her face twisted as if she were trying not to cry. A smile tugged at her mouth, though, and the look she gave me was droll. "I was thinking of my brother," she admitted, "not about the castle at all. When I was eight he dared me to walk across the moat one winter. I stepped on the ice and there was a cracking sound. I hesitated, Jean gave me a shove and I slipped and fell on my rear, sliding right out into the moat. At that moment, Richard came running through the snow, yelling at me not to move and for Jean to grab my cloak. The ice gave away just as Jean took my arm, and I pulled him right in with me.

"Richard fished us out and dragged us to the kitchen where we were undressed and sat right in the chimney. Cook gave us broth and Dame Blanche was fetched from her chambers and scolded for not watching us. She fluttered around the kitchen like a nervous chicken and finally went to get us our dry clothes.

"Everyone treated Jean like a hero. Richard saw him grab for me and thought he dove in after me. I was the fool who tried to walk on thin ice. Mother, of course, covered Jean with kisses for being so brave and saving his little sister. I was made to sit in the corner of the chimney all day."

Her voice faded and she gave a little laugh. "The strange thing is, it never occurred to me to tell anyone that Jean pushed me out on the ice. It seemed normal to me that Jean was a hero. He was always mine. People loved him and fussed over him, and I was never jealous because I was sure he deserved it." Her mouth quirked and tears sparkled on her lashes. "I miss him terribly. Will you tell me about him? You were with him this past year, what did he do? What did he say when you first met him? Will you tell me?"

I nodded slowly. "I saw Jean for the first time in the middle of a barn. He stood with a group of lads, but it seemed he stood alone. He was taller than they were and stood straight. He looked like a young eagle. His green eyes were the first things I loved about him." I smiled and shook my head. "You and your father have those same eyes. It disconcerts me. Especially when you gaze at me from beneath your lashes, as if you're weighing each of my words and finding them wanting."

Elaine gave a short laugh. "It's a family trait, I'm afraid. We all seem terribly critical, but I think it's only nearsightedness. Now you know our darkest secret."

I smiled. "Another thing you share with your brother is your lightness of spirit. Nothing could keep Jean down for long. He bounced back from each misfortune with a smile and a joke.

The only other person I met like that was Prince Jean-Tristan. His death was a terrible blow for Jean. He grieved a long time for his friend."

Our mules were tied together. We sat on a sort of wooden platform lashed across their backs and cushioned with a thick carpet. A wooden frame could be inserted into its four corners to make a covered litter, but the weather was fair and we enjoyed the sun.

It never occurred to me to glance behind us. If I had, I would have seen François. As it was, I didn't see him until after my story, and by then, it was too late.

"Why did he say he'd gone on the crusade?" asked Elaine in a low voice. Her hand plucked nervously at the rug.

I bit my lip but answered honestly. "He never really told me why, but he did say he was at odds with your father. Whenever I begged him to turn around and go back, he answered that he wouldn't until he could prove to his father that he was a man."

"You begged him to go back home?" Elaine frowned. "I didn't know you wanted to turn back."

I cast a desperate look at Charles, but he was too far ahead of us to hear our conversation. I cleared my throat. "I wanted to go back because I was afraid he would die."

"You knew he would die?" Elaine leaned forward, and her eyes narrowed. "Was it a premonition?"

Her words made me nervous. "No, nothing like that. The whole voyage seemed unlucky. First, the ship with my family was lost, along with our fortune. Then there was the fever, and Jean-Tristan died so suddenly. King Louis, too. All I wanted to do was go back to France."

"The crusade was ill-fated. Perhaps you're clairvoyant." Elaine stuck her palm at me. "Can you read my future?"

"No!" I pushed her hand away. "Don't let Père Martin see you do that. He'll think I'm a witch." I shuddered as I said that, and Elaine turned pale.

"Tell me more about Jean. Why was he angry with Father?"

"He said that he'd never shown any interest in him."

Elaine looked troubled. "Mother gave him so much attention no one could compete. Father was always away, hunting or at the court. Then Jean was sent to school." She shook her head. "Jean wanted to become a knight. He begged for a horse and armor, but all Father did was give him his grandfather's armor and told him to joust with Richard's sons. It was a blow to Jean's ego, because Jean-Tristan was training to be a knight, and he wrote him letters telling about his fights. Jean wanted more than anything to be able to take part in a tournament. He dreamed of winning a joust and fighting in battle."

"He got his wish," I said sadly. "He fought in a battle. Two, actually."

"He fought two battles? Tell me!" cried Elaine.

"The first was at Jean-Tristan's side. They won easily, and Jean came back that evening looking as if the sun shone out of his eyes." I smiled, remembering the scrap of underwear on his helmet. "He was so happy that day, and I found out I was pregnant."

Elaine gave a small start. "It's so strange. I see you, yet I can't imagine you with Jean, and I have the hardest time imagining that Aurore is truly his baby. When Father got Jean's letter informing us you were expecting a child, he was livid!" She laughed, then sobered. "No one was angrier than I was, though. I'd gone out of my way to help Jean run away so he could marry a wealthy woman, and he married a nobody."

"Thank you," I said dryly.

She had the grace to blush. "Sometimes I feel Jean is dead by my fault, and other times I feel it's Father's fault for betrothing me to Robert d'Artois. If that hadn't happened, Jean would still be here, and so would Mother." Her voice turned venomous. "Father loved Mother, you know. You're just a pretty *divertissement* for him. He wouldn't dream of marrying someone with no fortune. If he does marry you, I'll never speak to him again."

Her comment caught me by surprise and I felt my cheeks grow hot. At that moment, I glanced behind us and saw François.

Our eyes met. What my face looked like, I don't know, but his face was drawn so tightly the bones showed white beneath his skin. I spun around, facing frontward again, and my breath came fast.

"What is it?" Elaine looked back. "Oh! Father…" but her words died in her throat as François kicked his horse and galloped by us.

The platform lurched as our mules shied sideways. Elaine grabbed at my arm. It wasn't a long drop, but my robes hampered my legs and Elaine, by grasping my sleeve, hindered rather than helped me. I couldn't put my hands out to save myself, and I landed on my head. There was a flash of light, the breath was knocked out of my chest and the day grew strangely dark.

I opened my eyes. Sharp pain chased itself around my skull, and I moaned. Immediately someone took my hand. "Are you awake?" Charles asked.

I blinked, but the darkness was so deep and inky I could see nothing. "What happened?" Then I remembered. "I fell off the litter, didn't I? Have I been unconscious long?"

"A few hours. Do you remember falling?"

"Yes." I spoke quietly. "I'm sorry. Did I wake you?"

There was a confused silence, and Charles said, "No," rather hesitantly. Then he said, "Would you like some water?"

I was parched. "Yes, please." I struggled to a sitting position, my head aching horribly. White points of light danced in front of my eyes and I blinked hard to clear my vision, which remained black. Where was the glow of embers in the fireplace or glimmer of stars in the sky? I squinted toward the sky.

"Here." It was Charles.

I turned toward the sound of his voice and frowned. "Where are you?" My head hurt so much that tears leaked down my cheeks. I could feel each heartbeat in my skull like a blow. I heard more footsteps and the swishing sound of a tent flap being opened.

"I'm right here." Charles sounded anxious.

I reached my hand out, blundering into the goblet he held. Liquid spilled over my hands and I gave a little cry. "Perhaps you should light tinder. It's so dark in here that I can't see anything. What time is it?"

"It's just past vespers." Charles' voice was high with fright.

I turned my head toward the sound of his breathing. "What did you say?"

"It's sunset," said Charles.

Fear iced my blood. I felt as if I'd just been dropped into a well. I lay back down, slowly, for the pain was dire, and reached a hand to my head. A bandage swathed my forehead, but my eyes were uncovered. I opened and shut my fingers, right in front of my eyes. Nothing. I moved my hand over my face, strangely numb, and dried blood flaked beneath my fingers. I traced a line from my forehead to chin and noted that my cheekbones felt as if they'd been shot with anesthesia. So did the bridge of my nose.

My hair prickled. "I can't see," I whispered.

A choking cry sounded behind Charles, and I recognized Elaine's voice.

"Elaine?"

"I'm here." She swallowed hard. I heard her.

"Where is François?" I was afraid to ask, but I had to.

"I'm here." His voice came from next to me, and his hand took mine. It was large and warm. I felt some of the ice thaw.

I used François' hand to pull myself to a seated position. "It's just a nerve," I said, trying to ignore the sharp pain every movement cost me. "I fell on my forehead and damaged the optic nerve. Perhaps there's a small bruise in my brain, and the pressure is causing blindness. It could go away when the bleeding is absorbed." I babbled from sheer nerves.

There was a rather uncomfortable silence, and François said, "It was my fault." His voice was raw.

Elaine started to speak, but he shushed her. "I'll look after you, Isobel, and you shall want for nothing, I promise." His hand trembled a bit. I could picture his face. His eyes would be downcast, their emerald green hidden by long lashes. His mouth would be drawn in that thin line I'd come to know so well. That line of frustration, of simmering anger against life in general. François was not one to accept anything gracefully. I think discovering his beloved Elaine blamed him for everything had shocked him as did hearing his son blamed him as well. Our words had wounded him.

I put my hand out to search for his face. He caught it before I could touch him.

"No," he said. "I don't want your pity." His words were so low I doubt anyone in the tent heard them except me. His face was close to mine, and I felt his warm breath on my neck.

My hand tightened on his. "I don't want your pity, either," I whispered. My headache reached a crescendo, and I thought I'd probably pass out in another minute, or die, but I had to do something first. I turned my head, guided by instinct more than anything else, and pulled him to me. My lips brushed against his, and I pressed closer. Our kiss deepened, but only for a moment.

Elaine's sharp cry knifed between us. "What are you doing?" she shrieked. "Isobel is Jean's wife!"

François pulled away from me as if he was burned. I didn't care. I fainted, I think.

* * * * *

I would have loved to have seen Navarre in the summertime. All I could do was hear it and smell it. I knew from maps that the kingdom was small, niched between Spain and France, and reached from the mountains to the sea. It was a powerful little kingdom, affiliated to France through blood and marriage but independent by religion and government. Even without sight I could measure the gentle climate, with orchards and vineyards on the mountain slopes. Hot springs dotted the countryside.

On one side was France and on the other was the Moorish kingdom of Cordovan, with Spain next to that. My studies in prison had confirmed Navarre contained a mixture of culture and learning that existed nowhere else on Earth at that time. The city of Alacanté was the biggest capital in the world, and traders and minstrels roamed through both the city and the kingdom. It was the passageway from north to south, east to west. A cool breeze greeted me, redolent of orange blossoms, spices and mountain snows. The first moment my feet crossed the border, I felt as if I was coming home.

At first, we stayed in the city of Pamplune, at the court. The king of Navarre was in his northern holds when we arrived, so we didn't meet him. We spent a few days at the court while François searched for suitable lodgings. He found us a small manor, and we moved in the first week of July.

\* \* \* \* \*

I was in severe pain most of the time and stayed bedridden. Noise hurt my head, and I begged Nurse to take Aurore away when she cried. She was teething, so the poor baby whimpered frequently. Charles was my constant companion those days. He would sit by my side so silently I would fear he'd left, and my hand would grope for him. He was always there, though, and he brought me food and small tidbits of gossip of those I knew from the crusade. Everyone who had accompanied the king was now in Paris with his court. The rumor was he would remarry in the fall.

Charles was silent while I thought about this bit of news. After a moment, I sighed. "It's better for him. He must be so lonely."

"Are you thinking about the king?" Charles asked quietly.

"Who else would I be thinking about?" I asked, but he wouldn't answer.

I wanted to explore the manor and experience the countryside, but my pain was such that I stayed in a room with my head swathed in heavy cloth to keep it still. When I think back on that time, it seems as if everything is colored by that pain. It was dark, of course, and it was darkness made heavier by suffering. Movement brought stabbing pains so I lay still even when I felt I might go mad from restiveness. I was afraid of damaging my eyes, so I had Nurse keep the curtains drawn. The resulting stuffiness made me feel trapped in some terrible nightmare. I slept fitfully, never sure what time it was. My sense of time shifted so much I was often wide-awake while the household slept. Only in those quiet hours could I imagine that my pain grew fainter, and I could think about other things.

Other things being François.

When had I fallen in love with him? The first time I'd seen him, astride his restless horse and looking down upon me, his face had been cold, hard. I hadn't loved him then. Nor had it been when he'd questioned me, gazing into the distance, as if what I said interested him not in the least.

Perhaps it was when he'd bent over Aurore that first morning of her existence. For a minute his guard had fallen, and I'd seen something glow in his eyes. He'd turned to me and his face held some of the wonder he'd felt. It stirred something in my breast that no one had touched, not Jean, not my former fiancé. No one. I knew, suddenly, that he was vulnerable, that his frown was his shield and that his icy stare was a sham. It was only a matter of time before those thoughts crystallized in my mind, and I recognized what I felt to be love.

It was easier for me to recognize love now that I had Aurore. She had opened the gates to my heart. I felt silly, sometimes, with these thoughts mingling with the pain in my skull, but they kept me from sliding into the depths of melancholy. I'd found something to cling to—perhaps, someday, François could learn to love me too.

\* \* \* \* \*

A week before he left for Bruges, François visited my room. I still remember each word he said, each nuance of his voice, and even the faint air currents his movements stirred as he moved around my room.

He was a pacer. He could rarely stay still. His hands moved and he leaned forward when he spoke. He would often get up in the middle of a phrase and walk around. He'd go to the window or the chimney to prod the embers. When he came to my room, he first knocked softly, and then leaned in to see if I was awake.

Charles sat by my side, as usual. "I'll go now," he said. His voice was carefully neutral. He had guessed what I felt but had no idea what François wanted. Neither did I, so with his entrance my heart pounded and my face warmed. I hoped that the curtains were drawn so that shadow would hide my flushed cheeks.

François sat on the stool Charles vacated. I heard it creak and he took my hand. "How are you feeling?"

I tried to guess what he was about by the grip of his hand. It was firm, yet gentle. His skin was warm and slightly rough. I felt the strongest tingling in my hand and wondered how he could miss it. Perhaps he felt it too, because his hand tightened. "I'm feeling much better," I said.

"You say that each time I ask."

I smiled. "It's true, though. If there were more light, I could see a bit. My vision is slowly returning. And I can move my head without much pain."

"Is your vision truly returning?" He sounded doubtful.

"I promise."

"I still feel dreadful about the accident."

"I wish you wouldn't." I was trembling now. The mere feel of his hand in mine was so intense it was as if my whole being was condensed in our simple touch. I had the strongest longing to run my hand up his arm, over his broad shoulders, and trace the firm lines of his neck and chin. I couldn't see him anymore, but I knew the tilt of his head, each swooping line that drew his face, and the soft curve of his lips.

"François," I whispered.

He touched my cheek. His fingers tickled over my own face. He took a ragged breath and leaned toward me. Our lips touched for just a second, so lightly that I'm still not sure if I imagined it. Then he gently disengaged his hand from mine and stood up. "I'll see you in a few weeks, Isobel." My name was a caress when he said it.

"Where are you going?"

"I have some business to look into." I could hear him walk across the room. Then his footsteps stopped near the doorway. "Don't worry about Elaine," he said, and left.

Those words were the ones I clung to—they were the only ones to give me any hope at all.

That evening, when everyone was asleep, I crept out of my bed and walked on bare feet across my chamber. In the dark, my eyes could pick out dim places where moonlight shone through the window. I pressed my forehead to the glass and stared at the sky. I saw a faint, fuzzy circle that I took to be the moon. From Nurse's side of the room, I heard her snores muffled behind thick curtains. I glided to Aurore's bed and leaned down, but I could see nothing. I could hear her soft breathing, and I touched her rose-petal cheek with one finger. Then I straightened, drew a deep breath and eased my door open.

The hallway was dark, and I had to feel my way along, hands outstretched, groping carefully as I walked, counting the doorways. One, two, three. I hesitated then lifted the wooden latch. It made a little sighing sound, and the person in the bed stirred. I closed the door behind me and made my way toward the broad expanse of white I could just make out with my ruined eyes. Sliding my hands along the linen sheets, I encountered a warm shoulder.

Quick as a snake, a hand grabbed my wrist and pinned me down. Then I heard a rapid intake of breath. I thought he would say something, but he didn't. My heart hammered in my chest. Would he push me away?

No. Gently, he drew me into the bed with him and smoothed my hair from my face. I saw shadow loom as he reared over me, then the shadow blotted out the faint light.

We sighed as we came together. He buried his face in my neck and I heard his breathing deepen and quicken. He was tender. Each touch was featherlight, each kiss was a whisper. I urged him on in the end, a little cry escaping my lips. He chuckled softly and pulled me to him, curling around me and holding me close. "Isobel?"

"Yes, François?" My voice was a whisper.

"Why did you come tonight?" His hands tightened around my waist.

"You're leaving tomorrow. I'll miss you."

"I'll miss you too, Isobel." There was a definite chuckle in his voice now.

"I wish I'd come sooner," I said. Then I turned around and kissed him. I waited until he'd fallen asleep again, and I crept out of his warm bed and made my blind way back to my room.

The next day François left before dawn. He took Lucian with him. No one was up to see him off, except Richard. For no reason I understood, Elaine was in a furious mood after her father left. She made everyone in the manor miserable for a week by changing all the furniture and rooms around ten times a day to her liking. Eventually she calmed, and life went back to normal.

# Chapter Fifteen

**જ**

The month of August arrived with the first rumors of war, which I knew King Philip would soon quell.

For years, France had managed to keep her neighbors at bay, first with Philip August's careful politics then by force, as he won decisive victories against Spain and Burgundy. King Louis had had a peaceful reign, except for the two forays into the Holy Land that cost France so much money and so many lives. War was just a whisper yet, so the people tilled their fields, went to church and prayed for peace and prosperity.

I was lucky, or unlucky, enough to be there to witness some of the first signs of the changes that would shape the country over the next centuries. Some changes were good, like our larder stocked with fresh produce that the farmers, taking advantage of the newfound peace, sold at the markets. And some changes were hints of conflicts to come as the Church sought more power.

In cold weather, the peasants often brought their animals to church with them. They held them on their laps, to keep warm. Services could last three or four hours and the churches were built of stone, and freezing cold. Holes in the roofs leaked rain and snow, and cracks in walls meant drafts. Peasants held their chickens tightly in their arms, rested their feet on the backs of pigs, or sat with a goat firmly wedged between them. Afterwards we'd often find the pigs or chickens for sale in the Sunday market, which was where I was when the messenger came, announcing one of these coming changes.

"No more animals allowed in church," cried the messenger. According to Charles, standing at my elbow, the messenger stood very straight, held a rolled parchment which he didn't even glance at and shouted to everyone in the marketplace.

The noise quieted as the people mulled over that command. It was part of a longer edict issued by the Church and backed by the government. Part of it dealt with taxes, and the other half contained new policies relating to the Church.

The messenger repeated the new rule. "No animals in church and by order of the University of Paris, anyone caught reading pamphlets or reciting prose by Thomas Aquinas will be persecuted by the Church's Inquisition."

I turned to Charles, "And so the dark ages were ushered in with a rule against chickens in church."

He didn't laugh. Instead, his husky voice was pensive as he said, "The dark ages? Is that what they call this time period?"

"I'm afraid so," I answered.

He nodded and sighed. "I would have liked to see the world you lived in."

"It wasn't much different from this one," I lied. "People still live and die, and the world still revolves around the sun."

"The world turns around the sun?"

"Yes, it does. The idea you have now of everything revolving around the Earth came from the ancient Greeks, but in a few hundred years people will learn the true nature of the universe."

Charles gave a ghost of a laugh. "Don't let Père Martin hear you speaking thus, or he'll cry heresy. The Earth is the center of the universe, and it is quite flat, don't forget." He spoke wryly.

After I told him about my true purpose, Charles frequently questioned me when we were alone, but never when there was a chance of being overheard by anyone. Even so, as I lived there longer and began to accept the possibility I'd somehow accomplished my task, I wasn't as cautious as I should have been. Luckily he was my shadow and gave me a sharp jab with his elbow if I started to sound outlandish.

Like today, when we chanced to be in the market and hear the messenger. I suppose I was giddy with relief that I could leave the house now. My vision was slowly creeping back, although it was painful, and I could see vague, shadowy forms against the light. Migraines were constant companions. The only thing that helped was when I wrapped a linen bandage around my eyes and let Charles lead me about.

The villagers got used to seeing me blind, and they all shifted over when I got to church and make room for me in the front. The old priest had died two days after we arrived in the village and to my relief, Père Martin had become the new priest and was no longer underfoot at the house all day.

Père Martin always managed to be at my side, taking my hand to pray, and I hated hearing his heavy breathing. It annoyed me, but who could I complain to? Even with him gone most of the time, I didn't dare arouse his ire by avoiding him. Confession was now an obligation, and every day, it seemed, new edicts from the Church arrived. So, one by one, Elaine, Nurse, Dame Blanche and I confessed every day, kneeling on the hard floor while Père Martin breathed loudly through his mouth.

I didn't have much to say, so I usually invented some minor sin, just to get it over with.

"Forgive me my Father, for I have sinned," I said.

"What was it?" His voice gave me the chills. I hated not being able to see him as he sat by my side. Some days his cassock rustled so much that I wondered if he had fleas.

"I was angry at Elaine. I felt that she had a finer robe than I." The sin of envy was a handy sin. Père Martin would be able to concentrate on one thing, and his sermon would be over sooner. I settled myself as comfortably as I could on the stones and gritted my teeth. I had to be careful of my expressions. I couldn't see, but Père Martin could.

Today, though, his sermon was briefer than usual. After the absolving of my sin, he muttered, "Your sins are forgiven, my daughter. Try not to envy those placed above you, and be charitable to those below you on the great wheel of life."

I nodded, stifled a yawn and began to rise to my feet. Père Martin put his hand on my arm, ostensibly to help me rise.

"Thank you," I said, stepping away. I hoped Charles would come and lead me to my room, as I wanted to lie down a bit.

"Isobel." Père Martin's voice was oily. "Your blindness is a terrible handicap. In the future, you'll want a protector, someone to look after you in your need." His hands closed around my arms and he drew me near. "I'd like you to think of me as a friend, Dame Isobel. A very intimate friend who will take you in when you have nowhere to turn."

"Pardon?" Blind, I whipped my head around. My mouth must have been open in shock, but I managed not to cringe as he pawed at me.

"Sir François cannot keep you forever. He is seeking a new wife, and she'll be the head of the household. She won't want you around, will she?"

"Who told you that?"

"Lady Elaine." He sounded smug. He probably knew Elaine was furious with me, especially if he heard her confessions. She hadn't spoken a word to me since she'd seen her father kiss me. What she would have done if she'd seen me creeping out of his room didn't bear thinking about.

"I don't know what to say." A man of the cloth, making a pass at me? Did the clergy at this time have kept women? I knew they didn't marry, but had my history books mentioned whether or not they kept mistresses? I was too stunned to recall.

His hand ran up my arm. "You need someone to take care of you, Isobel."

"I...I'll think about it." I heard Charles' light footsteps. "Good day, Père Martin."

"Good day to you, Lady Isobel." His fat fingers brushed across my breasts, and I jerked backwards. "A shy creature, aren't you?" He spoke in a thick whisper, and his breath came fast.

Charles took my arm just then, and I left without replying.

"What was that all about?" Charles asked me, when we were safely out of earshot.

"He wants me as his mistress," I said. I shivered in disgust. "I think I'm about to be sick."

There was a stunned silence from Charles, then, "What did you say?"

"Oh God, Charles, I'd rather die."

"You didn't tell him that, did you?" Humor crept into his voice and I smiled.

"No, of course not. Is it true François is looking for a new wife?"

Another silence, then, "I don't know. Elaine won't speak to me either."

"What can I do?" I sighed. "I love him, you know."

"I know." I could practically hear Charles shrug. "You must miss him."

"I do. I wish he'd come back. He left so soon after we settled here, and there's been no news from him, or none Elaine will share. I wish she wasn't so angry with me." I bit my lip and put my hand out as Charles warned me of the doorway. "Will she ever forgive me?"

"Ask me something I know," he said.

"Is it rainy today?"

"No, it's sunny."

"Will you take me to town later?"

"We'll go after you rest. Lie down, Isobel. Your face is so white it looks transparent. You look more and more like the marble angels carved in the churches. It frightens me, sometimes, to see you."

"How is Aurore?"

"She's fine. Nurse says she'll bring her to you this evening. Now sleep, please." Charles stroked my forehead. "I'll try and find out what François has said to Elaine. Perhaps Dame Blanche will know something." He left and shut the door quietly behind him.

I lay awake for a long while, thinking about what Père Martin's proposal meant and what it would mean if François did find a new wife. I wouldn't be able to stay if he came back with someone else. Elaine, I thought, was counting on that fact.

Worry kept me from sleeping. I tried to think about something more pleasant until I drifted off. What was good about this time? Aurore, obviously, and Charles, and my feelings for François. I also loved to go to the village. It was a prosperous place, directly beneath the fortress being built on the hills. We weren't far from Pamplune, the capitol of Navarre. The mountains soared above us, their shoulders sometimes frosted with snow even in the summer. To the west was the Atlantic Ocean — the great sea. No one knew what lay beyond it. We were still in the in-between times, caught between the demise of the Roman Empire and the beginning of the Renaissance. The dark ages had just begun, and the Inquisition was an ominous whisper on the horizon.

* * * * *

"Do I hear a chicken?"

The congregation suddenly became very still. Père Martin had taken the animal edict very seriously. Now anyone bringing an animal into the church was liable to pay a fine to the priest. In the tiny church, a faint clucking could clearly be heard. Someone shifted, then everyone turned about and craned their heads to see who the offender was.

I choked back a nervous giggle. Charles, at my side, dug his elbow into my ribs. "He's looking at you," he hissed out of the corner of his mouth.

"I don't see why. I don't have a chicken," I whispered back. I didn't have to ask who "he" was. Since Père Martin had made his intentions clear, he was almost always present, either in my room or at my side when we dined. In church, he often referred obliquely to a woman's obligations. His sermons shifted from fire and brimstone to the importance of duty and obedience. Especially a woman's obedience toward men.

"Who has the chicken?" Père Martin lowered his voice dramatically. "Bring him forth!"

I shook in a desperate effort not to giggle. The "Bring him forth!" was too much. I exploded in a peal of laughter.

There was a second of stunned silence before some of the congregation, restless from a two-hour sermon about duty, tittered as well. Charles tugged on my sleeve.

"Hush, Isobel, please!" His voice was strained.

I pressed my hands to my mouth and leaned over to stifle the laughter bubbling out of my throat. In front of us, I heard Elaine whisper, "Really!" in an aggrieved voice.

Père Martin thumped his fist on the pulpit. "Be quiet!" he thundered.

All tittering ceased, and all giggles were hastily choked.

"That's better," he said.

Then the chicken let out a loud cackle, and the entire congregation burst into gales of laughter.

The sermon was over. Père Martin never found the chicken, and everyone surged out of the church at once without waiting for the benediction, which was not forthcoming since the priest was too angry. Charles pulled me out of the church and pushed his way through the crowd. I followed blindly, tripped and hastily grasped at my skirt.

"Slow down," I said.

"We'd better get back to the manor before Père Martin sees you. He kept looking at you all through the sermon. It was very queer. He had one hand in his pocket the whole time as if he had something there."

I giggled nervously. "Something?"

"He's on the far side of the market now." Charles stopped and I crashed into him. "Damn, he's headed this way. Quick, into the marketplace. Hopefully we'll get away from him."

"Why bother?" I tripped again on a cobblestone. "Damn these streets! Why don't they fix the holes? I can't see well enough to avoid them."

"His face is so red it looks like a boiled beet," said Charles, tugging on my arm.

"I can't run away forever. I'll just tell him I have a cold."

"He's seen us." Charles said mournfully. Then he stiffened. "He has some sort of letter in his hand that he's waving at us."

"Maybe it's from François!" I cried.

"Elaine is at his heels." Charles' hand tightened on my arm. "I don't like the looks of this."

"Isobel!" Père Martin's voice rose above the bustle in the marketplace. "Isobel! Stay right where you are! I have here a letter from the queen's confessor, Père Denis." He arrived in front of us, puffing like bellows, and he fanned the paper at my face. I blinked. "It says you were exempted from the year of mourning. The queen, Isabella, expressed her wishes to her confessor that you should marry as soon as your child was born. It's been over a year since your husband died."

"The queen, God rest her soul, meant to choose the suitor herself," Charles retorted in his dry, rasping voice.

"Unfortunately she died before she could," I said.

"It still means you can marry right away." Elaine's voice had a note of triumph in it, and a note of spite. I wished I could see her face, so that I could slap it.

"And if not marry, you can open your heart to other things," Père Martin added. I could hear the gloating in his words. "No need to mourn for your deceased husband forever."

"I prefer to wait, thank you," I said stiffly. I gathered my skirts in one hand and nudged Charles with the other. "If you'll excuse me, I wish to go back to the house and see my child."

"You can't see anything." Elaine's voice was bright with anger. "You're blind. You're simply another mouth to feed. We've no more money, and I've decided to get rid of excess expenses. Like you."

I was stunned. "You can't do this. François won't let you throw me out of his home."

"My father sent me a letter giving me power to do whatever I liked with the household. He's looking for another wife in Paris, and he won't be back until he finds someone."

"I'd like to see that letter," I said, keeping my voice steady.

"See it?" She laughed. "Look all you want."

A piece of paper was thrust into my hand. I pushed the linen bandage off my eyes and peered at the blur in front of me. I could vaguely make out a glow where the sunlight hit the paper and darkness where shadows fell from my fingers, but the words were totally lost to me. I'd never be able to read it, and I doubted they'd let Charles read it to me. I lowered my hand. The paper was snatched away.

"If you don't want to marry, that's fine," Elaine said. "You can leave any time you wish, the sooner the better. Just know that you're no longer welcome in my household." I heard the wooden heels of Elaine's shoes tapping a staccato on the stone street as she left.

Père Martin cleared his throat. "I believe that, under the circumstances, we should discuss your plans." I heard the sound of his palms rubbing together. "I can get an apartment for you in town."

"What shall I do?" I asked Charles, when the swish of the priest's robes vanished into the busy marketplace.

"I saw the letter," he said. "Elaine held it toward me. She doesn't know I can read."

"Was it from François?"

"Yes." My heart sank, but Charles patted my arm. "I didn't see the word 'wife' written anywhere, but one thing was clear. The king refused to extend his credit, and he sold the last of their land in Tours. He told her to do what she could with the money he left her and get rid of useless and frivolous expenses."

"To Elaine I am useless," I said.

"Don't sound so bitter." Charles and I wandered through the market. On my left, I heard hens cackling and I grinned briefly. Charles cleared his throat. "Do you suppose she means to keep Aurore?"

That was something that hadn't occurred to me, but it was entirely possible. Legally, in those times the family of the father would have the right to the child, especially if the wife were cast out.

"Lord, I don't know! François won't take it lightly if Elaine sent away his granddaughter. I'd like to think he'd mind if I were sent away, but perhaps not, if he plans to find a wife." I shivered and cold despair settled over me. How could I leave Aurore? Simply put, I couldn't. I couldn't possibly. If I married Père Martin, I might be allowed to keep her, but he hadn't offered marriage. And if Elaine cast me out, I'd have to leave her behind. My heart pounded with a sudden onset of panic. "Maybe you're right. Maybe François doesn't care for me."

"I didn't say that," Charles protested.

"I know. I wish I knew where he was so I could go to him." I said. Then I stopped walking. "That's it! We'll go to Paris!"

"Isobel!"

"Please, we'll go to Paris and find François."

"You think we can?" Charles sounded wry. "I'll lead you all the way to Paris, tripping and stumbling on your skirt?"

I jerked angrily upright. "I didn't say that. I'll ride."

"Blind?"

"I won't be Père Martin's paramour. I'd rather die," I said rashly. But was it preferable to leaving my daughter behind? I didn't know.

Charles heaved a great sigh. "Isobel, I think you'd better speak to Elaine. She holds the only chance you have of staying at the house until François comes home. I didn't see the end of the letter, so I don't know if he said he'd return soon."

"If you didn't see the end of the letter, how do you know he didn't write of getting a new wife?" My voice wavered. "Perhaps I'll be obliged to move into an apartment and be Père Martin's kept woman. Otherwise I'll be cast out of the house, and I'll never see Aurore again."

It was too much. My legs were trembling so hard I had to stop walking. I still had one gold piece sewed into my skirt, and the silver. I could live for at least a year on that, but still, without Aurore… A little sob surprised me by creeping out of my throat.

Charles sighed again and tugged my hand. "Come, we'd best go home and see what Elaine has in mind. Then we can make plans."

It sounded like a sensible idea, so I followed him quietly. Inwardly I seethed with anger at Elaine, fear that I'd be separated from my daughter and despair that I'd never see François again.

A few paces further I stopped again and sniffed the air. "Charles, what is that heavenly smell?" I turned my head this way and that to locate the scent I'd caught on the breeze.

He gave a loud sniff. "Linden blossoms, if I'm not mistaken."

"How wonderful! They smell like a combination of the sweetest honey and the deepest rose. Are they for sale in the marketplace?"

"No, they are blooming on a linden tree, not far from here. I think I saw one as we came up the crest of the hill. They're very easy to spot, as tall as they are wide."

"Tell me what they look like."

Charles sighed with impatience, but he humored me. "The tree leaves are heart-shaped. The flowers small, pale green, and are dried and used as infusions. Dame Blanche always has an infusion of them at night, before she sleeps. I take them to her."

I bit my lip, frowning. "Do they make you work very hard?"

I felt his shrug. His raspy voice was resigned. "No, not very hard. Less so than Madame Latrainée when I was in Chartres. But I tire of forever running errands, and it seems as though I can't sit still two minutes without someone having a chore for me to do."

"At least you're useful," I said.

"At least you still have your sense of humor," he replied.

"Please take me to the tree. The scent is marvelous, even borne on the wind." I wanted to take some flowers back to Aurore and Nurse.

"From too close it will be overpowering, but I'll take you. Come on, and watch your step. We're heading into the meadow now. There's a path, but it's narrow. Take my belt and follow me."

I did as he said, and he led me into a fragrant meadow where a great linden tree spread its shade over a burbling brook.

I took the bandage off my eyes and peered up at the tree. The dappled light filtered through its branches, turning my white apron green. I smiled then, tears leaking from my weakened eyes. "It's beautiful. I can see a bit better here in the shade."

Charles' face was a white blur, and a darker blur was the tree trunk behind him. I put my hand out and caught a branch. Drawing it toward me, I saw two pale, narrow leaves framing a double flower. It looked like a fuzzy miniature cherry with its stems and pom-poms. The leaves of the linden tree were larger than my hand, and, as Charles said, nearly heart-shaped. The scent of the blossoms was intoxicating and the whole tree sang with the heady buzzing of bees.

"What part do they dry for tea?" I asked.

"The little round flowers and their stems. The narrow leaves are discarded." Charles' finger poked the bloom in my hand.

"Will you ask Dame Blanche if I can try some tonight?"

"Of course. Here, if we pick some, we can dry it. It's easy to do, and Dame Blanche told me it keeps for years if you keep it in a covered jar."

We filled my apron with the blossoms, and I carried them back to the manor. I kept the bandage off my eyes because I wanted to exercise them and because I wanted Elaine to know my sight was nigh on to restored. I paid for my vanity with a violent headache that evening, but the scent of linden blossoms soothed me.

# Chapter Sixteen

છ

I tried to speak to Elaine soon thereafter. The fear of losing my daughter spurred me on. I couldn't imagine becoming Père Martin's mistress. I made my way to her room, my hand on the wall for guidance and balance, my heart pounding in my chest. I rapped on her door, and she called out, "Come in, Dame Blanche!"

"It's Isobel," I said, opening her door. My voice was husky with nerves so I cleared my throat a bit.

I couldn't see her, but I heard her swift intake of breath. "Why are you here?"

"I want to talk to you." I wasn't sure where to start. "You've been avoiding me, and I thought perhaps you were angry with me for some reason." I knew why she was angry, but I wanted to hear it from her lips.

"I want you to leave," she said, her voice angry. If only I could see her face clearly! She rose from her bed to stand stiffly in front of the window, blocking the light.

"I don't want to leave, and I won't leave Aurore," I said.

"You'd best stay in Père Martin's good graces then." Spite turned her voice into a jab of hate.

"I don't want to be with him, I'm not in love with him and you know it. I love your father."

"Get out," she spat. "Get out! I know what you're about. I realize now what kind of viper you are. Get out of my room, you scheming whore."

I wasn't prepared for her venom. I reeled backwards but caught myself on the doorway. My shock made me forget myself. "No, I love him, I need him!" I cried. I suppose I wasn't brave enough to stand up to her. I'd misjudged her anger and my strength.

"You don't love him, you're using him, just as you used my brother. When your parents lost their fortune, you saw Jean as a way to hoist yourself back to riches. When he died, you decided to seduce my father. You're nothing but a leech, a parasite—of course you need him! You're blind! If we cast you away, you'll be nothing but a beggar!"

"I'm not blind." I tried to steady my voice. "It will pass."

"There you go with your prophesying again. Beware…if Père Martin hears you, he'll think you're a witch. Then not even he will stand by you." She gave a bitter laugh. "I knew you were trouble the minute I saw you. How much older than Jean are you? That didn't stop you from seducing him, did it?"

I took a wavering breath then let it out slowly. She was right, in a way. I never should have been involved with Jean. That had been a weakness on my part, and a mistake. "I'm sorry he's dead," I said. "I wish he hadn't died." There wasn't a day gone by that I didn't wish Jean still alive and back home. The image of François' face came to me, and I realized, not for the first time, that whatever I'd felt about Jean, it paled to nothing next to my feelings for François. But I still wished Jean were alive.

"Get out," Elaine said. Her blurred figure grew larger as she walked toward me, and her hands pushed me off the door. When I was in the hallway, she slammed it in my face.

I stood there for a long while, trying to sort out my feelings. I was too confused to understand why I'd fallen in love with a man I barely knew. Suppose he didn't care for me? Suppose his promise that he'd see to my needs ended when he got himself a wife? I put my hands over my face and shuddered. I almost wished the sky would crack open and the TCF would erase me and my pain from the face of the earth. If I were gone, I wouldn't care anymore about François or agonize about my baby.

* * * * *

The day after I'd gathered linden blossoms and had the disastrous talk with Elaine, I decided to sort laundry. I suppose I wanted to prove I was "useful". The laundry room was vast and dark, perfect for my tired eyes. Charles came to see if he could help, and I put the sheet I was folding carefully into a basket and nodded. I had a question to ask him, and in this private place, I could speak without worrying about anyone overhearing.

"Charles, will you do something for me?"

I had debated with myself for hours before making up my mind. It wouldn't be easy, and his life would be in danger if he were caught.

"Yes, I'd do anything for you." He looked up at me, and I caught a hint of a question in his eyes. My sight was coming back and each day I saw more clearly. I could make out faces when they were as close as Charles' was.

"I know that, but weigh what I ask you carefully. I want you to go to Elaine's room and get the letter that François sent her. If there are several, take them all. We won't steal them," I hastened to add. "We'll simply borrow them. I need to read them and find out what I must do."

Charles pondered my words. "I will," he decided. "I'll take them just after she leaves her room for breakfast. If I can, I'll bring the letters to your room. Then, when she goes to vespers, I'll put them back."

"We must hope she won't spot the missing letters."

"Then perhaps we'd better do it today, before she gets more mail to tuck into her box," said Charles. He was quiet again, helping me fold and sort the clean laundry. When the baskets were full, we carried them to their respective owners. Elaine had the most laundry because she insisted on changing her sheets three times a week. Dame Blanche had a multitude of shifts, and Aurore had two dozen linen diapers that I washed endlessly. Père Martin still lived with us, and he had several smocks and vests to wash. That was no problem, though. It was feeding him that cost Elaine the most.

I knocked on his door and then set his basket just outside of it. He was probably out visiting the poor and comforting the sick. He wasn't a completely bad man, and I gathered that he took his priestly duties far more seriously than many village priests did at that time. Plus he was honest. Most of the money from the pardons he sold went to the church coffers, which were collected twice a year by the king's own men. Père Martin was fond of jewelry, though, and I often caught sight of a new bauble glinting from his fingers or strung around his neck.

I returned to the laundry room. My eyes were tired, and by the time I made the second trip with Dame Blanche's laundry, my head ached and I knew I must put my linen bandage back on or suffer sharper pain.

Dame Blanche was gone as well, and I wondered where everyone was that afternoon. The sun was bright and fine, so perhaps they were in the orchards or in the village.

In my room, the window was open, and the sweet scents of summer, along with the ripe odor of the manure pile, floated on the breeze. I knew I was lucky to live in such luxury in this age. Most people lived in single-roomed houses, rife with fleas and diseases. Even the wealthy often slept all massed together in the main dining room, everyone curled in the rushes along with the dogs, cats and geese.

The manor we lived in was new and had a stone foundation and first floor, with a stucco and beam second story. There were fireplaces in the main rooms, and the bedrooms were built just above them, sharing the heat from the brick chimney conduit. The kitchen was in a separate building, as wont in a century with wooden houses and no fire department. The stables and barn were the north and east walls of the courtyard, and the main house was an 'L' shape facing south and west. Everyone had his own room except the cook and Charles, who shared a room over the kitchen. Richard and his family slept in rooms over the stables. They had no fireplace, but the animals kept the building warm. The north-facing walls were twice as thick as the other walls and had no windows.

Windows were a luxury at that time, yet our manor had beautiful windows with small, round glass panes thick enough to keep the cold at bay and let in floods of warm sunlight. My room was small, and a curtain separated it from Nurse's half of the room, where she shared a bed with Aurore now that she'd grown out of her little cradle. They were out too, most likely taking advantage of the balmy weather.

As I wrapped my eyes with linen, I thought I should be proud to have survived so far, but what was the use of surviving if I couldn't live happily? Why struggle and half-starve simply to live a miserable life as Père Martin's kept woman? If I couldn't have my daughter living with me nor be near the man I loved, why bother to live? Or was this my punishment for killing someone else's child?

I recognized the dark feelings of depression settling on my shoulders, pushing me down into the depths of my own mind. Stress, like a bitter taste in my throat, rose to seize me around the chest. My breathing quickened. I struggled to the window where I leaned out to get some fresh air. My eyes strained toward the light, and my hands clenched the sill as the blur brightened, like headlights swinging around the bend in the road.

A child stared up at me. His face was white in the light, white against the shining blacktop, white and frozen with shock. He held a filmy net in one hand and a glass jar flashed in the other. All those things I saw so clearly and so slowly. Time is not arbitrary. It follows rules of its own making. It can slow down, or speed up. That night, it had been as slow as molasses. Right now, it was even slower.

There was no sound. When time is warped, sound escapes, or is erased, it seems. I wrenched the steering wheel around, swerving away from the small, pale form caught in the headlights. There was a shock as the car hit the child. A jolt that I felt through my hands, feet, skull... Oh Lord. The tree loomed huge and black and swallowed the car. I didn't care. All I could think about was the shock and its implications, and the sight of the child's pale face turned toward me, mouth open.

The jar shattered, sparkling, or maybe it was the windshield. I flew, but not for long. When the sound came back, I heard a scream, a mother's scream for her child, and for the first time, a thousand years away, I knew just what she felt.

Depression always hit me too fast for me to ward it off. One minute I would be fine, and the next, I would be incapable of speech, locked in a world where my own heartbeat frightened me, where all I could think about was death and the blessed silence it could bring.

I leaned further out the window.

"Isobel!"

Charles dragged me back from doom. I didn't struggle. I longed for death, but it was a rabbit's longing, weak, quivering and incapable of decisive movement. My hands were nerveless. I lay on my bed and trembled. Charles felt my pulse, touched my neck and pulled the covers over me. "I'll go to Isobel's room now," he said. "She's gone to the village, and afterwards there is vespers in the chapel. Père Martin has been speaking about his plans to install you in a little love nest in town. Dame Blanche is all aflutter about that."

He meant to make me smile, but I could only see shadows.

He patted my hand. "I'll be back. Try to sleep, please?"

I didn't answer, and a few moments later the door shut.

* * * * *

"Dear daughter, today I have seen the king. He has granted me exemption from the dime this year in regards to Jean because he was on the crusade, and because he fought alongside Jean-Tristan. However, he will not grant me an extension of credit, and I have had to go to the moneylenders in the city. There is one, an Italian, whom I trust.

"There is enough in the coffer to get us through this year and to buy the manor outright, which I have done. The papers will be sent along shortly. Put them in my silver chest. I have been to Bruges to see about buying part of a new dye business there, and I will tell you about it when I return. However, I think we will stay near Pamplune for now, as there are rumors that France will soon be at war again. You must be careful of expenses, Elaine. I charge you with running the household and grant you the right to make whatever decisions are needed while I am absent.

"Make sure that Dame Blanche and Nurse receive their pay at the end of each week so that they may send it to their families. In addition, I want Richard to sell Isobel's two ponies. Use that money toward household expenses. I am counting on you, daughter, to do away with all unnecessary expenses. Do not be frivolous. I will try to return as soon as I finish business in Bruges.

"Affectionately, your father, François de Bourbon-Dampierre de Navarre."

Charles read in a careful, slow voice, sounding the words out as he went along. I listened carefully, concentrating on each syllable.

"He said nothing about a new wife," I said.

I heard paper being folded and a rustle as Charles tucked the missive back into his shirt. "He'll be home soon," he said. "The letter is dated nearly a month ago."

"Soon?"

"In a month, maybe less."

"Oh, that soon." I tried to grin, to fight the heavy sadness that weighed upon me. "When did Elaine say I was to leave?"

"In three weeks."

"That's cutting it a bit fine," I said. "If I refuse to become the priest's woman, do you think he'll make trouble for me?"

"I don't know." Charles sounded troubled. "Ask me…"

"Something you know," I finished for him. I took a shaky breath. "I must make peace with Elaine."

"I'm going to return the letter." Charles hesitated. "There were other notes there. I had to sift through them to see which was the latest François had sent. One is addressed to François from the late queen Isabella ." He swallowed nervously. "I took that one too. Would you like me to read it to you?"

I gave a small laugh. "Might as well be hung for a sheep as for a…"

"Hush." His voice was strained as he read. "To François and Eleanéor de Bourbon-Dampierre. Greetings from Isabella, wife of Philip, crown prince of France. I am writing this from Italy, after a harrowing voyage to the Holy Land. Alas, the crusade was a failure, although perhaps some would not deem it so, the king's brother having negotiated a truce with the King of Tunis just as we were leaving.

"By now, you have heard the terrible news of King Louis' death. May God rest his soul and that of his son, Jean-Tristan, dead of the flux in Tunis. This brings me to the most difficult part of my missive, the death of your own son, Jean. I am writing this to you because I have taken your daughter-in-law under my protection for the time being. She is expecting a child, your grandchild. I hope this news eases somewhat your burden of grief. Your son fought boldly at my brother-in-law's side and died on the battlefield, unlike so many others, struck down by pestilence.

"Your new daughter-in-law will be traveling with us to Paris. If you wish, you could meet us on the road. I would like to keep her as my lady-in-waiting, though, and have her in court with me. I have also decided to find a new husband for her so that you won't be burdened financially. I know that these affairs are delicate to speak about, but I have always believed in frankness, and so I will be blunt. As long as Isobel remains with me as my lady-in-waiting, I will pay her a salary. When I find her a suitable husband, you will be exempt from paying a dowry, as her salary will go to that end.

"May God be with you, Isabella."

Charles finished reading and folded the letter carefully. "What do you think?" he asked.

"I don't know. For some reason, I don't think it pleased François that I was to be Isabella's lady-in-waiting."

"At least not after he saw you," said Charles. "But he didn't dare ask the queen to let you go."

I thought back to the day she'd died, and his haste to take me away. "You'd better put the letters back in their place. The bells for vespers will ring soon."

"Are you feeling better?" Charles asked.

I nodded and turned my face away from him. "Leave me now," I told him. His eyes were far too sharp. Sometimes I was afraid of what he would see.

Charles managed to put the letters back, and Elaine never noticed they'd been taken. I felt a few pangs of guilt for reading her mail, but they didn't last long.

* * * * *

The week went by slowly. My daily confessions with the Père Martin were still the worst part of the day. Finally, I decided I had to tell him the truth.

"My sight is coming back," I told him.

"Isobel, that isn't possible," he said pompously. "Cease your delusions. The blind cannot see, unless the Lord wills it."

"Then He must have willed it," I answered.

He didn't seem to hear me. "Don't worry, I won't let you starve."

"How kind," I said between clenched teeth. Emboldened by my compliment he put his hands on my bosom.

"A man needs a woman and a woman needs a man," he said. His voice got a bit strangled.

I pushed his hands away. "I don't want to become anyone's mistress."

He huffed noisily. "I'm offering you a comfortable life," he said. "No one else will do the same. You're blind and a burden to this household. Lady Elaine doesn't want you under her roof. She won't hesitate to cast you into the street, and in your condition, you'd have but one option—to beg. I cannot let that happen to you."

"Père Martin, I keep telling you that my blindness is temporary. Do you truly believe that François, Sir Dampierre, will let his daughter throw me out of his house? I'm not worried about that. I am the mother of his dear granddaughter."

His hands went back to my breasts and he gave them a lecherous squeeze. "Sir François won't keep you around forever, though he'll keep his grandchild, of course. You'll end up a beggar on the street."

"I'm trying to tell you that my sight is returning. In two or three weeks I'll be able to see clearly." Right now he was nothing but a blur. A red-faced blur. But I wasn't about to say that. I slapped at his hands angrily and he drew his breath in with a hiss.

"Beware, Isobel. The Church does not like those who prophesy. It's considered black magic. If you continue, I shall have to report you as a witch."

"I'm not prophesying, and I'm not a witch," I sputtered.

"Don't argue. A woman needs…"

"I don't need anything but to be left alone," I cried, thoroughly out of patience now.

Furious, he muttered a few Latin phrases, absolving me of my sins, and then Charles came to lead me back to my room.

# Chapter Seventeen

**಄**

My sight grew slowly clearer, and two weeks later it came back in a rush. One day, I could look out my window and see the tops of the houses in the village down in the valley. I could make out people's faces, and even tell from across a room who I looked at.

Now I watched Père Martin as he strode across the courtyard from the kitchen toward the main house. His robes flapped as he walked, as it was a blustery day. Clouds scudded across the sky, seeming to shred themselves on the trees. He glanced up and saw me. I waved, and his face was a study in surprise and outright shock. I don't think anyone but Charles believed my sight was truly returning.

He stopped and gathered his robe tighter around himself. He waved at me hesitantly.

"Good day, Père Martin," I called cheerfully. The clouds were a blessing for my eyes, too sensitive by far in the sunlight yet.

"You can see me?" He took a step backwards. "Can you really see me?"

"Yes!" I smiled. "I told you it was just temporary."

He hastily traced a cross in the air in front of him. "Sorcery!" he cried.

"Not at all." I laughed at his horrified expression. His eyes were so wide he looked like an owl. "It was the shock of the fall, but the nerve has healed. An Arab surgeon would have known."

"Infidels!" he choked. "Infidels and sorcery!"

"Don't be ridiculous," I said. "The queen Isabella, God rest her soul, favored an Arab doctor while were in Tunis."

"I shall write to the Holy See this afternoon. They must hear about this," he muttered to himself, but I heard him. My keen ears were not affected by my accident. He looked once more at my window, his face a study in confusion and fear, then he crossed himself and hurried off.

I giggled and pulled my head back in my room. Nurse was bouncing Aurore on her knee, and Aurore burbled little baby noises and tried to catch Nurse's ribbon with her chubby fist.

"Are you my little angel?" I asked my daughter, chucking her under the chin.

"Arrooo!" she agreed. A bright string of drool dripped downwards.

"She get tooth," said Nurse, in her rusty, succinct speech. After our first conversation she spoke to me sometimes, but she never said a single word more than necessary to convey her message.

"I can see that!" I cried. "I can see!" The relief of getting my vision back made me giddy. I spun around, twirled my skirt out and laughed aloud. "I have my sight back, and Père Martin is having second thoughts about me. He's starting to think that perhaps I won't be the tractable, obedient mistress he'd like."

I laughed again, but Nurse drew her brows down in a ferocious scowl. "Be careful," she said. She leaned forward and caught my wrist, searching for words. Her mouth opened, but no sound came out. Frustrated, she let go of my arm and shook her head. "H-he thinks evil thoughts," she finally managed to stutter.

I raised my eyebrows. "Impure thoughts? Oh ho! And him a man of the cloth." I smiled. "Don't worry about him. He won't try to hurt me. The worst he does is paw my breasts and pant. That doesn't bother me, rest assured. Shall I take Aurore for a while? Now that I can see better, perhaps we can go for a walk in the village."

"No."

"Why not? Are you afraid I'll fall down? I can see now!" Hope bubbled within me. With the return of my sight, I could be useful again and Elaine would have no reason to cast me out.

She shook her head. "Rain," she said.

I looked out the window and uttered a cry of annoyance. "You're right, the sky has darkened." I shut the window and scratched my head. "I have a feeling it's going to storm. Look at my arms, all gooseflesh."

Nurse didn't reply, and soon Aurore fell asleep. Nurse retrieved her basket of mending, but my eyes weren't strong enough for sewing, so I wandered about the room, quietly so as not to wake my napping child. The storm drew near, thunder growled in the distance and I lit a small lamp so that Nurse could see her work. There was nothing for me to do except take a nap myself, but I wasn't tired. I was in the mood for talking, but a glance at Nurse's face told me that she didn't share my good humor. I sighed and touched my hair again. It was dirty, a normal state for it to be in, as there was no shampoo. I thought that as long as it was raining, I'd go to the laundry room and get a piece of soap to wash myself.

I stripped in the laundry room then went outside and stood under the deluge, letting the rainwater cleanse me. I scrubbed my hair and skin, thankful for the late summer's sultry weather. The water ran off the slate roof in a steady stream, enabling me to rinse all the soap out of my hair. At the far corner of the stables, I noticed that Richard's family was also taking advantage of the rain to wash themselves.

Dame Blanche came naked out the laundry-room door, clutching a cake of soap.

"How are you?" she cried, over the pounding rain.

"Wonderful!" I enthused and moved over to make room. "I'm almost done."

"Take your time." She stood with her hands clasped modestly in front of her bosom.

I finished but stayed outside, enjoying the summer shower. The water that fell was nearly as warm as bath water and soft as dew. I opened my arms and tipped my face to the sky, for the sheer joy of feeling the rain on my skin. My hair whipped my back, and I laughed again. There was mud underfoot, but even that felt fine.

Elaine came outside then and washed in a stony silence. Dame Blanche joined me in the rain, and we linked arms and twirled each other about. She was a sprightly woman and loved to dance. At first Elaine glowered at us, but the spirit of the warm rain was infectious and she ended up joining our rain dance. Though she didn't smile at me, only at Dame Blanche, I hoped she was thawing toward me. Perhaps thinking I was going to accept Père Martin's offer helped her hate me less. Let her believe it! That thought made me laugh aloud again.

A flash of lightning was followed by a clap of thunder, and everyone dashed inside.

"How wonderful!" I grabbed a linen towel and rubbed myself until my skin glowed.

Elaine stared at me for a moment. "It's true. You can see again." Her words came out slowly, as if she was reluctant to speak to me.

"Of course!" I was amused. "I told you." I finished drying my hair and shrugged a clean tunic over my shoulders. I tied my apron on over it and used my towel to tie my hair in a turban. "Can't we cry peace, Elaine?" I begged. "Please? Can you forget your anger and…"

"Why did you kiss him? Why did you try to seduce my father?" Her voice was low, but her eyes flashed in anger.

I shook my head. "I didn't seduce anyone. I fell in love with him."

"Père Martin is buying an apartment for you."

"I don't think he wants me after all," I said. "I wouldn't make a good mistress for him, and he knows that. I think he just pitied my blindness and lusted after my body. Now that I can see, he doesn't seem to feel the same way about me. Besides, I love your father."

Elaine stared at me for a moment before her eyes dropped. A blush spread over her cheeks. "I don't believe you're capable of loving anyone," she said. She spun on her heel and left the laundry room.

* * * * *

During the next three days, I sensed a queer tension in the household. Père Martin was gone on a short trip, and Elaine stayed out of my way. At first, I was relieved. My eyes were getting better and I took advantage of it to go to the market with Nurse and Aurore. I recognized the fruit merchant and bought some oranges from him. They were the first of the season, and I couldn't wait to give one to Nurse.

"Hello, Dame Isobel," he said, smiling brightly at me and Aurore. "I bet you can't guess what I have for you!"

"I can too, oranges! I'd like two please."

When I pointed straight to the oranges, he gasped. "How…how did you know?"

"My sight has returned," I said, too pleased to notice his terrified gaze at first. He sold me two oranges, then stepped back, when usually he stayed beside me to chat about the weather and his trips to Spain. What was wrong? I didn't understand, and Nurse was so enthralled with her first orange she didn't notice. But I didn't like the suspicious looks the merchant cast at me.

"Gaëtan, what is it?" I asked him. Aurore, sitting at my feet, gurgled happily at the orange I'd handed her.

"Go away now, witch!" His voice was loud, and he crossed himself.

At first, the people in the marketplace didn't hear, but when he repeated it, heads turned.

"My eyes got better, that's all," I said in an attempt to soothe him.

"The blind cannot see!" he cried. "Now leave, and don't return!" He made a sign of warding off the evil, and the people nearby backed away and muttered. I sensed the mood of the crowd turning ugly, and so did Nurse, for she pocketed her precious orange and grabbed my arm.

"We go," she said urgently.

I snatched up Aurore in my arms and hurried from the marketplace, fleeing the angry hissing and fearful looks.

Once back at the manor, I sought Dame Blanche. Perhaps she could give me some advice. She sat with Elaine in the solar, and as I arrived, Elaine gave a stiff curtsey and excused herself, saying she couldn't stay in the same room with a whore.

Dame Blanche patted my arm gently. "Don't heed her. When she gets angry, she says things she doesn't mean." Her words were sure, but a frown creased her face. "I am glad she left, for I must speak with you. I saw how François looked at you, and so did Elaine. It made her fearfully jealous and worried her father won't marry a wealthy woman. I think she wants to get even."

"Has she done something?" I asked.

"She sent a message yesterday, but she wouldn't tell me where she sent it."

"You know who she sent it to," I prompted.

"Yes, I think I do." Her voice dropped to a whisper. "She sent a letter to the Holy See."

"That's two messages they'll be receiving, then, about me," I said.

Dame Blanche shook her head. "It's not a laughing matter, my child. It was only a few years ago that all the Cathari were exterminated. In some villages, there are people who point and call out "Cathari!" and that's enough to cause the suspect to be imprisoned and tried as a heretic."

"I didn't realize that the hatred was still so strong," I said. Worry assailed me. The people in the marketplace had whispered that I was a witch. Was that better or worse than the Cathari? I had no idea.

"Some believe that King Louis was killed by the infidel, and some say it was a heretic spy amongst the crusaders." Dame Blanche pulled her apron over her head and tied it around her waist. "I'd be careful if I were you, Isobel. Your ways are strange sometimes, and it's no ordinary thing to be healed from blindness. Perhaps people in Marseilles are more tolerant. Your parents were certainly good folk and would have been saddened to see suspicious fingers pointed at their daughter."

"When we traveled through Italy, there were people who threw charred fish bones at us. They thought to appease the demons they believed accompanied the body of King Louis. No matter who you are, there will always be some who dislike you or even fear you."

"I know, child." Dame Blanche paused. "But Elaine has done something foolish."

"How foolish?" I asked.

"I fear that she denounced you to the Inquisition," she said. "She won't say if it's true, but I suspect it. Her temper has always been her biggest fault, and you angered her beyond measure. First her beloved brother, then her father, whom she adores. She feels as if you've stolen both of them from her."

"The Inquisition?" I raised my eyebrows. "That's a bit dramatic, isn't it? Do you think they'll even bother? They must get hundreds of complaints."

"They've become powerful, thanks to the war against the Cathari."

"I was in the marketplace this morning," I said, not sure how to tell Dame Blanche of my experience. I was half-embarrassed, half-frightened about the whole event. "I'm afraid the fruit merchant thinks I'm a witch."

Dame Blanche gave a sharp cry. "What happened? Tell me!"

I did, and she shook her head. To my shock, tears rolled down her cheeks. "My poor Isobel, things are very grave. Not only Père Martin and Elaine have denounced you, but the villagers as well."

"What should I do?"

Dame Blanche hesitated and inspected her embroidery for a long moment. "I'm afraid you must leave," she said finally. "Go back to your own city. You must have some family left."

"I can't do that!" I cried, stunned. "Leave? What will become of Aurore?"

"Your daughter will be raised as a princess, Sir Dampierre will see to that. She's related by blood and marriage to the king, and no one can take that from her."

"I'm her mother!"

Dame Blanche saw my mutinous expression and took a hold of my arm. Her voice was pleading. She was truly worried. "You must be gone before the Inquisition comes. Père Martin thinks your sight was recovered through sorcery. If he's gone to send a message to the Holy See, they'll look into the matter and if they speak with the villagers and Elaine..." Her voice trailed off and she gave a nervous cough. "I'll help you if you need money for the journey. I have some saved, I don't need it and Elaine sees I lack nothing. Take what I offer and leave, please!"

"No!" I cried, pushing her away. "How can you ask me to leave? How can I leave my baby?"

"Don't you understand? If you're condemned, your child will be condemned along with you and burned. The family Dampierre will lose its influence and respect. If you're not afraid for your own skin, think of others."

"It's absurd! I'm no Cathari and certainly not a witch!"

"Even a hint of suspicion will ruin François." Dame Blanche shook her head sorrowfully. "You can't pretend you don't care for him, but your love is doomed, my child. He will not be able to wed a woman questioned by the Inquisition—the king will not allow it. Not with the Cathari war so fresh in our memories."

I stared at her. When she didn't lower her eyes, I dropped my gaze. "I'll think about it," I whispered. I couldn't put my child's life in danger. If I were accused of sorcery or thought to be a heretic the Inquisition would kill her too. I hadn't realized that before. A cold arrow shot through my heart.

"You must leave as soon as possible so that they have no chance to catch up to you."

"I need to see François before I can make a decision," I said.

"It's impossible. He won't be back for another month, at least." Dame Blanche spoke firmly.

"My hands are cold, feel them," I said inanely. I felt as if my extremities had turned to ice.

"You poor child. Here, come sit by the fire. I'll go fetch some spiced wine and a parchment. We must write to your family and tell them you're coming."

"I have no more family. I want to write to a lawyer."

"A lawyer?" She looked as scandalized as if I'd said I want to write to the devil.

"Burn the heart and liver of a fish," I murmured.

"What's that?" Dame Blanche leaned closer.

"Nothing. An incantation against demons," I said. Then I put my face in my hands and I cried.

\* \* \* \* \*

Charles and I left three days later, early in the morning. We were on foot, leading our donkey, and my eyes were bandaged again. I'd strained them in an effort to write a letter and to draw Aurore.

I had no camera, of course, so I used a piece of charcoal to draw my daughter. I am no artist, and the first results landed in the fireplace. Finally I managed a decent sketch of my sleeping daughter. Meanwhile, Charles packed our meager belongings and set about plotting our route. We'd follow the coast after taking the winding road that led through the mountains. Once past Navarre, we'd enter the region of France that had been devastated during the war against the Cathari. Few people lived there now, and food would likely be scarce. We had to leave before autumn set in or risk starvation.

Our hasty departure was also a lonely one. Richard and Dame Blanche waved us off. Cook came and pressed another cheese into Charles' hands, and Nurse wept with great, choking sobs. Aurore cried as well, but I could hardly look at her. The pain in my chest was too sharp.

We left just after dawn. The little donkey set its hooves down delicately, Charles walked steadily and I dragged my feet in an effort to keep moving. Behind us was the manor, and I could hear my child wailing hysterically. Each sob shattered my heart further until it was nothing but dust. Elaine hid in her room and Père Martin, the hypocrite, knelt in the doorway, praying for my soul. Ahead of us, there was nothing but winding road and blue mountains fragrant with oranges.

In my pocket was a letter to a certain Maître Houdebert, *Avocat de Cour*. I prayed that he was still our friend, and that he would help me now that I had no one else to turn to. Perhaps he could clear my name and help me get custody of my daughter. Why hadn't I studied medieval law? I knew nothing about what could legally happen to me.

The road was clearly marked. As the days passed in numbing sameness, we trod through small stone villages and old, wooden fortresses. People in the villages asked us for news. Some took pity on us. I wrapped white linen around my eyes during the day, and kindhearted folk offered us shelter. Mostly we slept in haystacks or beneath dense hedges.

Charles kept up a lively chatter to keep my mind off my sorrow. At first, the voyage was easy. There were many villages along the way, most of the people were kind and we had plenty of fresh milk and walnuts. When the road narrowed and grew steep, we entered the land of the Catheris, which had been scoured by war. We were alone. Houses stood abandoned, graves dotted the hillsides and we saw packs of wild dogs in the distance.

I grew melancholy and even Charles couldn't make me smile. The higher we climbed, the more pronounced my depression grew, until I could no longer speak. My throat too was tight with grief. Each step was another step away from my daughter and from François.

Ghosts accompanied me across the mountains. White, round faces would suddenly loom out of the darkness and scream silently. The child I'd killed would rouse me out of my sleep, and the silent scream would burst out of my raw throat.

Jean rode beside me, sometimes. He never spoke. When he tipped his head down to smile at me, my underwear slipped down his helmet and covered his eyes. I wanted to see their green sparkle, but they were hidden behind a white cloth. My eyes, too, remained hidden. The sun was bright, the stones on the road sparkled and the light stabbed my head like knives. I wrapped my linen around my eyes, took hold of the donkey's tail and shuffled along, my ghosts following me.

When I was blindfolded, I saw the child. When I wasn't, Jean appeared, and sometimes at night, there were others whom I'd never seen. They floated out of the evening sky, settled around the flickering fire and stared at me with great, saucer eyes.

Charles followed my terrified glances but saw nothing, and I wouldn't frighten him with the visions that haunted me. He'd believe I was losing my mind.

Perhaps, I thought at times, this was the erasure. I was slowly being sucked into half-world where the dead wandered. One day I'd disappear entirely, perhaps fading like mist, and the world I glimpsed would open up like a rent in space and suck me into it. My hands, when I looked at them, seemed to be fading into nothing. My fingers became transparent, the bones showing up as if on an x-ray film.

Part of me realized that it was nothing more than grief playing tricks on my mind. My limits had at last been broken. Ironically, it was now I reflected on the fact that the TCF had long hesitated about sending me on this mission. It had been written in large type on the top of my admission sheet — "subject to manic depression". The nurses whispered about it, and my psychologist spoke to me for hours, telling me what to do when I felt the first signs. I'd been able to rise above it before. Now it submerged me.

"Aurore," I whispered, trying to conjure her image. My whole body ached with longing for my child, adding to my misery.

"Isobel?" Charles prodded my shoulder.

Where were we? What day was it? I uncurled my body and sat up. I pushed the linen off my eyes and blinked, trying to focus on his face. It wavered in the pale light before me, as if unattached to his head.

I blinked harder and he snapped into focus. "What is it?" I whispered. My voice was rusty, strained with choking back screams. I shuddered as Jean surged out of the mist behind Charles. The vision was so real, so clear, I gasped, and then the blood drained from my face.

Charles turned, and, incredibly, he smiled. "François came after us!"

I dared look again. It wasn't Jean standing behind Charles, looking down at me with a face grown white with fatigue. It was François, and he held a parchment in hands that shook. Behind him, I heard horses' hooves, and Lucien appeared too, leading three cobs by their reins.

"Richard gave me the letter," François said.

I let out the breath I'd been holding in a sigh. "Thank God," I said, and then I lay down again because my head spun so much I thought I would faint. I had given a letter to Richard for François, but I hadn't dared let myself hope that he'd come after me. My eyes filled with tears of joy.

Lucien and Charles went to fetch wood while François sat beside me. He looked at me then averted his gaze toward the flinty road where we'd been heading. "Elaine is sorry," he said after a while.

"I'll forgive her." I found I couldn't stop smiling. Tears trickled down my cheeks, and still I couldn't stop smiling. "I am so happy to see you, François."

"You can truly see me?"

"You're holding two fingers up and waving them around. Stop, you look silly." I ran a thin hand through my hair, where it got stuck in the grime of days. I winced. "When Lucien and Charles return, will you ask them to fetch and heat water for me? I need to bathe."

"Bathe? You look fine to me, though a bit peaked." His jaw clenched and unclenched as his eyes devoured me. Then he pulled me into his arms and hugged me so hard my ribs creaked. "When I saw you had gone, I nearly went mad. Don't ever leave me again, promise."

"I won't. Please tell me, how is Aurore?" I asked. I could let myself think of my daughter again. Fresh tears coursed down my cheeks.

"She's fine and healthy and misses her mother. She'll be overjoyed to see you." He nuzzled my neck, his arms still holding me tightly. "I missed you too."

"I want to start anew." My voice was firm. "François, I love you."

He blushed. Green eyes sparkled behind long, black lashes. "Dame Blanche was quite explicit about that," he said, a chuckle at the end of the phrase. "She worried about you."

"She said that the Inquisition wanted to question me."

"The Inquisition wants to question a certain Isobel, but she fled. I think I'll wed a widow in Montpellier and bring her back to Navarre. Her name is Isault, and she's as lovely as an angel. I hear you know of a lawyer there. Perhaps he'll draw up the wedding certificate."

When his meaning became clear, I slumped with relief. "Will Père Martin say anything?"

"He's been sent to Avignon. The Church means to make a cardinal of our dear priest. No, I'm free to wed a certain Isault. Will you be my wife, Isault?"

"I will." I closed my eyes and concentrated, but the face that had stared at me in horror so many times was now smiling at me. Peace surrounded it in a nimbus. I knew it wasn't real, that it was simply my own mind putting this particular ghost to rest, but it made my heart swell. A warm glow surrounded me. I opened my eyes and saw it was François, who draped his cape over my shoulders.

"We will live in Navarre and raise Aurore together."

"There will be more." I snuggled into his embrace. "Sons and daughters, with green eyes and dimples at the corners of their mouths."

"My eyes, your dimples, what else could we ask for?" His voice tickled my ear.

"I could ask for nothing more, now that you've found me." I held my hands in front of my face and looked at them. They seemed more substantial now – the light had ceased to render them transparent. I had come to this world, and I would stay.

# Epilogue

*Ten years later…*

ରୁ

The manor echoes with the shouts of three little boys chasing after their older sister. I lean out the window to tell them to put the frog down and leave Aurore alone. She grows more beautiful each day, and François never tires of telling me she looks like her mother.

François has gone into the wool business and has a dye shop in Bruges, so we travel back and forth twice a year to Bruges from Navarre. When we pass through Paris, we stay with Elaine, who has married and has four children already, two girls and two boys. She and I are friends now, and our children spend summers together in the manor in Navarre.

Charles married a girl from the village and François put him in charge of the dye shop in Bruges. He's turned into quite a good merchant and when we are alone together I tell him how to invest the money, what commodities will thrive, and what to avoid. He is the only person I have ever told about my past life, and I will never tell François, no matter how much I love him. Loving someone means not hurting them, and the truth would only hurt my husband. He and I are happy as we are and I make sure that our family prospers and stays out of political conflicts. My history lessons served me well, in the end.

Today the linden trees are in blossom and Aurore and I will gather the flowers and lay them to dry on clean sheets. My three boys, Jean-Marie, Thomas and Luke, will come with us and most likely hinder more than help. Nurse will keep them in line, though she's getting on in years. The boys are just excited because their cousins will arrive any day now.

I'm excited too, for François is accompanying them and I haven't seen him in a month. After I gather the linden blossoms, I will get our room ready. My heart is light. The sun is shining, the linden trees perfume the balmy air and François will soon be home.

Life is sweet, and I am more deeply in love with François each passing year. When I think of my other life somewhere in the future, it's like a bad dream that I've woken from and I give thanks each day that the TCF chose me to save the crown of France.

I'm still not sure how our family will be linked with the kingdom of France, though I know that it shall someday. We sometimes go to the court in Navarre and the queen has offered to take Aurore as a lady-in-waiting when she turns fifteen. Jean-Marie sometimes plays with the young prince of Navarre, and he told me that the prince thought Aurore was beautiful, so perhaps she's the key that unlocks the puzzle of time and sets everything back on its track.

Somewhere in the future a quartz-crystal book sits in the middle of an ice-blue beam of light. Written on its pages are the names of the kings and queens of France and all their descendants. Jean de Bourbon-Dampierre's name is there, and so, perhaps, is Aurore's.

Children's laughter brings me back to the present. Right now sun is streaming through the casement windows and I hear the sound of hoofbeats in the courtyard. My beloved François is home, and I will go and greet him. The linden blossoms will wait.

# Why an electronic book?

We live in the Information Age—an exciting time in the history of human civilization, in which technology rules supreme and continues to progress in leaps and bounds every minute of every day. For a multitude of reasons, more and more avid literary fans are opting to purchase e-books instead of paper books. The question from those not yet initiated into the world of electronic reading is simply: *Why?*

1.  ***Price.*** An electronic title at Ellora's Cave Publishing and Cerridwen Press runs anywhere from 40% to 75% less than the cover price of the exact same title in paperback format. Why? Basic mathematics and cost. It is less expensive to publish an e-book (no paper and printing, no warehousing and shipping) than it is to publish a paperback, so the savings are passed along to the consumer.

2.  ***Space.*** Running out of room in your house for your books? That is one worry you will never have with electronic books. For a low one-time cost, you can purchase a handheld device specifically designed for e-reading. Many e-readers have large, convenient screens for viewing. Better yet, hundreds of titles can be stored within your new library—on a single microchip. There are a variety of e-readers from different manufacturers. You can also read e-books on your PC or laptop computer. (Please note that Ellora's

Cave does not endorse any specific brands. You can check our websites at www.ellorascave.com or www.cerridwenpress.com for information we make available to new consumers.)

3. *Mobility.* Because your new e-library consists of only a microchip within a small, easily transportable e-reader, your entire cache of books can be taken with you wherever you go.

4. *Personal Viewing Preferences.* Are the words you are currently reading too small? Too large? Too... ANNOYING? Paperback books cannot be modified according to personal preferences, but e-books can.

5. *Instant Gratification.* Is it the middle of the night and all the bookstores near you are closed? Are you tired of waiting days, sometimes weeks, for bookstores to ship the novels you bought? Ellora's Cave Publishing sells instantaneous downloads twenty-four hours a day, seven days a week, every day of the year. Our webstore is never closed. Our e-book delivery system is 100% automated, meaning your order is filled as soon as you pay for it.

Those are a few of the top reasons why electronic books are replacing paperbacks for many avid readers.

As always, Ellora's Cave and Cerridwen Press welcome your questions and comments. We invite you to email us at Comments@ellorascave.com or write to us directly at Ellora's Cave Publishing Inc., 1056 Home Avenue, Akron, OH 44310-3502.

# Cerridwen Press
## Monthly Newsletter

News
Author Appearances
Book Signings
New Releases
Contests
Author Profiles
Feature Articles

Available online at
www.CerridwenPress.com

# CERRIDWEN PRESS

Cerridwen, the Celtic goddess of wisdom, was the muse who brought inspiration to storytellers and those in the creative arts.

Cerridwen Press encompasses the best and most innovative stories in all genres of today's fiction.

Visit our website and discover the newest titles by talented authors who still get inspired — much like the ancient storytellers did...

once upon a time.

www.cerridwenpress.com